REDEMPTION

DISCONNECTED #3

G.A. EVERETT

EVERETT OSTRICHES PUBLISHING

Copyright © 2021 by Everett Ostriches Publishing

The moral right of the author has been asserted.

All rights reserved.

No part of this book may be reproduced in any form or by any electronic or mechanical means, including information storage and retrieval systems, without written permission from the author, except for the use of brief quotations in a book review.

You do have the author's full permission to encourage every single person you know to purchase a copy of this novel and then recommend it to everybody they know. Spread the word, good friends!

Cover design by Stuart Bache

This is a work of fiction. Names, characters, businesses, places, events and incidents are either the products of the author's imagination or used in a fictitious manner. Any resemblance to actual persons, living or dead, or actual events is purely coincidental. The author acknowledges the trademarked status and trademark owners of various products referenced in this work of fiction.

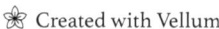 Created with Vellum

THANK YOU

Huzzah! You have stumbled upon my novel. This makes YOU the person I used to dream about, hoping would someday pick up a copy of one of my novels and dive willingly into its world.

If you do enjoy my work, and you fancy following along with what I'm up to, you can visit my website gaeverett.com to sign up to my newsletter and receive a FREE BOOK.

You may have come to this novel because you chanced upon it, you liked the cover, the premise, or even because somebody recommended it to you (one can dream). Reading, for me, was always a thoroughly enjoyable pastime, along with music, film and theatre, in which I could escape from my everyday life to go on adventures, uncover crimes, slay dragons, or fall in love, if just for a moment. Whatever your reason for choosing my novel, I hope you enjoy reading it as much as I did writing it.

Happy reading.

NOVELS BY G.A. EVERETT

Hunted (Disconnected series prequel)
Artificial (Disconnected #1)
Blackout (Disconnected #2)
Redemption (Disconnected #3)

Downfall (Queen of the Unworthy #1)

1

'What's that?' Mia said, pointing to something off in the distance as they walked along the road.

Returning from the daydream he'd been indulging in while plodding ever onwards in the midday heat, Dylan turned to see what Mia was looking at. It was indeed quite odd. Some kind of rock formation, by the looks of it. A strange one. It could almost be man-made.

For once she had genuinely stumped him. He was used to coming across the destroyed remnants of the world from before the Blackout, the world he had never known. But those buildings had a certain style to them. Mostly they were made of brick and glass, although finding one with glass intact was almost impossible now. He'd never seen anything made purely out of rock. It seemed to him a completely mundane structure. His curiosity was piqued.

Usually, Mia's constant barrage of questions over the last few weeks had been about simpler things; a tool she'd never seen before, or some kind of remnant of the old world that she'd never come across in her sheltered life, having been cooped up in one enclosed settlement since childhood. Like cars. She'd never seen the rusted steel carcasses sitting out on roads before. Her settlement had cleared them out long before she'd been born. Dylan had had a hard time explaining them to her, since he had no understanding of what they were beyond the steel shells that sat there doing nothing. His mother had once explained to him that they used to carry people from place to place, like mechanical animals, at speeds no animal could match. Lacking his own first-hand experience, he'd tried his best to communicate her explanation from memory.

Mia had never ventured out into the 'real world'. Not like Dylan had. She was ignorant of its ways. She hadn't grown up in a forest dwelling like he had. Hadn't moved around parts of the country like his family had. She'd never needed to. *Oh, to be so lucky.* She had been part of something bigger: a community large enough that people were assigned roles and responsibilities, some being scouts, others medics, cooks, fighters and so forth. Her job had been to look after some of the settlement's internal responsibilities. She'd learned skills such as stock control and sewing wounds.

Dylan's childhood could not have been more different. As part of a small family, he and his brother had grown up sharing all the same tasks as their parents. Every responsibility was owned equally by each family member. As such, he'd spent time venturing out before they'd been captured and taken to Mia's settlement.

But this was what their adventure was all about. And besides, he found that he quite enjoyed explaining these new discoveries to her. It made him seem knowledgeable. Worldly, even, if that were possible. Having recently survived a battle in which he had been shot by his own brother, he felt ready to go out and confront the unknown; to have experiences beyond simple everyday survival. To try and live like people had back then. Not like he and everyone he knew did now, with their whole lives about making it from one day to the next.

Dylan had always been fascinated by stories of the pre-Blackout world. He found the evidence of it intriguing. It was all there, right in front of him. Plain as day, yet a mystery all the same. Something to be uncovered. It was there in the crumbling buildings losing their battle with nature, the machines and devices that no longer worked, and in the weapons that still did, however scarce they were these days.

For three weeks he and Mia had been heading east from the settlement known as Taunton, onwards towards London, the fabled big city, and hopefully even beyond that to the continent across the sea, where the books he'd collected from time to time told of white sandy beaches, something neither Dylan nor Mia had ever seen. It seemed to him a whole other world.

Progress had been slow as they tried to keep themselves out of danger, or stopped to discover something new. The trip was, after all, about new experiences. And this was definitely something new. 'Let's go have a look,' he said, wondering what this rock formation could be.

It was laid out in a circle: a ring of tall standing stones, each one easily more than twice his height.

'Stonehenge,' Mia said, reading from a barely legible rusted sign as they approached.

The name meant nothing to Dylan.

'Do you know it?' she said.

'Afraid not.'

'It's so different to everything else we've come across.'

'That it is. It seems older, much older.'

'What do you think its purpose was?'

Dylan looked around the structure as he lifted his heavy rucksack off his back and dropped it to the ground, along with his rifle, bow and quiver, grateful to allow his sweating shoulders a chance to breathe. Some stones seemed to be missing. The pattern of the circle was obvious, with pillars spaced fairly evenly apart and other stones laid across on top like beams, but there were many gaps. Like everything in the world he had grown up in, this too was something destroyed before his time. His was a world of leftovers; a world in tatters. 'Not a clue,' he said.

'It's pretty,' Mia said. 'At least, compared to the buildings we usually come across.'

'No arguments there.'

'Do you think they built things just to be pretty?'

'No idea. Mum always said they did everything they thought possible except do a single thing they actually needed to.'

'I hope they did.'

'You hope they what?' Dylan said.

'Build things just to be pretty. I like the idea of building something just to be appreciated, you know? Not a fence to keep others out, or a den to store weapons.'

'Or traps to kill intruders,' Dylan said, remembering some that he and his family used to lay around the perimeter of their forest dwelling back before he and his brother were captured.

'Charming,' Mia said. 'Speaking of traps, shall we eat?'

'Good idea.' Dylan removed the leftover strips of hare he'd saved from the capture earlier that morning. In the last few weeks he'd been getting back to his old ways of setting traps at night before they went to sleep. He wasn't as good as his younger brother Jake had been, but still, every other day or so he found one of the traps full as they journeyed east. The success rate was pretty good, as far as he was concerned.

They sat in the centre of the stone circle, enjoying the slight shade offered by a couple of pillars. The shadows weren't much at this time of day, with the sun almost at its zenith, but any shade was good shade in this heat. Dylan found himself looking forward to the coming winter. If the changing colour of the foliage was anything to go by, these hot days were numbered.

'How long do you think until we reach the coast?' Mia said.

'I don't know,' Dylan said, recalling what his mother had said. She'd suggested following all the signs to London, after which they could apparently follow the roads to a place called Dover. From there, assuming they were still alive and hadn't given up on their adventure to turn back, she reckoned they could commandeer a boat, if they were lucky, and head to the continent. 'It doesn't matter,' he said. 'I'm just enjoying our adventure.'

'Me too,' she said, her face lighting up from behind the flask of water she was draining. 'And thank you.'

'For what?'

'For keeping your promise.'

'I said we'd see the world, didn't I?'

'You did. It's just ... after everything that happened back home, I thought maybe you'd want to stay.'

'It made me want to get out of there even more.'

'You don't think we made a mistake leaving town?'

'The way I see it,' he said, 'any place is as dangerous as the next. What we survived, taking on Frank's crew, it almost cost us our lives. But it's only worth it if we then get to enjoy the freedom we fought for. Staying back home just because the town was liberated wouldn't be a life well lived. I want to see what's out there.'

'Okay,' she said.

Trying to gauge her response, Dylan sipped from his own flask. When he'd proposed the idea of breaking out of town to her, she'd been tentative at first, then thrilled. She'd wanted to go see the world beyond the only walls she'd ever known. He tried to put himself in her shoes. To understand what it must feel like to be farther from home than she'd ever been, with a guy she hadn't known particularly long. Now that he thought about it, it must be terrifying. But she *had* wanted it. And he was glad to have her with him. There was no way he could have stayed. The town only brought back the nightmares of his family's capture. Of watching his brother fall for Mia first. Of watching his brother's allegiance shift to Frank, that evil sonofabitch who lorded it over the townsfolk and had once whipped Dylan to within an inch of his life as punishment for trying to escape. No, there was nothing back there he wanted to stay for. He wanted to move on, not look back. Hopefully, somewhere out towards the horizon, he'd finally be able to get his brother out of his mind.

'Do you think your brother is still alive?' Mia said.

Admiring her ability to read his every thought, Dylan nodded. 'Jake survived the fall, didn't he?'

'Yes, but we waited weeks before we left town. He never showed. Do you think he might have succumbed to his injuries?'

'It's possible. I don't think so, though. Something tells me he's out there. I can feel it.'

'Do you want to see him again?'

'Well, last time he shot me and accused me of stealing you, so I'm in no rush, if that's what you're asking.'

'I'm nobody's to steal,' she said, her tone defiant.

'Couldn't agree more, but Jake was angry. He was confused. Frank got in his head. We can't be held accountable for nature taking its course. Jake needs to find his own way now, whatever that is. It's his life. We, on the other hand, need to get a move on.'

'In a rush to take me somewhere, mister?'

Playing it off as best he could, Dylan shook his head. 'Nah, no rush,' he said. The last thing he wanted was to seed the beginnings of panic, but he had a sneaking suspicion they were being watched. What was worse, he'd felt it for over a week now. Like someone was out there trailing them, waiting for the moment to strike. There was no way he could explain it without sounding like he'd lost the plot entirely, but the feeling had been nagging at him all the while. Sometimes he thought he'd caught the blur of a silhouette in the distance, peering out momentarily from behind a tree or rock formation. Other times it was a rustle in the long grass or the snap of a dry twig in the night. Every night, before they'd found a place to sleep, Dylan had created some kind of warning system around their perimeter, laying out rows of twigs that, if stepped on, would make a noise. Sometimes he ran string from tree to tree, with empty tin cans attached that clanged together when disturbed. Problem with those was how easy it was for a windy night to drive his paranoia to unbearable levels. When Mia had asked why he'd become so serious about this ritual every evening, he'd just explained that it was better to be safe than sorry. He'd told her about the various traps they used to lay out when he'd grown up in the forest with his family, how trespassers might come through their territory unaware. In this world, outside of safe settlements like the one she'd grown up in, surprises like that were unwelcome, and often led to bloodshed. Mia didn't argue. She was used to scouts and security teams running to schedules in her town, Dylan figured. The systems he created made her feel safer, she'd said. He only wished they had the same effect on him.

They finished up their meal and washed their hands with the water from their flasks. As he slipped his rucksack back on, with the bow and quiver, and went to pick up his rifle, Dylan saw the figures step out from behind the stone pillars surrounding them.

'I wouldn't touch that if I were you,' the man in front said.

2

The morning light shone on Jake's face, waking him from his slumber and releasing him from the nightmares that tormented him. Every time he closed his eyes, there they were. Scenes of the battle a few weeks ago, playing over and over until he woke, exhausted, angry and fearful. In the nightmares he felt the grip of a wiry arm around his neck, Frank using him as a shield. The man in whom he had put his trust, betraying him when the moment became a life-or-death matter. Jake felt the guilt at seeing his mother, whom he'd presumed dead, burst through the door across the room, pointing a gun at them, her friend lying prone on the ground with her crossbow. He recalled the heartbreak in his mother's eyes. The pain as her body shook, trying to keep her aim steady. She had not wanted to shoot him, he thought. But she had pointed the shotgun at him all the same. He had to live with that knowledge. Then the flash. The whip of air as her friend's crossbow fired. Each time he relived it, the experience felt as real as the first time. The feeling of shock as the bolt just missed his face, only to strike Frank behind him. Then the pull as Frank stumbled backwards to the tower ledge, taking Jake with him over the edge. No, Jake couldn't forgive it. His family had made their choice. They had been willing to end him because of their differences.

Bastards.

He wiped the sheen of sweat from his arms as he shook the nightmares off, allowing the sun to thaw the ice running through his veins. Slowly, feeling returned. The fresh morning air cleared his mind. On a branch above, a robin peered inquisitively down at him, its red breast puffed out as it twisted its head to the side. Drawing some strength from the fearless little creature, Jake set his mind to the day ahead. Would today be the day? Time would tell.

With his nightmares vanquished and his newfound determination in place, Jake packed up his things and put his rucksack on his back. He checked his traps.

Nothing.

All were empty. *No matter. Today might be the day.* Taking great care to keep quiet as he moved about, Jake set off through the trees. When he got to the camp, he found it empty. *Where the hell are they?* Surely they hadn't set off already? When he'd spied on them the night before, they'd made no mention of an early start. No matter what he did, they were always one step ahead. He wondered if Dylan knew he was being followed. Perhaps his older brother had spotted him the day before? Jake recalled popping his head out from behind a tree at just the wrong moment. He thought he'd been far enough away so as not to be seen, but now he was not so sure. His brother appeared to be upping his security measures with each passing day.

First it was twigs. Then it was tin cans on string tied between trees and covered in foliage to blend in. Once in a while, Dylan and Mia took it in turns to take watch all through the night. That had really caught Jake off guard the first time it happened. The two lovebirds were usually so keen to get their heads down. Although there were other reasons for that. Those nights weren't worth spying on. It only fuelled his rage to think of his brother with the girl he had fallen for. His half-brother, really. Jake had never really thought Dylan to be different from him in childhood, despite their contrasting skin colours. But recently, putting his brother in his true light, as the son of another man other than Jake's own father, helped immensely. It provided the separation he needed. No real brother could do what he did. No real brother would have tormented him so, not listening when Jake didn't want to attempt an escape from Frank's gang. A real brother would have listened to his sibling, would have made the decisions together. Not Dylan, though. No, he was only ever out for himself. His being with Mia now was proof enough of that.

Jake moved on from the camp. *They can't have gone far.* Having trailed them for three weeks now, he knew that they never headed in any direction with purpose. Despite their gradual move east, the pair had covered remarkably little ground in that time if one were to measure it in a straight line. Instead they spent their days gallivanting after each and every possible distraction. Jake knew Mia had never left her settlement. She had grown up in the Blackout knowing only one group of people, one patch of land. He figured she was therefore loving her little adventure with his older brother. Every day must be a new experience to her. Often he found them investigating the most mundane of pre-Blackout relics. Once he had seen them standing in a building, staring at the black box in the corner. Televisions, his mother had told him they were called when he had first stumbled upon one as a kid.

Presumably Mia had never seen the plastic and glass boxes before either. She and Dylan had stared at the thing for an age, Dylan waxing lyrical on the world that once was, as if he were some great orator. Jake had watched as Dylan gesticulated before the box, stepping in front of it and turning to face Mia, as if he were coming out of it. It was the same presentation their mother had once given them, explaining how the boxes used to have moving pictures of people within. He had been fascinated by the concept of sitting around and watching other people pretending to do other tasks, while not getting on with their own lives. When he'd asked how they had found the time to gather food, or prepare for winters, she had explained that back then, those were the most trivial of concerns to the populace, who were far more concerned by the moving pictures. Some kind of escape from their lives, apparently. A distraction to keep them occupied. Had they needed an escape from their lives, they surely had only to step outside and take in the world on their doorstep, Jake had suggested, but Claire had said it wasn't that simple. Everything about the old world seemed so complicated to him.

Knowing that Dylan and Mia were generally heading east, Jake picked up their trail soon enough. He found them walking on the main road once more, moving hand in hand without a care in the world as they cut through the countryside. There weren't many buildings in the area but Jake was still amazed by their brazenness. They moved forwards so boldly. Jake watched as his brother scanned the horizon from time to time with minimal concern. How could he be so arrogant? Even out here, with almost nobody around. There could be wolves, or traps, or scouts looking for unsuspecting prey. And yet his brother was only concerned with the girl holding his hand. It was like he was begging to be taught a lesson.

Jake followed in the long grass beside the road, choosing the more difficult route with more cover. If he stayed on the road, his brother had only to turn his head and Jake would be discovered. All his hard work would be lost in an instant. The weeks of trailing them as he built up the courage to do what needed to be done. The long nights spent listening to their conversations. The torturous days of hunger where Jake had to give up on a trap or a hunt because his brother had moved on and he couldn't let him out of his sight for too long. No, he was not about to waste all the effort he had put in to seek vengeance for his brother's betrayal. Besides, their final confrontation was getting nearer. He could feel it. Like an itch beneath his skin growing in its ferocity. He wanted to scratch at it. To feel the satisfying release of pent-up desire. A catharsis he longed for. *Soon. Perhaps even before the day is out.*

All morning he followed, keeping a half-mile or so behind. Far enough back that he could duck down into the grass if needed and not be seen, but not so far back that he couldn't see what they were up to. He wanted to know everything they did. The thought gnawed at him that his brother might be well aware of Jake's presence and Jake didn't want any surprises. If Dylan was going to round on him at any point, he wanted to be ready to take action. To do so, he needed to keep his brother close enough to know every little thing he did. And so he followed, bitterly resenting the way Dylan and Mia held hands.

He wanted to be angry at her, too. It was she, after all, who had chosen her brother over him. Even after Jake and Mia had spent time getting to know each other back in her settlement. After Frank had captured Jake and his brother.

He had met her first. He had gone round to her place for dinner one night. She had seemed into him. At the end of the date she'd even kissed him. He hadn't been wrong. And yet, once she met Dylan, her loyalties had changed. Jake knew why. His brother was physically more impressive than him. Dylan was taller than Jake by about a head. He had broader shoulders and an impressive physique. All that running around and leaping off waterfalls. His endless energy seemed to know no bounds. He was charming and fun-loving, too. It was part of what made Jake so drawn to his older brother. He had once liked how Dylan's reckless pursuit of fun pulled him out of his own shell. Jake had preferred a quieter life. He liked to work on his traps. To read books from the old world whenever he found them. But the one thing he didn't like to admit, even back then, was how much he had relied on his brother to provide a distraction from his solitude. Of course Mia would have gone for Dylan. Jake knew that by comparison, he was nothing more than a weedy, insecure mess.

And yet, he could not find it within himself to be as angry with Mia as he was with his brother. Perhaps it was a lifetime of envy manifesting itself in something more ugly. All his resentment now had a reason upon which to feed. His brother had wronged him. But it wasn't just about the girl. No, perhaps that was why he was less angry about her. It was about everything Dylan had done.

After they had been captured, Dylan had made all the decisions, getting them into more and more trouble with Frank and his gang despite Jake trying to take a more tactful approach. His brother was reckless, with no ability to play the long game. And when Jake had tried to prove to him that Frank wasn't so bad, that New Britain's settlement might actually provide them with a future, with food and friends and security, his brother had not listened. Dylan had dismissed Jake as nonchalantly as he had dismissed most of Jake's suggestions when they were kids. *You won't dismiss me today, brother. Today we finally have it out.*

Around midday, as the sun beat down, turning Dylan and Mia into water-like mirages up ahead, Jake watched as they turned off and headed in the direction of a rock formation to the left. They were stopping to rest and eat, it seemed. Jake found himself intrigued by the rock formation. It seemed unnatural. Clearly made by men in a time gone by. But the structure was unlike anything he'd ever come across. The stone pillars looked nothing like the brick houses from the old world which he'd spent his life ransacking for supplies. Moving in closer, as much to get a better view of the stones as to spy on his brother and Mia, Jake saw to his horror a group of people appear in the long grass. He was too far away, and each one of them carried weapons. There was nothing he could do but watch as his brother was surrounded.

3

Claire looked across her desk into the eyes of the town's latest arrivals as the sun coming through her office window warmed her back. They looked haggard and gaunt, starved and terrified. A mother clutched two young children to her waist, desperately trying to show strength where clearly she had none left. The attempt at bravery, even now, when she had lost everything, endeared her to Claire. The woman reminded her of herself and the recent ordeal she had been through to save her two sons after they had been captured by the local tyrant.

'Don't be afraid,' she said to the woman. 'I know how you feel.' The woman clutched her children closer. 'I can only imagine what you've been through. What brought you here?'

'We heard rumours that New Britain had been defeated; that Frank no longer ruled over this area. Is it true?' the woman said.

'It is,' Claire said. 'Frank is dead. The town is free now. You don't need to worry about New Britain ever again.'

'How can you be sure?'

'Because I was there when Frank was killed.'

'You killed him?'

'No, but I was beside the woman who did. He is gone. The rumours are true. Taunton is safe now, as is the whole surrounding area. We are open for trade. If you wish, you and your children are welcome to live here.'

'At what cost?'

'What do you mean?' Claire said.

The woman looked down at her feet. She seemed broken by whatever she had been through. All faith in the world a distant and shattered memory. 'Nobody does anything for free. Not before the Blackout and certainly not now.'

'You will find a way to contribute,' Claire said. 'But you'll have time to figure out how. I'm not going to force you to do anything you're incapable of. The town has only been free a matter of weeks. We're rebuilding. There are plenty of jobs to go round. The more hands we have, the sooner we can turn this place into something worth talking about.' Claire knelt down so that she was eye level with the two kids, their dust-covered faces stained with long streaks of black where tears had washed through the dirt. She thought of her own sons and what she had found herself capable of when saving them. Whatever this woman had done, she'd kept her kids alive. And that, in this world, was something. This family would be an asset to the town. Of that she had no doubt.

She pulled a couple of hard-boiled sweets from her back pocket. Chipo had found a pack on her last scouting mission and, knowing Claire's love of all things sweet, had given them to her. Claire handed one each to the little boy and his sister and watched as their eyes lit up when the sugar hit their tongues. 'Don't crunch them,' she said. 'Savour them.

Treats like these are so rare these days.' The two heads nodded furiously, beaming smiles now stretched across their faces as Claire stood once more to address their mother. 'It's safe here, I promise. We have people working on the fences. We have scouts out in the surrounding areas. This place will be something special soon enough. We've all suffered for too long. It's about time we rebuilt this world, before we've all entirely lost our humanity. You and your children are a part of that future now, if you want. Now go rest. We'll have time to discuss roles and responsibilities another time.'

'Thank you,' the woman said.

After she'd gone, Claire returned to her desk and sat down, placing her head in her hands. Seeing the mother holding her kids so tight had struck a nerve within. She wanted desperately to know where her two boys were. Dylan and his girlfriend, Mia, had been gone for three weeks now. She wondered how far they'd gone, what adventures they might be having. Wherever they were, she hoped they were safe. It had taken all her strength not to deny them their request to go out into the world. She knew that ultimately, she had no say in the matter. Regardless of how ridiculous it might seem to her that anybody would want to leave the safety of their community, the decision was theirs to make. Besides, they had grown up knowing only the world after the Blackout. They had not had the privileged childhood she had. They had never seen other countries or even other cities. Survival had been the only thing on her mind when she'd raised her boys. *At least they have each other. Dylan will be less reckless with Mia around. If it gets too dangerous out there, they know they can return.*

Jake was a different story, though. Claire had no idea where he was. No idea whether he was alive or not. The last time she'd seen him was when she had mounted an attack on a nearby school to rescue him from Frank's clutches, only to watch him disown her. She recalled the moment Chipo's crossbow bolt had almost killed her son as he stood there in the school tower, helpless in Frank's grip as the bolt killed Frank, taking them both over the ledge and out onto the roof below. Claire had run to the ledge, her heart in her throat, but the relief she'd felt at seeing her son alive had dissipated when she saw the hatred written upon his face. He'd taken the assault on Frank as one on himself. A betrayal of sorts, even though Frank was the one who had killed the boy's father and abducted him. Somehow the man had got his clutches into Jake. Had turned her sweet, impressionable son against his own family.

And now she had no idea whether her baby boy was alive or dead. Chipo's searches had been fruitless over the past few weeks. But Claire couldn't give up hope. No news was good news. It meant there was no dead body. It meant that he was out there somewhere, probably alone and scared. She could still save him. Could still piece her family back together. What was left of it, at least.

A knock at the door brought her back to reality. She pulled out a book and notepad from her desk before beckoning the guest in. Anything to look like she hadn't just been sat there fantasising over the impossible.

'Morning, Claire,' Billy said. The old man had his usual broad smile across his face. 'I wasn't disturbing, was I?'

'No, you're good, Billy. Just prepping the next class for the chapter I'm going to take them through.'

'You're not forcing Shakespeare on 'em, are you? I swear that bastard was the reason I never took up reading. Give 'em something exciting first.'

Claire closed her copy of *The Hobbit* so Billy could see the cover.

'Ah, a fine choice,' he said. 'Nothing like a dragon to set a child's imagination alight. It's a good thing you're doing, y'know, getting 'em all to read and write.'

'Yes, well, when we rebuild this world, we're going to rebuild the best parts of it.'

'Too right.'

'How's the fence coming?'

'Pretty good,' he said. 'Tatenda and his team brought back some more wire from their last trip spreading the news of our little liberation. Said there's more where it came from. We've extended the perimeter to include the old park now. Should be nice for the little ones to run around in. We're a long way from getting the fence around the golf course, but don't you worry, we'll have it secured soon enough.'

'Great to hear. Thanks, Billy.' One of the first things she'd asked Billy to do after they had liberated the town was expand the perimeter fencing beyond its initial placing along the town's high street. If they were going to turn the place into something worth living in, she wanted more than just a few old brick buildings and concrete to go on. She wanted open green spaces that could be tamed, unlike the wild overgrown world of outside. The park just off the town's centre was the first goal. Then the golf course beyond it. Billy's team had made good progress in the short time since the expansion had begun. It was fast becoming a town to be proud of and Claire had high hopes for its future.

As Claire was congratulating Billy on the success of his efforts, another knock came. Chipo popped her head round. 'Claire, can we talk?'

She sounded serious. Claire tried to quell the unease in

the pit of her stomach. *Please don't be bad news about Jake.* 'Sure thing, Chipo. Come on in. Please excuse us, Billy.'

'Of course.' He closed the door behind him, leaving Chipo standing across the desk from Claire.

'What is it?' Claire said, unsure of whether to stand or continue sitting. She knew that look on her friend's face.

'I think I found him,' Chipo said.

'What do you mean?'

'His trail.'

Claire hesitated to ask, knowing that to do so might break her world in two. 'Did you find—a body?'

'No.'

Thanking whomever or whatever it was that decided the fates of her children, Claire breathed out a heavy sigh. 'What did you find?'

'Just tracks.'

'How can you be sure they're Jake's?'

'A hunch,' Chipo said.

'That seems like a leap.'

'Call it an educated guess, then.'

'Where were the tracks leading?'

Chipo picked momentarily at a piece of grass buried in her dark, tightly-curled hair. She gestured for Claire to sit still, which Claire did reluctantly. 'The tracks were headed in the same direction that Dylan and Mia went in.'

Claire was glad not to be standing. Chipo's words knocked the strength out of her like a storm tearing a tree down. Her head began to spin. Jake was chasing after Dylan. There could only be one reason for that. He wanted revenge. 'How can you be sure?' she said.

Chipo sat in the chair across from Claire's desk. 'I followed the tracks for almost a day, just to be sure. It's him, Claire. I'm sure of it. When I first found them, the footprints were unevenly spread out, often with drags through the mud. Whoever they belong to was likely carrying an injury of sorts.'

'Like a hurt leg,' Claire said, thinking of how Jake had fallen from the school tower onto the roof of the main building below. The fall would not have been kind to his body. Likely he had limped for a few days after.

'Like a hurt leg, yes,' Chipo said. 'The longer I followed the tracks, the more regular the spacing got between the footprints. There was no blood. I think the person they belonged to was getting better as time passed. Now, I can't be sure about exact dates, but the tracks looked about as old as Dylan's and Mia's. Looked to me like the person following was within a day of them. I'm sorry, Claire. I think Jake's gone after his brother.'

4

Dylan pulled Mia behind him, shielding her from the men who had emerged from behind the stone pillars. The men looked feral, each one dirty, with torn clothes that had been badly repaired over the years. The cumbersome needlework was apparent, even beneath the dirt. Their weapons, however, looked well taken care of. The blond fella in front of Dylan was carrying a handmade machete. The simple blade had a makeshift handle of what Dylan figured was bits of torn inner tubing from a tyre, wrapped around the metal. Specks of dried blood could be seen on the flat of the blade. Dylan couldn't quite tell how old the man was. It was hard to see past the long, straw-like hair and bushy beard. The fear in the man's eyes he could decipher, though. He looked as skittish as a deer, like he didn't much want to be facing down a stranger. His three friends looked much the same. Every one of them was on edge, looking to each other for instruction.

Dylan decided to try his luck.

'Please,' he said. 'We mean you no harm. We were just passing through.'

'Weapons down,' the blond guy said.

Dylan couldn't think of a way to avoid doing as he was told. It was four against two. Not impossible odds. Had it been two against one, with just his life on the line, he might have risked it. But four on two, with one of those two being Mia, meant the choice was made. No way he was risking her life unnecessarily. He remembered the time his family had been attacked by New Britain in their forest dwelling. Frank's men had surrounded his family. Everything had seemed salvageable for a moment, and then Frank had killed Dylan's stepfather, Maxime. Right now, he didn't want a similar result. Better to acquiesce and see how everything played out. At least nobody was pointing a gun at them. If it came down to it and he changed his mind, his fists might do enough damage to allow them to escape. He looked back over his shoulder to Mia and nodded his head. Heard her place her bow on the ground as he looked back at the blond guy. 'My name's Dylan,' he said, placing his own bow on the ground. 'This is Mia. We didn't mean to trespass on your territory. Like I said, we're just passing through.'

'Passing through to where?'

Knowing that to say they were simply off to see the world might sound like a ridiculous fantasy, Dylan decided it was best to explain the other reason for their journey. 'We're spreading the word.'

'What word?'

'The good news,' Dylan said. 'New Britain has been defeated.' He let that point sink in for a moment. Saw the strangers' furrowed brows relax in surprise. One of them almost let slip a smile. In that moment he knew they weren't enemies. Likely this was just one of the many groups terrorised by Frank and his gang over the years.

'You best not be trying to trick us, kid. If we find out you're one of them, we'll skin you alive. I mean it.'

'We're not,' Dylan said. 'Frank attacked my family a while back. Even killed one of us. But we fought back. We took him down. His men, too. Now we're out here spreading the word that it's safe to enter what was his territory. Taunton is a safe town. You're free to trade there if you wish. My mother is running things there now.'

'Prove it.'

'Eh?'

The man stepped closer to Dylan. 'You don't think I'm taking you at your word, do you?'

Grateful for his mother's forethought, Dylan smiled his most submissive smile. 'I can. Look here—'

'Hold it,' the man said, pointing his knife at Dylan's chest as Dylan went to remove the rucksack from his shoulders.

'Sorry,' Dylan said. 'I was just ... It doesn't matter. You take a look. If you'll let me, I'll place my bag on the ground. Inside you'll find some hand-drawn maps.'

'What's so special about them?'

'Nothing, really,' Dylan said, 'but you'll understand when you see them. Can you read?' Instantly regretting the question, he held his hands up in surrender. 'Sorry, man. Look, it's a rare skill these days. Here.' Gesturing for Mia to step aside to allow him some space, Dylan removed his rucksack and placed it on the ground before taking a couple of steps back, his hands held up once more. 'Look inside, please.'

The man eyed Dylan for a moment. Seemed he was weighing something up in his mind. Trust didn't come too easy to these folks by the looks of it. Using his machete, the man lifted the flap open and peered inside.

'They'll be near the top,' Dylan said. 'Just pages torn from a book. They have black marker written all over them.'

The man found the pages and lifted them out. Dylan watched as he checked the pages, front and back, flipping each one to the back of the pile as he inspected the one below. 'Directions to Taunton,' he said, reading from the header Dylan had been instructed to write out a hundred times, 'the first truly free town. New Britain out. All now welcome. We look forward to meeting you, friend.' He looked up to Dylan once more. 'It's cute. You copy this down yourself?'

'A hundred times,' Dylan said, nodding. 'We've been handing them out as we've moved east. My mum hopes this is the beginning of something new. Something better.' Dylan felt the tension in the air ease. The man's posture relaxed, along with his crew's. The crudely copied maps he had drawn out on torn book pages had so far saved him and Mia three times already as they wandered through others' territories. Every group they had shown the maps to had been delighted to hear of New Britain's downfall. Prior to setting out on the journey, Dylan had been sceptical of Claire's great plan to unite the territories once more, but every time he handed someone one of these maps, he found their relief heartening. People really did need the community. Most people didn't want to fight anymore. He could see it in their eyes.

'Well, if that bastard Frank and the rest of his meatheads really are dead then that's a story I want to hear. Come on, kid. You've earned yourselves a dinner.' Folding one of the maps and placing it in his back pocket, the man put down his machete and proffered his hand to Dylan. 'Name's Harry. Them lot are Tom, Ed and Dafydd.'

'Dylan. And Mia. Pleased to meet you all,' Dylan said, breathing a sigh of relief at the sight of them all putting their weapons away. Harry led the way, with the others still surrounding Dylan and Mia, back to the main road where they walked east over a hill and down into a small village below, just off the main road and across a river. But for a few by the roadside, most of the buildings had long since fallen into disrepair. The roofs had been stripped for spares, leaving the walls overgrown with vines and covered in thick black mould. All the windows had long since been destroyed. Even in the few buildings still functional, the windows were now makeshift shutters composed of corrugated iron or wood. Harry took them to one of the bigger houses in good condition. Good was a stretch; in better condition than those in complete disrepair, perhaps. Its walls were covered in dirt, the shutters covering the windows were rusted, and the roof, though intact, was covered in moss, giving the whole building a green tinge.

Inside, Harry introduced them to his wife, Ellen. She looked older than Harry, her face creased with wrinkles that gave Dylan the impression she'd spent much of her life in a state of despair. She had a faraway look in her eyes which unsettled Dylan to his core. Thankfully, their arrival seemed to bring her back from whatever edge she'd been teetering over, and she set about preparing a pot of stew on her wood-burning Aga stove.

By the time they gathered around the candlelit table, the sun had plunged towards the horizon, leaving the sky a patchwork of pink and purple as Dylan stared out the shutters.

'So he's really gone?' Harry said, handing out some metal camping bowls.

Dylan nodded. 'He's really gone.'

'You hear that, Ellen? Frank finally met his end. I hope the bastard suffered.'

Given she was tending to the vegetable stew on the stove, Dylan couldn't read Ellen's reaction. If the tension in her shoulders was anything to go by, she didn't welcome the news. Something about Harry's delivery seemed off to Dylan. Like he was trying to walk a lit torch into a cave where all the air had been sucked out, taking the light with it. It was a feeble attempt. Like he'd expected the reaction. And yet, he'd tried all the same. 'You should see the town now,' Dylan said, trying to lighten the mood that seemed to be poisoning the room. 'My mother's really turning it around.'

'Like how?' Dafydd said, speaking up for the first time. Dafydd had a thick square head, covered in dark hair, and a badly kept beard. Although, it was a damned sight better kept than Harry's.

Nodding his thanks as Ellen slopped some stew into his bowl without looking him in the eye, Dylan turned to Dafydd and the others. 'Well, they're cleaning it up for one. They're also expanding the perimeter in preparation for a larger population. My mother wants to turn it into more than just a base for a small army. We've been gone a few weeks, so we can't be too sure how successful they've been, but when we left, they were looking to expand the wall around the nearby park. Somewhere safe for children to play and adults to watch. Then they were trying to move the local residents back off the high street to live in the buildings in the newly expanded area. That way the high street could be returned to its former glory as a place of trade. That's what she said, anyway.'

'What about supplies?' Tom said.

'Yeah,' Ed said. 'And weapons? And water? It's hard work

looking after a whole population, you know. Real fucking hard.' Ed shared a look with the others as Ellen wiped a tear away.

Dylan didn't feel comfortable asking. Whatever this group had been through, the scars still hurt. 'If there's anyone who can do it, it's my mother,' he said, trying to kill the black mood.

'And why would you want to leave all that?' Harry said.

Mia scraped her chair forward into the candlelight, her confidence apparently returned. 'Because I was tired of that town. It was the only place I'd ever known. Even with it changing hands, I wanted more. I wanted to see what the world had to offer beyond the gates.'

'The only thing on offer is a fucking shit-sandwich, like,' Dafydd said. 'You'd have been better off sticking to your tidy little town.'

'That can't be the only option,' Dylan said. 'I lived in a forest my whole life because my family was too afraid to go out into the world. We spent every waking moment living in fear of the next intruders. We set traps for them. We killed the ones who got past the traps. And even once we did, the next day only brought the paranoia back again. It was relentless. We never built a community. Never trusted anyone. That's no way to live.'

'That's the only way to live, I'm afraid,' Harry said. 'And even then, it might not be enough. The world is no longer a place for naive idealists.'

'That can't be it,' Mia said. 'I'm so tired of hearing people from the old world go on like this is the end. Some of us have only ever known this. It's all we have. We have to be allowed to dream. If our dreams die then so does our humanity. People have to be allowed to hope, to think of a future. To live like they're planning for one. Otherwise we're all just wasting our time, sitting around and waiting to die.'

'Excuse me,' Ellen said quietly. She got out of her chair and grabbed the stew off the stove. 'I need to feed the others before I go to bed.'

'I'm sorry if we offended her,' Dylan said to Harry after she'd left.

'Don't worry about it. She's still hurting. Your optimism just gave her a fright, that's all. What Frank did to us—well, I don't think I have the strength to repeat it. We're all trying to find our own ways to move on.'

'I'm sorry,' Dylan said. 'I'd hoped the news we brought would be some consolation.'

'It is, kid. It is. Just brought the old ghosts back, too, I guess. Anyway, you don't need to suffer our misery. We'll give you safe passage through our territory. How far are you going?'

'As far as we can,' Dylan said.

'Very well,' Harry said. 'Rest up. We'll get you going in the morning.'

5

Jake could barely believe his eyes. As he stood watching what he thought would be a slaughter amongst the stone pillars, he saw the group talking to his brother and Mia. *Talking!* Dylan and Mia had both dropped their weapons. But the usual violence that Jake expected from random encounters with strangers did not follow. It beggared belief. He couldn't understand why they hadn't been killed, or robbed and left to die. Instead, one of the group inspected Dylan's rucksack, pulling bits of paper out. The conversation went on for an age. All the while, Jake's temper worsened. Dylan was just out of reach, yet again. What was it about his big brother always getting the good luck? He got the physique, the confidence, the physical skills, the girls. Now he was making nice with complete strangers. *Prick.*

Eventually, the group moved off with Dylan and Mia in their ranks. On the upside, Jake had not had the chance to kill his brother taken from him. Unfortunately, he now had a larger group of people to contend with, all of whom had weapons of their own.

He settled in behind them, trailing far enough back that they wouldn't hear him, but close enough that if something happened, he could take action as needed. He was much closer than he had been in the last few weeks of following the pair. No way he was letting Dylan go this time. This group had sealed its own fate. They were in the way. Whatever happened next, they had it coming. This was simply the way of things.

After a while the group veered off the old motorway as it baked in the afternoon sun, and into a town beside a river. *Fucking towns.* There was no telling how big the population was. Could be that it consisted simply of the group who'd found his brother and Mia among the stone pillars. Could be there were fifty or more of them in there. Knowing he couldn't risk charging in, Jake remained on the outskirts, taking note of the building Dylan, Mia and the others entered. At a quick glance, he couldn't see many others walking around. Whatever this town's population, it was pretty small. There were no walls, no fences. Not even an outpost. *Amateurs.* Or maybe it didn't have a population. Perhaps the group was simply passing through. Jake had seen enough abandoned old settlements in his life. It was more common to find places from the old world unoccupied than otherwise. People naturally kept their distance from buildings. They might harbour other people, and that brought further risks, often violent in nature. His family had avoided buildings unless absolutely necessary. Even then, they only entered them to scavenge for supplies. Never to reside in. At least not for any length of time. But this lot had gone into a house. One of the ones in better condition. It even had a chimney with smoke gently billowing out. Somebody must have a fire going. Jake recalled the last time he'd seen a working fire inside a house. It had been on his first date with Mia. They had cooked dinner together. He spat on the ground, the distasteful memory unsettling him more than he cared to admit to himself. It was one thing to be angry. But hurt—that was just pathetic. Frank hadn't gone around acting hurt. He led with force. Strength was his only mantra. And so it had become Jake's.

Waiting until the sun began to go down, Jake took the time to scout the nearby area. He ate some blackberries from a nearby bush and cleaned his weapons. Then, as darkness set in, he moved closer to the edge of town. As the blanket of night swept over, the population of the small town became apparent. Flickers of light came from two buildings a few hundred yards apart, as well as from the one Dylan and the others had entered. Jake figured the two other buildings probably held smaller groups. Scouts or guards. Something of that sort. Prisoners tended to be taken to the main buildings within communities like this. At least, that's how it had been when he and Dylan had been captured by New Britain. Easy to keep an eye on, he guessed. Even if Dylan and Mia looked more like guests than prisoners, he figured the house they'd been taken to was indeed the main one.

Going straight for the biggest group might be foolish. Any screams would only bring the people from the two other buildings. *Best to take them out first. Or check them out, at least.* Once he had an understanding of the firepower of the residents, he could make an informed decision about an attack. If needed, he could wait them out. Dylan and Mia would be on the move eventually. It wasn't like he had anything else to do with his days.

Creeping round the edge of town, Jake kept to the tall

grass at its perimeter. Moving gently through it like a light breeze, he kept his eyes trained on the closest building with light emanating from its shutters. He stopped outside, creeping up to the nearest window shutter and sitting below it, listening intently for any telltale giveaways from within. There were three voices coming from inside. Sounded like relatively old folk. No youthful outbursts or high-pitched whispers. Just the gravelly bass of men sat around a table, playing at cards or something. Jake recalled the deck of cards his father had once brought home from a scavenging hunt. He'd taught Jake and Dylan various different games which kept them entertained for years, until the cards were lost in a rucksack when they'd been crossing a river.

He sneaked a peek up over the windowsill. The metal shutter blocked almost everything, but, through the makeshift hinge, Jake could see the silhouettes of the men sitting around a table with an oil lamp between them. On the backs of their chairs hung various guns: an AK-47, a shotgun, a rifle. On the table, beside the oil lamp, was a bottle of some kind of brown liquor. A rare find these days. Extremely rare. The only person Jake had known to consume alcohol with such reckless abandon was Frank, and he had been the leader of New Britain. All supplies had gone through him when brought into town. It made sense that he helped himself to any drink that got brought in. This lot, though. Their mood seemed a little darker. They weren't drinking because they were celebrating a recent find. To Jake, they seemed to be drinking to numb some pain. They way they talked, only discussing their hands as each new one got dealt, their heads bowed so as not to have to look one another in the eye. No conversation. This whole place creeped him out. The lack of fences or walls, the lacklustre security, the black mood of the people. They seemed to him a defeated people. He wondered if perhaps these were the last remnants of a bigger population. Their mood reminded him of his own in the days immediately after the death of his father. Like some demon lived there beneath the surface.

Given the dark mood of the trio and the presence of their weapons, Jake decided to check the other source of light out first. This lot he wanted to leave until the contents of that bottle of brown liquor had been significantly reduced. Its effect on their reactions would be a benefit to him.

Dropping down beneath the windowsill, he crouched on his haunches until he reached the next building, and then made his way to the other one with light coming out. Keeping his ears tuned to the sounds of the night, Jake looked for signs of others. There might well be one or two asleep who had not lit any fires. To miss them out would be a grave mistake. Checking a couple of buildings on the way, he found nothing. They were empty. Even the roofs had been stripped, leaving the buildings open to the moonlight above. There was no hope of chancing upon any supplies, he knew. These buildings had likely been cleared out years ago.

He moved to the other firelit building. Again he crept up to a windowsill, finding one with a rusted old shutter made from corrugated iron. Bits of the corners had rusted off completely, leaving the perfect peephole. Lifting his head tentatively up, Jake saw a man and woman sat reading books in front of a lit fireplace. Shadows danced about the room as the flames flickered. The two people were silent, fully engrossed in their books. Again, though, Jake saw weapons stashed beside their chairs. Two rifles. No booze in sight, either. These two would be alert and ready the second they heard a sound. In a flash, they could dispense with the books and reach for their weapons. There was no way he could get a clean shot of his bow through the shutter even if he wanted to. If he broke in, it would be two on one. The second a gun sounded, the rest of the people in the other two buildings would be alerted. A stealth attack was looking less and less favourable. He might have to wait them all out, until Dylan and Mia left the town. But that could be days. Already they'd spent significant time with some of the other groups they'd come across.

Deciding he would check the main building before giving up, Jake made his way back across town. An owl hooted nearby as he crept up to the building he'd seen his brother enter earlier. The noise coming from within sounded a little more lively. It was immediately clear to him that there were multiple people inside. At the very least, there must be the four people whom Dylan and Mia had come with, plus those two, of course. He heard the sound of a woman's voice, too. That made seven, at least. There wasn't a hope of getting through five others plus his brother and Mia. Even if he risked it all to go in and take Dylan out first, there was no guarantee he would be successful. He sat on the step outside the front door, listening to the conversation within. He heard his brother talk of how their mother was cleaning up their town, welcoming others from outside. *Of course she is. Always fucking saving the world.* As he listened, the conversation turned to the future. They talked of hopes and dreams. At least, Dylan and Mia did. The others seemed less convinced, from what he could tell. Deciding he'd heard enough, Jake stood up and turned to leave. There were simply too many people to take on. He could wait until Dylan and Mia left.

As he made to walk off, the door opened behind him, light cascading out into the night and then disappearing once more as it was shut again. He spun quickly to face his attacker, planting his blade in her throat before she'd had a chance to let out a gasp. Her eyes were frozen in fear as the life drained from her before she'd fully registered what had happened.

6

'Are you sure you want to do this?' Chipo said to Claire.

Claire didn't hesitate. 'I have to know.'

'We might not find him.'

'At least we'll have tried. It's better than sitting around here, wondering whether my boy is alive or not, waiting for you to come back with confirmation you've found his body.'

'Fair enough,' Chipo said. 'But you remember how we left things with Jake? Even if we do find him, he's more likely to want a fight than he is to want to come home.'

'I have to try,' Claire said. 'He's my boy. I have to stop him from doing something he regrets. I can still save him. I can still keep what's left of my family …' The thought trailed to an end. Claire wasn't sure how to finish the sentence. It was only in saying it that she questioned its very legitimacy. Had they ever truly been a family? The boys came from different fathers. She and Maxime were a consequence of circumstance, really. If Dylan's father, Matt, hadn't sacrificed himself to bring down the rogue artificial intelligence Adam

Tanatswa a couple of decades ago, she and Maxime might never have become an item.

No. She pushed the thought from her mind, cursing herself for her own insecurities. Of course they had been a family. Maxime was so much more than a happy coincidence. For twenty years he had been her everything. And now that he was gone, her boys were everything. Without them, what was she even trying to build? Her whole purpose had been to keep them alive. Recently, she had hoped to build a better world for them. One they deserved. One that could live on. Without them, her efforts to rebuild the town felt hollow. She'd had her head down on tasks for weeks, keeping herself completely preoccupied as she spent her days trying to convince herself she could live without them. And now, given the slightest hint at the possibility of going after them, she felt the old pull. The feeling was unlike anything she could describe. It didn't matter, though. She didn't need to describe it. Nobody needed to understand. All that mattered was that she got to them before one did anything to the other that couldn't be taken back. Somehow, she needed to keep what was left of her family intact.

'Okay,' said Chipo. 'We're going to have to move fast if we want to catch up with him.'

'We?' Claire said.

'You don't think I'm going to let you go alone, do you?'

Claire was at a loss for words. Chipo's unwavering loyalty had been the source of her strength for long enough. She hadn't wanted to think of what she'd do without her friend by her side. Luckily, as it turned out, she wouldn't have to. Lacking the ability to verbalise her gratitude, Claire embraced her friend.

'Come on,' Chipo said after an age. 'We need to make

sure the others know what they're to do until we get back. Then we need to stock up.'

'You think we'll be able to catch up to them?' Claire said.

'Well,' Chipo said, doing some mental arithmetic as she looked to the ceiling, 'they have a three-week head start on us, give or take a few days, so time is not on our side. That said, Dylan and Mia weren't exactly on a mission to get anywhere fast. They were tasked with speaking to everybody they came across and sharing the news of our liberation. Given that we've been receiving newcomers, I'd say they're doing a good job of that. Which means they're stopping a lot. Besides, they wanted to see the world. You remember what you were like at that age, walking hand in hand with some dreamy sod?'

'I do.'

'Exactly. I doubt they ever get more than a few feet without stopping to stare into each other's eyes. They probably took detours to go see sights. And for safety reasons, too. Then there's the sleeping and the hunting.'

'We're not going to sleep?' Claire said.

'Not like they do. We'll stock up on food. We still have some old canned goods lying around. My brother has been making some of his famous biltong from the last deer we caught. If we wake early, walk all day and night, then eat and rest up for a few hours, we can cover a lot of ground in a short space of time. After that we just rinse and repeat until we find them. We know Dylan and Mia are headed towards London. As long as we make a straight shot in that direction, we may be able to do it.'

Chipo's optimism lifted Claire's spirits. If her usually pragmatic friend thought they could do it, they just might actually manage it. Tatenda's jerky, or biltong, as he and Chipo called it, was surprisingly good. Chipo had once told

Claire that Tatenda liked to make it because it connected him to Africa. It gave him something of the past to hold onto. But that mattered little to Claire right now. The biltong would last days. That was the important factor. They would be able to live on it for a while if needed. Chipo was right about Dylan's movements, too. He and Mia likely hadn't been trying to cover too much ground each day. Theirs was a journey of discovery. Of fun and adventure. If Jake was indeed trailing them, he was likely moving at their pace, looking for tracks daily to figure out their trail. Either that or he'd already caught up with them.

Mentally quashing her fear, Claire smiled her bravest smile. 'Okay. If you actually think we can do it, I believe you.'

'Good.'

They went in search of the others. Finding Susie down by the river wall, critiquing the guards on duty, Claire called her back to the market house, which served as the town's centre. Chipo went off to find Billy and brought him back, too. Both sat in front of them in Claire's office as Claire and Chipo stood behind the desk.

'Everything all right?' Billy said.

'Yes,' Claire said. 'And no, I guess. Chipo thinks she might have found Jake.'

'Is he—'

'He's alive, we think. Although, if it is him, he seems to be going after Dylan and Mia.'

'I'm sorry, Claire.'

'Don't be. We'll get to them in time.'

'You're going after them?' Susie said, exasperated. 'They left weeks ago. You've no idea where they are now.'

'I have to try,' Claire said. 'I can't risk the boys hurting one another. This can still be stopped.'

'And who is going to keep this place running in your absence? You could be gone for months, assuming of course you live to even return.'

'That's why we called you both here. Billy—'

'I'm coming with you.'

'No, you're not,' Claire said, a smile creeping across her face as she took in the sincerity of his expression. 'You've put your life at risk on my behalf plenty already. But you can do me a favour.'

'Yeah, what's that?'

'Keep extending the perimeter. Keep building this town into something worthy of a future. Don't let anybody rest up. We know Dylan and Mia have been spreading word of our new beginning. Our numbers are growing. Knowing you're keeping at it while I'm out there will keep me going.'

'You'll return to a paradise, you have my word.'

'Thank you.' She turned to Susie, the woman who had been running a brothel before Claire had liberated the town. Susie had proved herself to be a formidable leader in the time since. She was a smart, shrewd woman whom Claire had come to greatly admire. 'There is nobody I'd rather leave in charge than you, Susie. I need you to look after this lot. Don't let on, but I've become rather fond of them all. Keep them safe.'

'I will.'

'And keep them occupied. Everybody needs a purpose. Just because things have been quiet for a few weeks doesn't mean it won't all turn to shit soon enough. Keep scouting for supplies. Keep everybody trained and fit.'

'Of course.'

'Thank you,' Claire said. 'We'll be back soon enough.'

'Good luck,' Susie said.

Claire didn't much like the pitiful smile on Susie's face,

like she expected this to be their final meeting. Shaking the shiver from her spine, Claire walked out with Chipo, leaving Susie and Billy to discuss their next steps. She didn't need to stick around for that. The town was theirs to run as they saw fit. She trusted them. The only thing she needed to do was ready herself for her own journey.

They found Tatenda in the butchery. It wasn't much. Certainly nothing like Claire had even known from her pre-Blackout days. But as far as a butchery could go in the current circumstances, she was quite proud of it. It was nothing more than a few kitchen tables kept for the dressing of flesh. Most animals arrived dead—hunted or caught in traps—so the space was used to prepare the cuts of meat to best feed the population.

As they entered, Tatenda was showing a couple of young kids how to cut fillets of meat from a recently killed deer into strips.

'Teaching them to make biltong?' Chipo said to her brother.

Tatenda looked up at them, his usual mischievous grin firmly in place. 'They must learn young.' Above him hung strips of drying meat on wire hooks.

'How much of that do you have in stock?' Claire said, pointing to the strips of biltong.

'Why do you ask?'

'We may need to take some on our journey.'

'You found Jake's trail?' he said, his excitement clear.

'We think so,' Claire said. 'We're heading out to confirm it. If it is him, we're going after him.'

Tatenda eyed the strips of meat, performing the mental arithmetic in just the way his sister had. 'For the three of us, if we stick to rations, and assuming the meat lasts out there, perhaps a week or so.'

'The three of us?' Claire said.

'You think I'm letting you or my sister out of my sight? No way. I'm coming with. Besides, you don't know what or who we're going to run into out there. Three of us will be better than two.'

'I can't ask you to take that risk.'

'I wasn't looking for your permission. Now come on, help me pack these away. There are some old bags we can wrap the meat in. It'll keep for longer that way.'

IT WAS ALMOST EVENING by the time they left town, having pulled together food, water and weapons. Claire didn't want to wait until the next day. If she was to have any hope of catching her boys in time, every second counted.

They walked late into the night, crossing over the old motorway and heading east towards London along the main road. It was slow going, even for progress on a road. A couple of decades of rain had created enough potholes to cause serious risk to one's life, or failing that, one's ankles, at the very least. Where the tarmac had cracked and split, grasses and plants grew up out of the gaps. Then there were the rusted remains of cars from the old world littered along the way. Moving in the dark, then, required close attention to be paid to the road. After almost snapping an ankle in her third pothole of the night, Claire wondered whether it might be safer to walk beside the road. Not wanting to slow things down by causing a fuss, she pushed on, ignoring Tatenda's proffered hand as she hopped around in frustrated agony on her one good foot. Now was not the time for sympathy. Neither was it the time to stop. She pushed on. It wasn't until Chipo and Tatenda both made firm repeated requests to stop for the night that she entertained the thought.

Chipo, proving herself once more to be one of the few people who could sway Claire, finally put it to her in a way that made sense. 'If we don't get a good sleep, we're only going to hamper our progress tomorrow. And if we do that, it'll likely have continued knock-on effects for every day. We could lose a lot of time by not being smart.'

'Okay,' Claire said, finally acknowledging her weariness. She ached from head to toe; her calves especially felt shot. Perhaps sleep was a good idea. She let Chipo guide her to a large tree twenty yards from the road. It was surrounded by blackberry bushes and tall grass. Any passers-by wouldn't know to look for them there, she figured. 'Let's get our heads down for a few hours. Who wants to take first watch?'

'I will,' Tatenda said. 'You two get some sleep. I'll wake you soon enough.'

All too soon Claire felt herself being nudged awake. She opened a weary eye to the grey light of dawn. A cool breeze rustled through the long grass. Summer was coming to an end. Soon it would be winter. Claire had no desire to spend the winter chasing after her sons. Winters had become increasingly harder to survive. In the first few years since the Blackout began, supplies were easier to come by. There was medicine to take and blankets to loot from old stores. But over the years, everything had disappeared. It had all been used up. Kids born since the Blackout had not been immunised against diseases, meaning that they were more susceptible to flu. They were more susceptible to everything. It was one of her biggest fears about living in a large population. She had not voiced these concerns to anyone back in town, but in truth, she was not looking forward to the winter ahead. One of the reasons she had wanted Billy to expand the town's base was so that she could encourage anybody who got sick to isolate. Any kind of virus or illness could sweep through town and destroy the population in days. In the blink of an eye, everything would be over. It was one of the many reasons she had brought the boys up in a forest dwelling, away from the dangers of other people. Away from their violence, their greed, their contagions. Isolation had been her safest method of ensuring their survival.

And right now she was back on the road heading towards London, a city with a once vast population. She wanted very much to ensure she caught up with her sons long before they got anywhere near London. While the city might be an exciting new location for them, it wasn't somewhere she wanted to return to. There was no telling what it looked like these days. Twenty years was an awfully long time in any life, let alone one in which the world had been brought to its knees. Having seen what became of the towns in the areas surrounding her old forest dwelling, Claire had no desire to see what London looked like now. In her mind it was still a bustling city, filled with the latest technology. She knew, of course, that this was no longer the case. She had been there when everything went to shit. The riots, the killings, the satellites crashing out of the sky—she'd seen it all. Whatever was left of the city, she had no desire to find out.

The city carried with it her ghosts, too. Ghosts she'd not really spoken about since. Memories came to mind of the Disconnected, the resistance group she'd joined when she realised something was very wrong with the company she'd worked for and the rogue artificial intelligence that had put humanity in danger. Matt's death came to mind. So too her memories of telling him she was pregnant. How he'd smiled when she told him. It pained her that Dylan had never met his father.

Urban environments were hard to survive in during the winters, too. The old buildings were mouldy, and there was not enough space to grow crops in the summer to prepare for scarcer times. And there was no telling what other violent people lived nearby. No, she had no desire to go back to London.

With that thought in mind, she packed up her things and set off with Tatenda and Chipo in tow. 'How far until we get to the site of Jake's tracks?'

'We should reach it by the end of the day,' Chipo said.

'And then we'll know.'

'Yes, and then we'll know.'

Not wanting to lose any time, they decided not to stop for lunch, choosing instead to eat as they walked. Tatenda handed each of them a strip of biltong from his rucksack. Claire had grown accustomed to his dried meats. The trick was to nibble at the strip until it came away and then tear off a piece in one long bite, going with the grain of the meat. Kind of like biting an envelope and tearing along its length to open it. The strip Tatenda had given her was roughly the length of her forearm and had been seasoned with a few herbs grown in town before being left to dry. It tasted like a mix between jerky, which she had tried on trips to America as a child, and prosciutto. Like a lean charcuterie. *What I'd give for a glass of wine and a charcuterie board now.* Savouring every bite, she felt her energy pick up.

As the sun began to descend, Chipo led them away from the road. They crested a hill and came to a stop in a thicket below.

'What are we looking for?' Claire said.

'You'll see in a sec. Jake camped here one night, I think.'

Claire looked around. It had been weeks since anybody

had set foot here. The grass had grown back over the depressions, making it almost impossible to decipher the footprints in the dirt. But underneath a tree she saw a small circle of stones with dirt in the middle. *Fireplace.* Whoever had made the fire had covered the coals with dirt, just as she had taught her boys to do. Beside the fire lay a makeshift bed of long grass cut to serve as a pillow. It was only big enough for one head, meaning it couldn't have been Dylan and Mia's campsite. She moved through the campsite, checking under bushes until she found what she was looking for. A makeshift trap. Every trapper had a telltale style, and her son Jake was one of the finest she'd ever come across. There were not many who could build such simple yet elegant designs. Yes, this was certainly Jake's work. He was still alive.

Her fleeting moment of joy was suppressed by the realisation that he was in fact heading after his brother. The two were headed for a collision. She needed to pick up the pace. This couldn't be the fate of her family. After twenty years of keeping them safe from others, the estranged brothers were now a danger to each other. *I can still stop this. I have to.* 'It's him,' she said, pointing to the trap. 'This is Jake's work.'

'Okay,' Tatenda said. 'Then we better get a move on.'

7

Jake watched the furore from a distance, behind the cover of a tree trunk. They were all standing in a huddle outside the house, the man with straw-like hair going off on one. He could still hear their voices. Although, to be fair, he probably still could have heard the shouting from another few hundred yards back. Clearly they were interrogating Dylan and Mia about the missing woman that Jake had stabbed the night before. None of them knew to check the river. It didn't matter anyway. Her body would be miles from here by now. At least, Jake hoped it was.

He hadn't known what to do at the time. Her presence had taken him completely by surprise. What happened next could only be considered instinct. How was he to know she'd be stepping out the house in the night while he was spying on the others? It was her fault, really. Her carelessness was now going to stay with him forever. All night he'd been unable to sleep, the image of her panicked eyes burned into his mind. The blood she'd spat up. The knife he'd had to clean. Dumping her in the river had been as much about trying to get her out of his mind as about getting rid of the evidence. If there was one thing he'd learned growing up in this world, it was that nothing good ever came from hanging around near a dead body.

But he couldn't leave. Couldn't run away. Not with his brother still here. If he lost sight of Dylan, he might not ever pick up his trail again. And then what would his purpose be?

He had only one mission: revenge.

Besides, maybe the woman was a test. A trial to check whether he had it in him to do what was necessary. Frank certainly would not have hesitated. As the leader of New Britain, Frank would have done whatever was necessary to maintain the advantage, no matter the cost. There was no line he wouldn't cross. To someone like Frank, killing an unsuspecting woman who had wandered unintentionally into his path would have been considered collateral damage. Her killing would not have warranted another moment of thought. Frank would simply have executed the deed and moved on.

Jake realised that perhaps he and Frank were not as alike as he'd hoped. Frank wouldn't have felt the sickening shame that he now did. There would have been no remorse. No need to justify the action. Surviving was justification enough for any action in the world. Jake's stomach swirled from within as anxiety got the better of him. Sweat broke out on his brow and blinding stars flashed in his vision as he clutched at his stomach. He could not decide whether he was going to be sick or pass out.

As it turned out, it was neither. But the torture continued. It was a good thing that Frank was no longer alive to witness Jake's turmoil. What would he have said? Would he have understood Jake's doubt? Called it natural? Would he have said that coming to terms with oneself as a killer was a road he himself was still on? Unlikely, Jake figured. Frank would most likely have slapped some sense into him. Told him to pull it together. To keep his focus on what needed doing, not get waylaid with unnecessary guilt over people who didn't matter. But then, would Frank have understood every struggle Jake faced? Like his internal battle against his familial ties. Jake knew he would not have dared to utter anything regarding the torment he was also going through over Dylan. In truth, talking about it would only seed more doubt. Not that he had any, he told himself. It was just that seeing Dylan and Mia walking through the countryside brought to mind the memories of his upbringing in a forest with his own family. Of the close bond he had had with them, each of them. At one time, they had been everything to him. Nothing else in the world mattered, besides them.

The effect of the memories was at odds with the tunnel vision he had applied in his pursuit of Dylan so far. Now it nagged at him. He wondered whether revenge would suffice. Whether, if he actually caught and killed the man he'd once called his brother, he would feel better about his family's betrayal. Whether it would provide any catharsis at all for the feelings of hurt at seeing them mount an attack against him. Or whether the killing would in fact exact an even worse pain. Like the loss he had felt when his father had been killed. His whole life was beginning to feel like an open wound that just would not heal. He could not conceive of a way to return to the happiness he had felt before Frank's arrival had turned his world upside down.

He was angry at them all, he realised. Including Frank. Frank, after all, had been the one who had attacked and killed his father. But that was not it. Jake had already struggled with that when Frank was still alive. Frank had explained the necessity of his actions. Of needing to maintain order within the region. Of showing no weakness, so that others would follow. Under Frank's stewardship, Jake had learned why the decision made sense.

Jake's anger at Frank, then, was something else. Frank had revealed the weakness in his family's survival strategy. Living out in the forest, away from other communities, had not given them the shelter they had thought. Frank's attack showed that their shelter was in fact non-existent. Ultimately, they had not been able to rely on a community. They had no group to back them up. Frank had shown Jake why New Britain's way was better. Safety in numbers. Frank had torn Jake from his quiet existence and then, in doing so, proved that Jake could never return to such a way of life. His way was the only way, whether or not Jake liked it. Admitting it to himself for the first time, Jake accepted that he hated Frank a little for that.

But he hated his family more. Dylan had not listened to him. Had not trusted him. Instead, the family had turned against him. For that, they could not be forgiven. Jake needed his vengeance. Nothing else would quell the storm of emotions battering him.

Jake slapped himself on the cheek. *Pull it together, man. Focus.*

He heard the straw-haired man say something about safe passage no longer being the case. Told them to get lost. It seemed Dylan and Mia were in the clear. The guards said that they'd have spotted them if they'd left the main house. Jake couldn't imagine how, though. He'd managed to sneak around all night unseen. The group seemed to accept that perhaps it was some outside force. Either the woman—Ellen, they called her—had wandered off and hurt herself, or some raider had come through and nabbed her while she was walking alone in the dark. Jake didn't like it that he now knew her name. It made everything more real. Now she was Ellen. Ellen clearly had all these people who loved her. She probably had passions and interests, too. *For fuck's sake, Ellen. Why did you have to step out into the night?*

The tension in the group eased as Jake watched on. Now that Dylan and Mia weren't suspects, the conversation turned from accusations to concern. The group were going to fan out and start a search for her. Dylan offered to stay and help. *Of course you would, Dylan.* Straw-man—Harry, if Jake had heard right—thanked him but declined. Said something about them needing to move on. If there was danger about, there was no need for him and Mia to get dragged in. Dylan protested, saying he wanted to help, but again Harry thanked him and declined. He said something about this being his own responsibility. He even said Ellen might come wandering back into town with a fresh catch any minute now. *Not a chance, mate. Sorry.*

That settled it. Dylan and Mia thanked the others, put their rucksacks on and accepted their weapons back before moving on. Still heading east by the looks of it. With the knowledge of his brother's direction confirmed, Jake started creeping away. He needed to get out of this little town before the others found him. No way he could just stroll through and go after Dylan. There were too many of the others. Best to give them all a wide berth. Moving as slowly as he could in his crouched position, he backed into the long grass.

The search took hours. Every single one of the bastards joined in. A couple climbed up onto the roof of a house and used binoculars to scan the horizon, forcing Jake to keep his head down. All the while knowing his brother was getting farther away from him again. There was nothing he could do, though. Every inch of ground was being checked.

Jake spent the day shuffling through the grass, only just avoiding the others. At one point, he thought he'd crawled himself into a trap he couldn't escape, but a strategic chuck of a stone when the guy had his head turned caused the oaf to go off in the other direction.

Jake waited until the cover of night before eventually slipping back to the main road and moving on.

IT WAS ALMOST a week before Jake caught up to Dylan and Mia again. Ellen's disappearance had seemingly stopped them from wanting to dawdle anymore. No longer were they pausing for long afternoons to swim in lakes or to make love beneath the shade of a tree. Based on the pace he was going at to stay on their trail, Jake figured they too must be walking late into the night and rising early every morning. By the time he had them fully in his sights again, London was only a few miles away, if the rusted old signs were anything to go by. HEATHROW AIRPORT, a sign read on the motorway upon which he walked. This Heathrow place was off the motorway, some distance presumably not too far from here. The rusted old sign had a bullet hole right where the distance marker should have been. Nevertheless, he'd seen Dylan and Mia take the off-ramp. Something they'd seen that they wanted to go take a look at, presumably. Either that or they'd seen something they wanted to distance themselves from. *Not me.* He was sure he'd stayed hidden. All day he'd been walking in the long grass at the motorway's edge, ensuring that they'd see nothing but the empty tarmac behind them if they turned around. And it wasn't like they'd known he was behind them the last few days. He'd been so far back that he'd wondered if he'd ever catch up. All week he'd followed their trail as it zigzagged east across the terrain, keeping their distance from sizable towns and settlements. Based on their trail, they'd stopped only once to hunt a deer, which they'd tracked a few miles away from the main road. They killed it in a clearing, stripping and cooking most of the animal and leaving the rest. Presumably they took only as much as they could carry, choosing mobility over full stomachs. Jake didn't care. It had saved him the need to find his own kill. The meat left on the animal had sustained him for the last three days. Only now, as he walked, did he hear his stomach grumble. Knowing there was nothing left, he ignored it. He had his brother in his sights again. That was more important than a meal. It was the only thing that mattered. Each day this ridiculous hunt continued, the more angry he got, resenting having to chase the prick across half the fucking country just to have his vengeance. *Never mind—when I have it, it will be sweet.*

He took the off-ramp he'd seen Dylan and Mia take, slaloming between the growing number of rusted mechanical carcasses littering the road. He had never seen so many cars before in his life. Big ones, small ones. Even machines that surely couldn't be called cars. They were much bigger. Some of the big ones even had cars strapped to them. *Machines carrying machines. What did humans do in the old world?* It seemed to him that with all the machines around, humans served relatively little purpose. He was beginning to understand what his mother had said of this life she'd lived before the Blackout.

Climbing the big one that carried the other cars, Jake scanned the horizon. In the distance he could see two silhouettes moving in the direction of this Heathrow Airport. Recalling his mother's stories of people flying like birds in machines that traversed the skies, Jake imagined as best he could some kind of metallic hawk cutting through the clouds above. Having never seen these fabled machines, even on the ground, Jake had a hard time imagining them. When he saw the metallic carcasses of the cars on the roads, he found it difficult to imagine them getting themselves up off the ground. Claire had said that these machines carried hundreds of people at a time. The sheer scale of it was beyond comprehension to Jake. He'd never laid eyes on a hundred people together on the ground. The closest he'd got was Frank's place, with all of New Britain in the town. But even then, it was nowhere near one hundred. The old world, despite all the evidence that lay strewn across the earth, was always inconceivable to him. And yet his discussions with Frank, before Dylan and his fucking ego destroyed everything, had given him hope of seeing something of this old world return. Frank had been dead set on rebuilding what he called an empire. Of training people to do certain functions, of getting some of the old machines going again. His talk had awakened something within Jake. An excitement. Anticipation of some great change. Yet it was not to be. Dylan's ridiculous insistence on escape had caused the battle that ended it all and showed Jake finally whose side his mother took when push came to shove. It had not been his own.

He spat on the ground, willing the thought away, and headed after his traitorous brother with his lip curled back in a snarl.

With all his focus trained on what he would do when he ran into his brother, Jake turned a corner and instantly regretted his negligence. Before him stood three men, each with a weapon in hand. One held a long pipe with barbed wire wrapped around it. Another held what Jake knew to be a cricket bat, stained rusty from contact with its many victims, no doubt, and the last held two small blades in his hands. He wore a sadistic grin. The ones with small weapons always did. Only someone having complete disregard for their own life would choose to use a weapon that required getting within a few inches of another, his mother had said. Although her weapon of choice had been a khukuri knife, so he'd always wondered whether it was more a self-critique than a commentary on others.

'Who are you?' Jake said in his bravest voice as his hands twitched by his side. They didn't have guns. At least, they weren't holding guns. Which meant that they'd either have to reach for them or go for him with what they had in hand. He, unfortunately, had nothing in his hands. Such had been his ridiculous pursuit of his brother that he'd forgotten the one rule of life in the Blackout: never, ever walk into a new territory without a weapon in hand. Often just the sight of a weapon was enough to defuse a situation. By being so reckless he'd robbed himself of the opportunity to make a safe getaway or, at the very least, defend himself. If he went for a weapon now, he'd probably be dead before he managed it. His rifle was over one shoulder. His bow over the other. The gun had a round in the chamber. It wasn't much comfort, though. No way he was slipping the thing off his shoulder, firing, and then making it far enough away to reload before the other two were on him. *What a fucking mess.*

It was with this thought that Jake's world went dark as something awfully hard connected with the back of his skull. He was out before he hit the tarmac.

8

Dylan pointed to the motorway exit. HEATHROW AIRPORT. 'Maybe we should get off this road here.'

'Why's that?' Mia said.

'Road's too big. Buildings up ahead. Anybody on lookout duty will spot us a mile off.'

'You don't think they'll spot us anyway on a smaller road?'

'Maybe, but then at least we might have more cover than on a road as wide as this. We can make a run for it if needed. I'd just feel safer is all.'

'Okay,' Mia said. 'Let's leave the road.'

With Dylan's arm around her shoulder as she leaned in, they walked down the road as one. He didn't want to tell her that his suspicion they were being followed was back. It had recurred a couple of days ago, eating away at him as they walked. He was as concerned by what or who might be behind them as by what they'd find in front. Then again, nobody had actually confronted them. And why the hell would somebody trail them across the country for weeks on end without attacking? The closest he'd got to having his suspicions confirmed was the incident with the people who'd given them shelter for the night back at Stonehenge. At first, Harry's crew had suspected him and Mia of being Ellen's killers, but thankfully Dylan had been able to dissuade them with the help of a couple of guards who insisted they'd have spotted him sneaking around at night. *They didn't spot the attacker, though.* Perhaps Ellen had just wandered off. For all he knew, she'd walked back into camp a few minutes after he and Mia had left. Something deep down in his gut told him this wasn't the case. *She didn't return. Someone got to her. Someone who might have been coming for me.*

He needed to be careful. His mother had told him that to be left alone with one's thoughts was often worse than any reality. She'd had a point. So often at night he'd get his head down, only to hear a sound in the far-off distance, and his mind would get to work thinking up every possible tragedy that might await him. A wolf that had crossed into his territory from up north. Their numbers had been growing his whole childhood. An attacker sneaking up to kill him and his family for supplies. A snake slithering through the undergrowth, seeking the warmth of a rock that might still retain heat from the day's sunshine. These possibilities came to him often before he'd had the chance to blink an eye. But his mother had told him that the mind always imagined something worse. To help him get over these concerns, she'd encouraged him to seek out the noises where possible. It served a dual purpose. If there really was something dangerous out there, then he could deal with it before it took him by surprise. And if there was nothing there, he could put his mind to rest once more. The trouble now was that he didn't want to backtrack for miles to confirm his suspicions. Besides, if someone really was tracking him and Mia for some reason, they'd be aware of his change of direction, meaning they'd just move out of the way if he did go looking, which wouldn't help his sanity one bit.

No, best to just keep going.

Besides, they needed to stay alert. His mother had said that London could be dangerous. It was a big city, she said. Bigger than anything he'd ever come across before. There was no way to explain its scale to him, apparently. Perhaps she was right. The towns had been getting bigger as they'd approached London. Because of this, they'd had to take a number of diversions to avoid any risks of running into more people. He didn't fancy dying in some decrepit hellhole without having managed to see much of the world. At least London was worth seeing. Books he'd read had often suggested there was some kind of aura about the city. Some kind of majesty. He wanted very much to see the places which he'd only imagined from the stories he'd read. Often he'd asked his mother to describe the places to him. When she spoke of the city, she too gave it some kind of reverence. He'd known for a long time that he'd wanted to visit it. Now it was so close he could almost taste it.

They turned off the motorway only to be met with another heading north. The M25, the barely legible signs called it. It was just as ridiculously big as the one they'd left, stretching ahead like a grey snake cutting through the wilderness. It was impossible to see anything through the trees on either side. The city was close, he knew, but how close he wasn't sure. And what he'd find, he was even less sure of. Before he'd left, Claire had guessed it would be one of two things. Either the city's great population had all died or fled the urban environment in search of more natural surroundings in which to grow food and hunt animals; or, and possibly the more likely by her estimation, there would be pockets of civilisation hiding out in various parts of the city, doing exactly as others did in the countryside: keeping their distance from one another except when raiding for supplies or trying to expand territories. It seemed plausible enough to Dylan. Why would these people, if there were any left, be any different to the ones where he'd grown up? Everybody was basically the same when you thought about it. They wanted shelter, food and safety. And preferably some loved ones to spend the time with.

'Did you hear that?' Mia said, spinning on her feet to look behind her.

Dylan turned to face the same direction. 'Hear what?' He lifted his bow off his shoulder and nocked an arrow, drawing the bowstring taut.

'In the trees,' Mia said.

'Which side?'

'I don't know. I heard something behind us. Over my right shoulder, I think.'

That meant their left now as they'd spun round. Dylan, using the arrowhead as his sights, surveyed the treeline. All he could see beneath the branches was a wall of black. What monsters lay hiding in the darkness, he did not know.

He waited.

Shimmers of heat rose up from the tarmac, causing his vision to blur ever so slightly. Wiping the sweat from his brow with his forearm as he held the arrow in place, he turned to the other side of the road, just to be safe. Nothing there, either. Perhaps Mia's mind was playing tricks on her just as his had been doing since they'd first left town. Then again, you never could be too sure.

Something didn't feel right. This time it wasn't just a case of wondering whether he was being followed. It was too quiet. Just like it was when he was on a hunt. The eerie calm before all hell broke loose. Whoever was out there, they were waiting to pounce. Pulling Mia behind him, he stood up, making sure nothing would hit her if weapons started flying. 'Show yourselves,' he said, tracing the undergrowth once more with his bow and arrow. He wondered whether he had time to reach for his gun. *Probably not.* Any kind of action like that would unsettle anybody watching. It would decide his fate. An arrow was something he could be talked out of pointing. Guns, though—they had a way of escalating tension unlike anything else. Itchy trigger fingers were like to cause mistakes. The kind that couldn't be taken back. Then again, sometimes they weren't mistakes, and being the only one still standing was vindication enough for the decision to pick up a gun.

Before he had a chance to go for it, a man stepped out from behind one of the trees. Then another on the other side of the road. *Shit.* They were everywhere. 'How many are there of you?'

'More than you can handle, mate,' the one on his left said. He was tall. Freakishly so. Like he'd been grabbed by the wrists and ankles by two different people who'd pulled until they had nothing left to pull. There wasn't much meat on him. Probably why he'd lasted so long, Dylan figured. What kind of animal would want to go for him? There was no reward. Same went for other people. Probably not a single other person could fit into this guy's clothes. There was nothing to gain by fighting him. That is, unless he was in the way. And right now, he was in Dylan's way.

'Not another step,' Dylan said. 'I'll still get a shot off before the rest of your boys take me out. You willing to risk that?'

'You got balls, man. I like that.' The man made a pretence of peering over Dylan's shoulder. 'Who's your friend? She wanna say hey?'

'She's fine where she is.'

'That's a whole lot of attitude for a guy with only one arrow ready.'

'I reload fast.'

'I bet you do, mate. I bet you do. Still, my boys are pretty quick, too.'

Dylan heard a light rustling as figures moved in the undergrowth on either side of the road. He counted another two on either side. That made six of them in total. The motorway was a big road, though. Very wide. Even with a gun, anybody taking a shot at him was just as likely to miss as they were to hit. Glancing back over his shoulder momentarily, he figured he was about ten paces or so from the remains of an old car. It wasn't much by way of defence but it might just be enough. Deciding he preferred everybody where they were—at a distance—he loosed his arrow at the tall guy.

It missed.

Didn't matter, though. The guy ducked out of the way, snarling something feral. Dylan pushed Mia ahead of him and they both dashed behind the rusted car. The others came running out of the trees at a sprint. Dylan loosed another arrow before ducking back down and facing Mia. 'You need to get out of here. Now.'

'I'm not leaving you.'

'Yes, you are. I can track you. I know your footprints. Leave clues for me. Cut small crosses into buildings.

Anything. Just go, now!' He shoved her in the direction of the treeline and turned to face the others once more. A gunshot boomed nearby as the bullet zinged off the car with a spark. Then another and another. Pretty soon it sounded like a rainstorm had descended on him as bullets collided with the vehicle. Dylan turned and faced the shooter. Took a deep breath and nocked another arrow. It let fly with a *whoosh*, striking the shooter in the arm and causing him to pirouette ungracefully to the ground in a wail of screams.

But that was all Dylan remembered. The blow to the skull caused everything to stop there.

WHEN HE AWOKE with a searing pain in his head, he was inside some weirdly shaped vehicle. Like a long metal tube with small windows. Outside the window nearest him he could see a long metal wing stretching out on the tarmac below. *Aeroplane.* This must be what his mother had been talking about all those years. Only this one didn't look like it was ready to do any flying. Inside, metal poles and barbed wire formed makeshift holding cells in which a number of people were sitting. Up ahead, the front of the aeroplane—if that was what this was—seemed to be missing, like it had been ripped clean off, exposing more tarmac below. He looked around for Mia but couldn't see her in any of the other cells. Hoping that was a good thing, he closed his eyes for a moment, offering a quiet plea to anything or anyone out there who might keep her safe until he found her.

Looking more closely at the other prisoners, he noticed a giant mountain of a man, far too big for his cell, with a gruff look about him and dark red hair streaked with silver. He had an even fiercer red and silver beard, and sat staring out at the front of the aeroplane as if he too was looking for some missing loved one.

Moving on from the man-mountain, Dylan looked over the other prisoners until his eyes came to a stop on a familiar face grinning back at him.

'Hello, brother,' Jake said.

9

'Do you think at any point we'll pass them and not know it?' Claire said as she, Chipo and Tatenda trudged along the road. They had covered a lot of ground in just a few days, hardly stopping for long enough to catch their breath. It had been a pretty straight shot across the countryside, sticking mostly to a couple of main roads heading east towards London. Knowing the direction both sons were headed, they'd decided not to spend too long trying to find tracks, hoping instead that by moving quickly they might catch up with the boys sooner.

Boys. How could she still think of them as boys? They'd been forced to grow up so much quicker than she had. Theirs was a cruel and unforgiving world. They were holding weapons almost as soon as they could walk, hunting animals and defending against trespassers on a daily basis. She had tried to preserve their childhoods as much as possible, ensuring they spent time playing and reading whichever books she found on her scavenging trips, but there was no denying it. They were capable of things that could not be attributed to boys. They were men. Good men, she thought. At least, she hoped they were still, somewhere deep down inside. No matter what had gone on when they'd been captured by New Britain. Whatever trauma they'd been put through that had resulted in the current animosity. Jake especially. Her baby. She hoped that whatever was causing him to hunt his older brother down hadn't become some core part of his being. If she could only catch up to him, she could bring him back. Remind him of the boy he'd been. The sweet, innocent child who'd followed his brother loyally, who'd struggled to come to terms with the cruelty of the world. He could still be saved.

'It's possible,' Chipo said, bringing Claire back from her thoughts, 'but I don't think so.'

'Agreed,' Tatenda said, pulling the last three strips of biltong from his rucksack and handing one to each of them. 'Eat up. After this, we're onto tins of food from a very long time ago. There's no telling whether what's inside is still edible or not.' He tore a strip from his own piece and savoured the taste for a moment. 'By my count, we've made twenty miles a day for the last three days, give or take a few. It's been good going, all things considered.'

'And you don't think we've overshot them?' Claire said. 'Dylan and Mia weren't trying to cover ground fast. They were just seeing the world. For all we know, they've changed direction and headed elsewhere.'

'Relax, Claire,' Tatenda said. 'They've been gone for weeks. Even if they were taking their sweet time, they're probably much farther on than here.'

'But what if they've changed direction? What if they had to run away from a group of bandits? What if something happened to them?'

'You can't think like that,' Chipo said. 'We know they were headed towards London, so that's the direction we go.

It's all we can do, so there's no point panicking about other possibilities. We'll find them soon enough, Claire. You have to believe it.'

'Okay,' Claire said, grateful she was not left alone with her own thoughts. Chipo and Tatenda were more than just extra hands to carry weapons; they were her source of strength right now. Without them she'd have been a ball of insecurity and paranoia.

Looking for something else upon which to focus her mind, she tucked into her biltong. Tatenda was right. There was no guarantee that the canned food had lasted for twenty years. They could well find it all inedible and have to resort to hunting. Although, she recalled reading stories of soldiers in wars eating canned foods from decades before and finding them to be more than satisfactory. She hoped this was the case for their supplies. Hunting would slow them down dramatically if they needed to leave the road.

As they walked along, a sight Claire had completely forgotten existed came into view. She came to a halt in the middle of the road, staring at the stone pillars to her left. 'I don't believe it. Is that—'

'Stonehenge,' Chipo said.

'I haven't seen it since I was a child,' Claire said. 'It's still standing.'

'It's in better nick than the rest of the world,' Tatenda said.

Claire looked across the field at the pillars, leaving the road to get a better view.

Chipo came after her. 'Claire, where are you going?'

'If my boys saw this, they'd have stopped to check it out. We might find some kind of detail or clue there.'

'Assuming nobody else has been there since,' Chipo

said. 'I don't like this. It looks like a good place for a trap. We could be walking into danger.'

'That's why I have you two with me. Keep watch.' She moved through the long grass, not taking her eyes off the pillars for one second. If anything was still standing in this world, she was glad it was them. She recalled visiting the site as a child, hearing the theories of how the monument had come to be. The debates over its purpose. Seeing it again now, she found herself in awe of humanity's capabilities once more. What people could achieve when they came together for a common cause. It had been what she was striving for since they'd liberated the town from New Britain's rule. To bring the people together once more. To create purpose. To inspire dreams and hope for the future. To move away from the descent into violence she'd witnessed over the last two decades. This was an example of what was possible. And here it was, still standing, defiant through it all.

A silence fell over the three of them as they walked up to the monument, admiring its majesty. It looked almost as Claire remembered from her childhood visit. The pillars were smaller than she remembered. Still huge, but not quite so awesome as when she had gazed up from a considerably lower height. The long wild grass all around took a bit off their height, too. When she had first visited the site, it had been well kept, with grass cut as short as on a sports pitch. Not so anymore, though. It made everything seem more natural. Like the stone circle really belonged now. Like it was part of the landscape, rather than an addition to it.

'Beautiful, isn't it?' came a male voice from behind her.

Claire turned to face its owner. He had long straw-like hair and an equally long beard. She could almost smell him from where he stood. He looked like he'd had a hard couple of days. Probably a hard couple of decades, if she was being realistic, but a hard couple of days in particular. His face was gaunt. Not the hungry kind. No, this was something worse. She knew that look well. She had carried it for days after Maxime, her love of twenty years, had been killed. The sunken bloodshot eyes hidden behind puffy cheeks. A far-off stare. Lips curled back as if ready to bite. This was a truly unhappy man. His three friends didn't look too friendly either, but this guy in particular—something wasn't quite right with him.

'It is,' she said eventually, not bothering to reach for a weapon. There was no point. The guy's friends had guns pointed at her, Chipo and Tatenda. Everything would end in the blink of an eye if she tried anything reckless. 'It's been a long time since I last saw it.'

'Still look the same?'

'Pretty much. The groundsman needs firing, though. Grass hasn't been trimmed in years.'

'I'll pass the feedback on.'

'Thanks.'

'What brings you all the way out here?' he said. 'You one of them New Britain lot?'

Tatenda tutted nearby. Claire stared daggers at him, willing him not to piss this guy off. 'I'm not,' she said. 'Neither are Tatenda and Chipo.'

'Nice names.'

'And I'm Claire, by the way. If we're dispensing with the formalities.'

'You didn't answer my question, Claire. What are you doing on my turf?'

'Looking for my sons,' she said. 'Well, one of them. I have a hunch the other one was trying to catch up to him, though. You haven't seen either of them, have you?'

'I've seen a lot of people. Normally from the end of my rifle. What did they look like?'

'Well, Dylan's a tall lad. Stocky, with broad shoulders—'

'Dylan?' one of this straw-haired man's mates said.

'Shut up, Dafydd,' Straw-man hissed.

'You seen him?' Claire said, her heart skipping a beat.

'Perhaps,' Straw-man said.

'Please, that's my son. He was travelling with a girl, Mia. They were headed east from our town. Chances are they passed this way.'

'That's them,' Dafydd said.

Ignoring his mate, Straw-man kept his gaze on Claire. 'Your town? That'd make you the one who brought New Britain down, if Dylan's stories are correct?'

'I had some help,' Claire said.

Straw-man smiled. 'Weapons down, boys,' he said, his tone becoming considerably more amicable. 'These here are friends, and they deserve a drink.'

'To the end of Frank's tyranny,' Straw-man said, holding up his steel mug. Harry, in fact, as he'd told Claire and the others while they walked from Stonehenge to his riverside village nearby. 'May he rot in hell forever.'

'I don't know about hell,' Claire said, 'but the prick managed to get himself impaled on a bunch of spikes after Chipo shot him through the head with her crossbow.'

'And rot he did,' Chipo added.

'Cheers to that,' Harry said.

They all raised their drinks. A collection of cups and mugs, mostly. Harry's collection of finery was about as good as anybody else's in the post-Blackout world, which was to say it had room for improvement, as Claire's mother would once have put it. The walk to Harry's village had not taken long. He and the others had kept the conversation to a relative minimum, explaining only that a young lad named Dylan and a young woman named Mia had passed through only a couple of nights before. Harry had promised the rest of the details at dinner, stating that the world had lost much of its civility in twenty years, and that he would do what he could to uphold the efforts of generations of progress. Claire did not argue. Something about him, perhaps the deep sense of loss, perhaps the civility, put her at ease. At least, a lot more so than when she'd first crossed his path. She did not get that feeling she often got when coming across others, where she felt like they might be waiting for an opportune moment to rob her or kill her. Whatever Harry's deal, it was not bloodlust. She accepted his hospitality with genuine appreciation, revelling in the opportunity to rest her weary legs for a few hours. If what Harry had said was true, Dylan and Mia weren't far off. She hadn't passed them, nor was she too far behind. His confirmation that they'd stayed with him only a couple of nights before meant that as of two days ago, at least, they were still alive. Wherever Jake was, he had not got to them just yet. *I still have a chance.*

Returning her attention to the group, she sipped her homemade ale. It tasted foul, but then, to be fair, it was no worse than much else she'd tasted of late. Even water took forever to purify these days, and unless it was pure rainwater, it still didn't taste quite right. In twenty years, no matter how much she had acclimated to this way of life, she had never forgotten what a cool glass of fresh tap water tasted like. How it quenched a parched throat. How the body zinged with life after a sip, almost drunk on its purity. Not so anymore. But this homemade ale was not all bad. Once the initial kick to the teeth was over, the aftertaste was almost pleasant.

'So,' Harry said, 'your son.'

'How did he look?' Claire said.

'Quite well.' Harry scratched at his beard for a moment. 'He was a nice chap, actually. Not too many of them going around these days. Mia was nice, too. You really think it's a good idea letting two kids as nice as them go gallivanting around this disaster of a world?'

Claire stared into her drink. Harry was right. Sort of. His reaction had been much like her own. But it was only right from the point of view of safety. It wasn't right to force people to stay in one place. It wasn't right to deny others the chance to dream, to go out and make something of their lives. Even in the world as it currently was, she had to let them be who they were.

'I struggled with it for a long time,' she said. 'Really struggled. Had they been given a perfect upbringing in the old world, I still would have struggled to see my child leave home. That's just the way of it. But with the world being what it is now, something could have taken them in the night from under my nose just as easily as something might happen to them out on the road. Could be a snake. Perhaps a wolf. Where we were, we'd had a few venturing south. Been running into them more and more over the last few years. It could also be something as simple and pathetic as a broken limb. Perhaps one day my boy slips in the mud and his ankle goes. And then I've never let him out for what? So that he can be taken by accident? No, I had to accept that nothing is a guarantee in this life. Safety is a fallacy. Something people strive for but truly have no control over. I accepted that my boys had their own lives to live. I didn't want to cage them like animals under any false pretence.'

'And now you're chasing after them—why?'

'Something happened in our town. My boys were taken from me.'

'New Britain?'

'Yes. Frank. He killed my partner, took the boys and left me to die. By the time I went to save them, Frank had turned one of them. Not Dylan; the younger one, Jake. He indoctrinated him into his ways. Somehow, he made Jake believe that his mission was righteous, that Jake's own family was against that, and therefore, against him.'

'I'm sorry to hear that,' Harry said. 'Frank has a lot to answer for.'

'Had,' Claire said. 'He *had* a lot to answer for. He's gone now and he's not coming back. But the ramifications of his actions live on. Dylan and Mia don't know it, but Jake is on a mission to take them out. We've been following his tracks as best we can. He's been heading this way, not far behind them.'

'This Jake,' Harry said, a look passing between him and his own men, 'he dangerous?'

'He's a boy.'

'He strong enough to hold a weapon?'

'Of course.'

'Then maybe he's dangerous.'

'Why do you ask?' Claire said, not quite liking Harry's tone.

'Because the night Dylan and Mia stayed here was also the night my wife Ellen was killed. We think, anyway. It was the night she went missing, at least. Could have been the following morning that it actually happened. We found her body downstream a little later the next day.'

Oh, no. Fighting the sickening sensation she felt in the pit of her stomach, she shook her head. 'Not Jake. Not my

Jake. He would never kill someone in cold blood. To protect himself, maybe, but—'

'The world brings out the worst in all of us,' Harry said. 'For your family's sake, I hope you're right. Somebody killed my Ellen, though.'

Harry's face looked to Claire like that of someone who was holding their breath for too long. His cheeks were puffed out, a vein in his forehead pulsating as he tried unsuccessfully to keep his composure. 'I'm so sorry,' she said, knowing it was of no comfort. She wanted desperately to move on as quickly as she could. The tension in the room had increased like a thick fog rolling in, clogging up the tranquillity. Tatenda and Chipo sat rigidly nearby as everybody in the room said with their eyes what they were too cautious to say out loud.

Harry finished his drink and let out a long sigh. 'It's probably for the best. At least now Ellen can be with our own kids. Frank took them from us when we wouldn't hand them over to him. Carrying on without them was too painful for her anyway. You go find your kids, Claire. I hope you never have to experience what Ellen and I did.'

'Thank you,' Claire said. 'For everything.'

She, Tatenda and Chipo decided it would be best if they didn't wait until morning. For Tatenda and Chipo, it was simply a desire not to outstay their welcome. For Claire, though, it was a feeling she could not shake. Time was running out. They thanked Harry and his people and left in the night.

10

'Jake!' Dylan realised he'd spoken too loudly, disturbing the other prisoners in the fuselage-cum-prison. Shaking off his light-headedness, he looked at his brother opposite him. Jake was gaunt. His toffee-coloured skin had a lifeless grey sheen to it. His hair was a mess, with bits of grass and small twigs caught up in the disaster, making it look more like a bird's nest than anything. But worst of all were his eyes. They looked lifeless. Like the fire behind them had been put out. Some spark in Jake had died and it made Dylan feel very queasy. 'You're alive.'

'No thanks to you.'

Dylan thought back to their standoff, when their mother had come to save them. Jake had shot him, leaving him gasping for his life. That had been the last Dylan had known of the battle. Had Mia not saved his life with her usual quick thinking and medical prowess, he likely wouldn't have survived. It had been a long while before he'd found out that his brother had fled after falling from a tower and had not been seen since.

It all made sense to Dylan now. The nasty sensation of being followed had been justified. There really had been someone after him. At least, it seemed that way. Although, if that was the case, how had Jake beaten him here? 'It was you, wasn't it?' he said. 'Following Mia and me from Taunton.'

'You didn't think I'd let you get away with it, did you?'

Dylan's queasiness got worse, bringing on a headache as he struggled to wrap his mind around his brother's words. Something about the person in the cell opposite him didn't feel right. It wasn't the companion he'd grown up with. Not the guy he'd built traps with, jumped off waterfalls with or hunted with. This was something else. 'Get away with what, exactly?'

'Everything.' Jake's teeth flashed like a wolf's in the low light. His voice a low growl, etched with fury, ready to snap. 'I told you Frank was onto something. He showed us another way to live. A life without the need to hide like scared deer in a forest, always quaking at the sound of any other forms of life passing by. But you couldn't fucking listen, could you? No, not Dylan, the great and precious one—'

'If anyone was the precious one—'

'See! There you go again. Always just having it your own way. Never listening to me. Never listening to anybody else. Does that ego allow anything besides your own voice to get through those ears? Or is it that you're too fucking stupid to comprehend a single thought that isn't your own perceived genius—'

'If you two muckers don't stop your blasted nattering, you'll have us all in the doghouse, and then it'll be me yeh answer to.'

Dylan turned to see the owner of the gruff voice. It was

the burly man-mountain. His eyes were buried behind his big, bushy red and silver hair and even bushier beard, but their intensity still sent a shiver down Dylan's spine. He didn't look like the kind of guy who liked repeating himself, even if his jovial accent was at odds with the severity of his words. The accent was familiar. Definitely from Dylan's part of the world. This guy wasn't from this part of town. At least, not originally. Putting on his best please-don't-eat-me-big-monster-man look, Dylan bowed his head. 'Sorry.'

'That's better, innit?' The man-mountain's accent was such that most of his Ts appeared to have been lost somewhere, along with any personal grooming kit, so that it came out, 'Thass be- er, innit.' His Rs, too, were more pronounced.

The cell he'd been put in was much too small for a man of his stature and Dylan found himself wondering how many people it had taken to bring the man-mountain down. More than a few, he guessed.

A loud bang on the fuselage warned Dylan that his captors were entering. The door opened and a man Dylan had not seen before entered. How big was this crew if none of the ones from the road were needed for general security? It was his experience that any population sizable enough for people to be assigned specific roles was a formidable one. It had once been Jake's argument to Dylan as to why they should give up on their secluded forest way of life and accept the strength and safety that came with being a part of New Britain.

Dylan assessed the man. He was big. Not as big as the man-mountain, but a lot bigger than Dylan. The guy's frame had that thick sturdiness to it, whereby it was apparent that despite a lack of cosmetic physicality, what lay beneath was pure brute strength. A real thug, as his mother would have put it. The thug was bald, with pale skin, reminding Dylan of a freshly washed potato, dotted with beady eyes and a sinister frown.

'Ah, another fresh recruit,' the thug said, looking at Dylan. He levelled the pistol in his hand and flashed an unsettling smile. 'You can call me Joe. And you are?'

'Dylan.'

'Right, Dylan, the rules here are simple. You'll do exactly as I say when I say or it'll be the last thing you do. Any questions?'

'No.'

'I like you already, kid.' As he walked into the fuselage, all the other prisoners moved to the back of their makeshift cells. Dylan took the hint. 'There's a good lad,' Joe said. He proceeded to unlock each cell and then led the prisoners out onto the tarmac below.

It took Dylan a moment for his eyes to adjust. 'Woah,' he said, looking at the remains of hundreds of aeroplanes scattered across the runway. It was hard to imagine all these huge metal frames being up in the air. Harder than imagining the things his mother had called cars moving along the roads. Surely these machines were impossible to get off the ground? Looking towards the big building in front of him, presumably the Heathrow airport that the road signs had alluded to, he saw that most of it had been severely damaged in a fire. Fairly recently, by the look of it. On one wall was a large spray-painted logo which looked like a cross between the planes on the ground and some kind of bird. SILVER EAGLES, the text below read. Much of the glass exterior had been smashed and what remained was blackened from smoke. Peering inside, Dylan could only see black. He'd come across many old homes before that had been burned, but he'd never seen anything on this scale before. The fire must have been huge. Circling the building and much of the landing strip was a makeshift fence, much like the one back home, made from steel poles, corrugated iron, wire and anything else that had been salvaged from nearby. Dylan figured trust issues were the same the world over.

'Now,' Joe said, 'I know you weren't a part of the bastard crew that attacked our base but you'll help clean up the mess, just like the rest of them.'

Dylan looked around at the man-mountain and the others, understanding a little of what had transpired here. This was a turf war, much like he'd witnessed back home. Presumably the man-mountain's faction had attempted to bring Joe's lot down and had been captured in the process. He understood now why the fuselage had been turned into a makeshift prison. There was nowhere in the building itself to house anybody. The structure looked like it might come crumbling down at any moment.

Dylan counted another five guards all around the group, each holding a weapon. Jake was no more than a few feet from him and Dylan realised that the guards might actually be a good thing right now. His brother's mind wasn't in the right place.

'Get to work,' Joe said, pointing towards the terminal in front of them.

Dylan followed the man-mountain, checking over his shoulder to see where Jake was, his mind racing all the while. He needed a weapon to defend himself, not necessarily from the guards but from his little brother who seemed hell-bent on some kind of revenge for what he perceived as Dylan's betrayal. He figured it had a lot to do with Frank and New Britain but probably a fair bit to do with Mia, too. He hoped that wherever she was, she was safe.

Following the other prisoners into the building, Dylan saw that the task was simple enough: clean-up. As penance for their transgressions, the prisoners who had been a part of the attack were charged with gutting the building of rubble, presumably to make it liveable again, although Dylan had his doubts about the prospects of that happening.

'Here,' the man-mountain said to Dylan, pointing to a pile of rubble. 'Help me start clearing this away.'

'Sure.'

'Name's Martin,' he said. Although, it came out as 'Mar'in.' 'Nice teh meet yeh.'

'Likewise, I guess.' They set to work as the guards watched over them. Martin's size and strength allowed him to pick up the heavier bits of rubble, which Dylan, as the next most physically capable of the prisoners, helped carry out of the old terminal onto the runway outside, whereby it would be sorted by the guards.

'What's with you and the other fella?' Martin said.

'He's my brother,' Dylan said, and then, noticing Martin's confusion, added, 'My half-brother. Different fathers.'

'Ah, that'll do it. Thought maybe you just didn't like the sun so much. What's got him so worked up about you?'

'A few things,' Dylan said. 'We were attacked a while back. Taken to a camp a lot like this one. I kept trying to break out. He ended up making nice with the leader and eventually wanted to stay. I guess that's where it started.'

'If you wanted different things, why not just go your separate ways?'

'There's a girl, too.'

Martin smiled. 'The world never changes much, does it?'

'If you say so.'

'Sounds like you two need to work it out before somebody gets hurt.'

'That's the thing,' Dylan said. 'I thought maybe he was dead. After he shot me—'

'He shot you?'

'Right here,' Dylan said, tapping the top of his chest near the shoulder. 'There was a big battle to liberate the town. The leader was killed and Jake went missing. I figured he might have died. Succumbed to an injury or something, you know?' Martin nodded. 'Anyway, I guess maybe he's been tracking me. Except he got here before me.'

'He was only brought in yesterday,' Martin said. 'Probably he was caught not far from where you were. He's been pretty quiet since he came in. Been in a mood ever since he was put in his cell. Bit of a temper on that one, if you ask me.'

Dylan laughed. It felt good to let off a little steam. This Martin guy seemed all right in his book.

As he bent down to pick up another piece of rubble, something whooshed over him where his head had been only a second ago. The object, a brick, hit the wall and cracked into pieces, releasing a small cloud of dust in the process. Then the yelling started.

Dylan turned just in time to register Jake's attack but, too slow to react, felt a crunch in his stomach as Jake tackled him. He slammed into Dylan with his shoulder, lifting him up off his feet, and speared him into the ground with a crunch that knocked the air out of him. It was all Dylan could do to lift his arms in a cross above his face to defend himself from the blows that followed.

'You ruined everything!' Jake screamed, delivering blow after blow to Dylan's head.

Dylan kept his arms up, desperately trying to shield

himself while he thought of a way to counter, but he realised he'd lost the fight the minute he'd been tackled. Every blow hit hard, surprising and scaring Dylan in equal measure. Jake was out for blood. One of his blows connected rather too well, bouncing the back of Dylan's skull off the ground. Everything went black after that.

When he came to, they were back in their cells in the fuselage of the old aeroplane. He groaned as his eyes struggled to open. It felt like they were being weighed down with rocks. Touching the back of his skull, Dylan reckoned it must be no better than a cracked egg, but thankfully, everything seemed in place.

'You're awake,' Martin said from the cell beside him. 'How do you feel?'

'Like my head just got caved in.'

'They were some hard blows, mind. Took me and three others to get Jake off of you.'

Dylan looked around for his brother. Jake sat sullen in the cell opposite him. 'Jake, I'm sorry. For everything. But whatever this is, we can sort it out later. Right now there's something more important and I need your help.' His brother didn't react. 'Mia's out there. I don't know where she is. You know this is the first time she's left home. She's probably terrified. We need to get out of here and go find her.'

'Why the hell would I want to help?' Jake said, his voice dripping with venom.

'Because,' Dylan said, 'whatever your issues with me, I know you don't want to see her hurt.'

Jake looked away for a moment. When his gaze returned, it looked to Dylan like his eyes were a little more watery than before. 'Have you noticed the cells we're in? Or the guards out there with weapons? This is exactly why I wanted us to be a part of New Britain. See what's out here? Nothing but fucking evil. Just people trying to kill each other. And here we are, trapped again. I fucking said that living in small numbers was a hopeless existence. You never listen. And now you've put someone else in danger. Nice one, man. Real fucking smooth, as ever.'

'If you two will give it a rest, maybe I can be of assistance,' Martin said.

Realising that it wasn't just him and his brother, Dylan turned to Martin. 'What do you mean?'

'You don't think I plan on staying here, too, do yeh?'

'I guess not.'

'Exactly. My people, we live in the city. If we can escape this shithole and get back to them, maybe I can help you find this Mia.'

'You'd do that?'

'You help us all break out of here and you have a deal, provided you two can keep yourselves from killing one another until then. I got no time for hot-headed young fools. The Silver Eagles are a vicious lot. And they ain't the only gang in London. This here's a city full of violent folks. Nasty factions in every direction you look. That Mia girl is bound to run into trouble sooner or later if you don't do something about it. Trust me, I've lost enough people over the years. We need to break out of this place before they end us all.'

Dylan tried to gauge his sincerity. They had hardly said more than a few words to each other, but to his credit, Martin had apparently stepped in to pull Jake off him. Not that Dylan was able to recall a single thing after his head got bounced off the ground like a freshly caught fish being put out of its misery. Still, Martin seemed like a nice enough bloke. There was something almost peaceful behind that rough exterior. And judging by the state of the other prisoners, Dylan figured Martin saw him as his best shot at overpowering a few of the other guards. It wasn't like Dylan had any other options. His brother had tried to kill him; there were guards aplenty, waiting to inflict further injury upon him; and somewhere, Mia was probably all alone. He needed to get back to her.

'Okay, you have my attention.' he said. 'How do you think we're going to break out of here? There's nothing but tarmac between here and the fence. We'd be shot to shit before we even get over it.'

'We're not going over the fence,' Martin said, his beard pulling back as a devilish grin flashed across his face.

11

Jake tried to put everything to the back of his mind as he worked. It was proving hard to do, though. Gutting the building of its rubble was a slow and thankless task. Every prisoner put in as little effort as they could get away with without being beaten by the guards. There was no need to work themselves to the bone willingly. The guards snapped on occasion, whenever their tempers were tested. Then the bats came out. Those and anything else that could inflict pain. Sometimes it was just fists. But then the work inevitably returned to its arduous pace and everybody ignored one another again.

This left Jake with nothing but his own thoughts to torment him. And torment him they did. Was there ever a prison so cruel as one's own mind? Having been a prisoner within two different factions now, he did not think so. No punishment inflicted was equal to what his own mind continued to put him through. The relentless rage, driving him to levels of madness in which his hatred of the world and those who had wronged him became a blinding force within, burning white-hot, followed only by crippling self-doubt and confusion that left him feeling hollow and unsure of everything. He simply could not get his mind to stop and leave him in peace. Not for a second.

The memory of having killed that woman, Ellen, still haunted him. The image of her eyes as he plunged the blade into her neck. She'd been as surprised as she had been terrified. As had he, if he was being honest. No matter what he'd told himself about it having been justified—about her being collateral damage, as Frank would have put it—it just didn't sit right with him. He had done something unforgivable. Against his nature. Something those who knew him would be ashamed to learn of. It was not how his parents had raised him. His father would have been appalled to find out that he'd killed somebody in cold blood. His mother, too. Despite the animosity he felt towards the surviving members of his family, he was ashamed to think of his mother and brother ever knowing of what he had done. The sheer cowardice of the attack. How he'd dumped her body in the river and hoped it would float downstream, never to bother his thoughts again.

How wrong he'd been about that.

Every moment since the slaying—there was no other word for it, if he truly thought about it—her image had been imprinted upon his mind. A part of him wanted to return and beg for forgiveness from those who had lost one of their own. They had lost a friend, a loved one, a companion through life. They alone knew the pain he had suffered at his own father's loss. Not that he wanted them to empathise. He was simply distraught over the idea that he was now a man who could kill and move on as if it were as mundane an action as hunting for food.

Nevertheless, he had not gone back. He had not apologised, to anyone. And so the image of her was there as he went about his business in the day, and it was there when he tried to close his eyes at night, haunting him every moment of every day until his mind went blank, incapable of handling the pain yet incapable of thinking about anything else. He almost wished he could take it all back.

Almost.

Then there was the matter of his having attacked Dylan. All things considered, how could he not have done? After what Dylan had done to turn against him, to take the girl he liked and disappear, he had it coming. It was simply the way of the world. Jake was perfectly entitled to exact his revenge. And now that they'd both been caught by the same faction, there was no telling if Jake would ever get another chance. They might not make it out of this prison alive. And if they did, Dylan might well disappear before Jake could do anything about it. Dylan had to pay for his betrayal somehow. Jake was only doing what was right.

Why, then, did he feel so upset? Again, he thought of how his parents might have reacted to such a sight. They would have been dismayed. Seeing the two brothers go at it would have been too troubling for them to even punish anyone. There wouldn't have been any verbal chastisement. No anger or physical outbursts from either of them. It would have been an action so upsetting to both his mother and father as to provoke the use of the single most cutting word a parent could utter to a child, at least in his experience: *disappointed*.

Regardless of all that he could and should rightly be angry at his family for, he just could not shake this feeling of guilt. Of shame. It gnawed at him like maggots preying upon a corpse. His actions were causing him to lose his understanding of who he was. Of what he stood for. It was all becoming so confusing, and he had a sneaking suspicion that he was beginning to dislike the person he was becoming. The ways he had learned to act from Frank were at odds with how he felt after such actions. He wondered whether perhaps Frank's preaching was really working for him. Whether that brute force approach, in which there was always an enemy to pit yourself against, was actually right for him. Just that fact that he was suffering such doubt would be an embarrassment to someone like Frank.

''Ere, mate, give us a hand, will ya?'

Jake turned to see Martin beside him, attempting to pick up some steel cabling lying in a pile of rubble. Grateful for the distraction, Jake grabbed one end of the cabling and lifted it out of the rubble on Martin's count. They dumped it in a trolley.

'What's with the black mood, kid?'

'Eh?'

'You got the kinda look people normally find at the bottom of a bottle, and there aren't many of those going around these days, so what's eating at you? Something to do with the theatrics between you and your brother?'

'That's a private matter.'

'Not if we're breaking out together, mate,' Martin whispered. 'Not a bloody chance in hell. Besides, it might do you good to get it off yer chest. Now, out with it.'

It couldn't be any worse than tormenting himself internally, Jake figured. But how could he trust this guy? And was the big oaf genuine about the breakout? Probably, considering the predicament they were all in together. Then again, that didn't mean he had to reveal all. 'How much time have you got?'

'If we stay captive in here, probably not much. And the way you went after your brother, I'm not sure either of you has much time left if you don't sort things out between you.

The Silver Eagles haven't let a single one of us avoid manual labour since we've been their prisoners, yet today your brother gets to stay in his cell. That's how hard you got him. Your man can barely stand right now. I've got to give it to you, kid, I haven't seen that kind of bloodlust from a lad of your stature in a long while. Your brother must have really pissed you off.'

'He did.'

Martin picked up a smaller piece of steel cabling and put it in the trolley with the rest. 'I've been angry, too, mate. Angry at the world. Angry at the people within it. Angry at myself.'

Jake, trying to appear indifferent, dug around the rubble for more cabling. 'Oh, yeah? Like what?'

'With myself? The attack on this place for one. Got a lot of my people killed. Good people. Those who've survived are in here with me, awaiting their deaths. That's on me, too. But that's just today's shame, if I'm being honest. When you get to being as old as me, there's more to regret than there is to be proud of.'

'You really think the Silver Eagles will kill all of the prisoners?'

'Killing's just a formality, kid. Prisoners are expensive to keep alive. They take up valuable resources. I'm just glad that if anybody caught my people, it was the Silver Eagles and not the Crows.'

'The Crows?'

'Them's the ones. I wouldn't wish the Crows upon my worst enemy.'

'Who are they?' Jake said, his curiosity piqued. 'Some other faction in this city?'

'Indeed. They're out east. Cruellest bunch of bastards I ever seen. They treat their own in ways I wouldn't treat a single enemy. There aren't many things that scare me in this world—oh, there's plenty I don't like—but seeing any of my people caught by them would terrify me to my core. This here's bad, but it ain't that. And so long as that's the case, we can hope to get out in one piece. Only problem is, the way you carry yourself worries me, too. And if the lives of my people and me are dependent on you and your brother breaking out with us, then we gotta work some of this out.'

Jake could see his point. Martin's mention of 'you and your brother' proved to him that there was perhaps a little more to it than just Martin looking out for Jake. It was Dylan's physical prowess Martin needed to launch an escape. Somebody big and hard, who could go toe to toe with the guards without backing down. Jake's inclusion was more by association. As a fellow prisoner, his advocacy of the plan was better for Martin and the others than resistance. Martin likely wanted him on side because he didn't want some other risk factor to worry about. Still, Jake appreciated that Martin was at least being somewhat tactful in his approach. And given the lack of allies Jake currently had in the world, he figured he may as well entertain Martin's offer of friendship. For now, anyway. 'You mentioned being angry a lot.'

'That I did.'

'You ever hang on to that anger, that bitterness, so intently that you let it consume you?'

'I have. And I can tell you that nothing good will come of it. Most of my regrets have come from places of anger. And regretting things is a wearisome business. It brings you down. Bitterness even more so.'

'So what do you do about it?'

'If I really knew the answer to that, I'd have settled happily decades ago and you wouldn't find the wreck you see before you now. As it is, I've spent twenty years being haunted by a mistake I made in anger. It's one I wish every day that I could take back, but I can't. Don't get me wrong, there are many more mistakes that haunt me each and every day, but there's one that really won't leave me alone. The worst part of it is that I still feel I was somewhat in the right to do what I did, but not enough, I suppose. I was in a situation I could see getting out of hand and I made a decision I thought was in the best interests of myself and somebody I loved. Turned out not to be a very good decision and so I continue to pay for it. But that's my burden. You don't have to tell me what's on your mind, lad. You're big enough and ugly enough to figure things out for yourself. At the end of the day, when you put your head down and close your eyes, the only person left for you to deal with is you. So you've got to figure out a way to be okay with who that person is. One little indiscretion can be forgiven without too much guilt. But you make enough of them, or make one so big you can't take it back, that's a slippery slope. You'll either numb yourself to the effects of guilt because of the sheer scale of it all, in which case you'll start to forget who you are, or you won't be able to live with what you've done. Neither is a particularly good option. The way I see it, whatever this war is you got going on in your head, you're headed for a cliff edge. It's a longer and harder road to turn around and walk yourself back than it is to just let go, but the chances of you getting out alive improve dramatically.'

Jake turned the trolley and started to push it back towards the crumbling building as Martin walked alongside him. It had been some time since he'd had a conversation like this with another. Getting another's perspective proved to be surprisingly insightful. It didn't mean Martin was right. The man still knew nothing about what Jake had been through. He couldn't truly appreciate Jake's own struggle and so his advice could not be taken without question. Nevertheless, he'd made some interesting points. 'Thanks. I guess I have some thinking to do.'

'Well, don't take too long, kid. I got no plans to hang around.'

12

Mia stopped running as she rounded a building and hunched over, resting her hands on her knees, her chest heaving and her vision blurring a little. Taking deep breaths which threatened to burst her lungs, she felt the ache in her muscles subside, if only a little. Her feet hurt from all the running. Her head hurt from all the panic. Her heart hurt from her separation from Dylan. Everything hurt. Terror had not gripped her so totally since the attack on New Britain, when Dylan had convinced her to join his side. Right now it wasn't looking like one of her better decisions. She was all alone, without a clue as to where she was or what she should do next. Dylan was gone. She had no idea if he was alive or not. Those thugs who'd attacked them could well have killed him by now, especially if he was doing something foolish to keep them from coming after her. If they hadn't killed him, they most likely had captured him. He had a bravery that to her often bordered on lunacy. Under Frank's rule, Dylan had taken multiple beatings in his attempts to keep his little brother safe. It was part of what had attracted her to him.

His willingness to do anything for those he loved. His earnestness. His dim-witted charm.

She wiped away the damp on her cheeks, unsure of what was sweat and what were tears. It didn't matter. Dylan was gone. She was on her own and far, far from home. Before meeting Dylan, she'd not left the New Britain base. Not properly, anyway. There had been no need. Beyond the walls lay danger, the others had told her.

How right they'd been.

As she caught her breath, she assessed her options. She could return to the site of the attack. *Probably not a good idea. They'll be expecting that.* She could give up and head home, but without Dylan, would it even be home anymore? After their last few weeks travelling east, she had grown so close to Dylan, begun to consider him the other half of a piece she hadn't known was missing. No, there was no way she was going anywhere without him. The best she could think to do was what Dylan had said: keep moving and leave clues for him to find her. He'd said she should mark buildings with little crosses, or something to that effect. She hadn't really been listening that well in the panic. And now she'd run for so long, changing direction so many times, she didn't have a clue where she was, or how to even go about figuring out where she was in relation to Dylan. It was all too much. Allowing herself a moment to be completely overwhelmed, she sat down against the wall and hugged her legs with her arms as she cried into her knees.

It felt good to let it out. The anxiety had made it difficult to breathe. Difficult to think straight, too. Now was not the time for rash decisions. Were Dylan in this situation, she knew he'd likely assess his options, pick whichever seemed most logical and stick with it. His calm stoicism had been a comfort to her all along their journey towards London. All she wanted was to be back by his side. But that was not possible. *Pull it together.*

All she had on her was her rucksack and a blade. Everything else had been dropped in the panic of the attack. If she were to find herself in another fight, her chances of surviving it were slim to none. Even with a weapon, she hated the idea of violence. It terrified her. Most of her formative years had been spent within the safety of New Britain's walls, taking care of supplies and providing medical treatment as best she could, not fighting others. Certainly not killing others. She needed to be careful. More than that, she needed to find something to eat and something to drink. The bottle of water clipped to her rucksack was almost empty. Taking a long swig, she emptied it, savouring every drop. It helped, a little. Gave her some of her strength back.

Looking at her surroundings, she realised the river must have burst its banks some time ago. In the distance, the water was level with the doors of some houses, so that the lawns were submerged, leaving the buildings looking like odd monstrosities, sticking out of the water as if they'd floated up from nowhere. On the up side, she reckoned it meant people were less likely to live nearby. *Who'd want to live in conditions like these?* She could see white watermarks on the walls where the water had clearly risen before. Anything inside was likely to have been ruined by the water years ago. There wouldn't be much point looking for supplies in there, she figured.

Gazing up towards the sun, she found east and decided it was the best course, given that was the direction she and Dylan had been heading. If he was able to break out, he would likely head in that direction, too. Besides, if she could find others who were against the gang that had attacked her, she might be able to convince them to help go back and free

Dylan. There might be others just like him who'd been captured under different scenarios.

As she considered everything, a thought popped into her mind: had he in fact been captured? He'd told her to run, and run she had. Endlessly. Until her body could run no more. She realised that she had not looked back over her shoulder. Not once. Such was the fear that had gripped her. Perhaps Dylan had managed to escape and was likely looking for her. Her nerves went into a spin, but she forced herself not to get her hopes up. Better to think like Dylan. Be logical. Play the situation out. Survive.

Walking along the streets, Mia did her best not to jump at every sound. Every time the nearby water lapped against a step, or a floating piece of debris crawled along the edge of a house, she would spin to face her phantom attacker, her palms sweating as she held her blade out in front of her. Then she would berate herself for her stupidity. If only she didn't have a mind that ran away with itself so easily. It amplified everything. Like a deer, her natural reaction was always a desire to flee. Panic seemed to be her primary state of mind. All she could do to quell such fantasies was close her eyes, take a couple of deep breaths, and wait. No monsters came, and so she would move on once more. She found herself wondering whether a human heart had a finite amount of beats in it. If so, she was burning through them with worrying speed.

As she moved, she made a point of stopping at every third house to carve an X into the wall with her blade. She was unsure of how big to carve them. Too big and any passers-by would start to speculate as to their meaning. Too small and Dylan might never see them. In the end, she decided to make them roughly the size of her hand. That way they were easily visible from the street but not so big that anyone who wasn't looking for them might have their eye drawn to them. Each cross took a few minutes to carve, which made progress slow. Using the palm of her hand as a hammer and the blade as a chisel, she'd tap into the wall until the line was a finger's width or so, and then she'd do the other. Despite the slow progress, carving the crosses into the walls helped settle her nerves a little. It gave her a purpose, a feeling that she was doing something that might actually help. There was a certain comfort to the methodical nature of the task. It gave her mind a few minutes' rest from the torment of rampant speculation as to the dangers she and Dylan might be in.

By the time the sun started going down, she was exhausted. It had been one of the worst days of her life, if not the worst. Her stomach gurgled as hunger set in, and her muscles ached, pleading with her to give them a rest. She filled her steel bottle full of river water and then set about starting a small fire in an overgrown back garden, sheltered by a fence, so that she could purify it. The water she'd collected didn't look like the water from a natural stream. She didn't want to take any chances. Breaking off slats from the fence and ripping some paper from a book she found on the ground, she got a fire going.

Something about tearing pages from a book still brought a great sense of loss to her. She had done it many times out of necessity but that didn't make it any easier. Besides the decrepit remains of buildings and machines, books were her only real connection to the old world. To any world, even the fictional ones. They allowed her to view life through the eyes of others. Those people's hopes and fears, the struggles they had to overcome, they way they so often chose kindness over cruelty; it was so unlike the world she had grown up in. Books were her chance to dream of something better.

Back home, she had hoarded a good many, but out here they were few and far between. Ripping the pages from yet another, she knew, was denying someone else the chance of seeing the world from another point of view. A chance to shape their mind. A chance to see something good and want to emulate it. Still, the temperature was dropping as the afternoon gave way to evening. She needed warmth and clean water, and the pages were the best way of getting a fire going.

The crackle of the small flame brought a familiar calm, and she held her hands out for warmth as the sun sank over the horizon, reducing her world to nothing but the fire before her. From her backpack she pulled out her purifier: a plastic bottle with the bottom cut off and turned upside down. It had been filled with a bit of cloth at its natural opening, then with layers of fine sand, coarse sand, and small pebbles. Holding the filter above the ground, she placed an empty plastic bottle beneath and proceeded to pour the river water through from her steel bottle. It was slow going. When it was done, she held the plastic bottle, now filled with water, up to the light of the fire and saw that it was clearer than it had been. Pouring it back into the steel bottle, she repeated the task a couple more times, checking each time that the water's clarity was improving. When she was satisfied that she had done all she could, she poured the water back into her steel water bottle and placed it in the coals at the edge of the fire. Then she pulled a small plastic tube from her rucksack and connected the plastic and the steel bottles, allowing the water that evaporated out to fill the clear plastic bottle once more.

She was almost asleep by the time the whole process was complete and the water had cooled sufficiently to drink. It was worth it, though. Was there ever anything as satisfying as a sip of water to a parched throat? She had let the fire go out, knowing that a bright flame in the darkness was not something she wanted to keep going. Then she lay beside the warm coals and closed her eyes.

But sleep never came.

At first she thought it might have been a fox. It sounded like a bark in the distance. However, upon second hearing, she knew it was a voice. A man's voice. Followed by a couple more. There was a group nearby. Whether patrolling or passing through, she didn't know. Didn't much matter, anyway. Her whole body tingled as her nerves fired. She got up, sitting on her haunches, and held her ear to the sky, trying to pinpoint the location, or at least direction, of the voices.

They were close.

She could almost make out what they were saying. It sounded like three voices. At least it wasn't a whole gang. But still, three men against her with just her knife as a weapon were not odds she considered favourable. Had it been one on one, she still wouldn't have liked her chances. Best thing she could do was stay out of their way. That left her with two choices: stay put and hope they passed without noticing her, or try and move in the opposite direction to them and put as much distance between these potential killers and herself as possible. She preferred the second option. Probably that deer mentality again, always wanting to flee, but she knew that brought with it its own risks. All it would take was for her to trip or stumble into something and the others might hear her. She decided to stay put until she knew exactly where they were. Then she could make her decision. Hopefully, it wouldn't be too late to react.

'Why the fuck are we out on patrol again?' one of the voices said.

'Because, dipshit, those fucking Disconnected might attack again,' another said. His voice was deeper, almost gravelly, like he was chewing on rocks as he spoke.

'They're not coming back. They must have lost half their numbers in that fire. I'm guessing they fled back to wherever their little hidey-hole is and they're licking their wounds, berating themselves for their piss-poor attempt of an attack.'

'I wouldn't say it was that piss-poor. They got a fair few of us, didn't they? And they burned down most of a terminal. If any of the other factions see that, they'll think something's up. If anybody gets a whiff of trouble on this end of town, that's it; there'll be a fucking war.'

'You reckon?'

'What if you saw the Wolves burning, wouldn't you want to move in and take the north?'

'Maybe. Maybe not. I reckon we're doing just fine out west. More greenery, more chance to grow food, more chance to find living food. What's so great about the Wolves's place?'

'I hear they've got supplies. The kind we haven't had for years.'

It sounded to Mia like they were almost upon her. They were on the road just outside her house. Balling her hands into fists, she closed her eyes and hoped they'd move on, but the bastards stopped for a drink. She couldn't stick around. She didn't trust herself to keep quiet enough. *I'll take my chances.*

She moved away back towards the water lapping the edge of the garden, figuring being cold and wet was better than being dead. If she could cross the river, she could be shot of this lot and find somewhere to dry off for the night. Their patrol was unlikely to cross the river, and hopefully there wouldn't be another patrol on the other side. *I guess I'll find out once I'm across.*

The water was ice cold as she waded in. A small gasp escaped her before she could stop it.

'You hear that?' the gravelly-voiced guy said.

Fuck, fuck, fuck! She dropped below the surface, rucksack and all, and swam through the dark, hoping they hadn't seen her.

13

'All right there, panda eyes?' Martin said.

Dylan blinked away the harshness of the morning light until the glare became tolerable. 'Panda?' His head still hurt from the fight with Jake. He figured Martin's comment had something to do with the state of his face, which still felt very much like a cracked egg.

'Fucking hell. Never mind. Guess no reason anyone should've ever explained something as irrelevant as that to you. Sometimes I forget just how much you young'uns don't know about before. Anyway, it doesn't matter. Not like you'd understand half of it if anyone tried to explain it to you. Best get your arse up—Joe and the others will be in shortly to get us to work.'

Dylan looked over at Jake in the cell opposite. It was hard to tell whether his brother still wanted to kill him or not. Jake didn't look at all happy about being near him, but Dylan's plea to help find Mia before she got into trouble seemed to have had some effect. Softened him a little, perhaps. Then again, perhaps he was just waiting patiently for the next moment to strike. Dylan gave him a curt nod and got nothing but a blank stare in return. *What the hell did Frank do to you?* How was his own brother, even if he was a half-brother, able to look at him with such disdain? No wonder Claire had tried to protect them from this world their whole lives. It hadn't taken much to break their fragile existence, and now the family was so fragmented as to be unrecognisable. Dylan wondered what his mother would do if she knew Jake was alive. She hadn't given up on searching for him, despite Jake turning against them. She had insisted he could still be saved, if he were still alive. They needed only to find him before the world got its claws into him and turned him forever. *I think we're too late, Mum.*

Dylan turned to Martin to pick up the conversation where they'd previously left off. 'So if we're not escaping over the wall—'

'Shh,' Martin said. 'Not here. Once we're at work, when we can see who's near us. Did no one ever tell yeh about walls and ears? There might be someone beneath the fuselage right now and we wouldn't know. Best not be too cavalier with our planning discussions.'

A familiar knock came from outside. Joe and his crew had arrived. Dylan and the others instinctively moved to the back of their cells and waited for Joe to let them out. The big potato-looking thug was carrying an old cricket bat today. It looked like an extension of his own arm, the way he swung it as he walked. Dylan didn't much like thinking about how Joe had grown to be so familiar with it. He didn't much like the rusty taint across the face of the bat, either.

They stepped out onto the runway and set to work just as they had done the day before, clearing rubble from within the burned building. Dylan found it odd that this faction had not bothered to introduce them to others within the group. Since he'd arrived, he'd only dealt with Joe and his crew. Nobody else. Not a single person had come to speak to him or interrogate him. Nothing. It made him question their intentions for their prisoners. Not bothering to even get to know them. Just making them work. That kind of apathy could only mean one thing by Dylan's estimation: the Silver Eagles planned on killing them pretty soon. Probably as soon as they'd finished gutting the ruined terminal. *We need to get out of here soon.*

It wasn't until the afternoon when Martin called on Dylan and Jake to help shift some of the rubble off-site that they got a real chance to talk. With a couple of guards trailing at a distance, they were allowed to exit the airport grounds to dump the rubble a short distance away, near an old reservoir. The guards were engrossed in their own conversation, giving Dylan the chance to speak quietly as he pushed his trolley of rubble along beside Martin's and Jake's. 'Why'd you attack the Silver Eagles anyway?' he said to Martin.

'Would you believe it if I said I was bored to tears?'

'No.'

'Fair play. Look, London's got a bunch of factions, all pesterin' each other as supplies run out. It's been getting more violent with every winter. With the next one on its way, we figured it was time to make a small stand. The fewer the Silver Eagles have to feed, the less likely they'd come looking for us when supplies run really low, you know?'

Dylan did know. Sort of, anyway. It was the same everywhere. Winters were hard. Some years they were real hard. He'd spent enough winters shivering in his family's makeshift wooden cabin, so mad with starvation he'd almost considered chopping a limb off just to have something to eat. And he'd lived in the forest, where food could be considered somewhat plentiful. Somehow, they'd always managed to find deer, or small animals, like hare. When that wasn't an option, they'd often managed to catch fish. And when there was nothing, they'd made do with whatever vegetation they could. He couldn't imagine what it must be like in a big concrete environment like this, with no large open spaces for wildlife to roam. Sure, the buildings were overgrown with plant life, and there were birds aplenty, but that wouldn't ever be enough. Surely they needed space to grow crops? Whatever they achieved here couldn't be enough. Especially with the other gangs all fighting for territory. He was surprised they hadn't all killed each other already.

'Tell me about the other factions,' he said, figuring knowledge was power here. If he could get an understanding, however biased, of the city's population, he could use that information in his search for Mia.

'Well,' Martin said, looking to the sky as he pondered where to start, 'you got the Silver Eagles here in the west. You ain't met 'em all but you underestimate 'em at your own peril, I tell you. Right bastards, the lot of 'em. They're pretty good at growing their own stuff, mind, so from time to time we come and liberate some of their excess for 'em. Most of West London can be considered theirs. Anywhere from here to about Hammersmith, although that shithole's been under water for years, so you won't find too many fighting over that part of town anytime soon. Probably the kindest thing you could've done to the place was sink it.' He chuckled to himself but it meant nothing to Dylan, who waited for Martin to continue. 'Then up north you got the Wolves. Nobody ventures up there. Not anybody who wants to survive the day, anyway. The rumours are always conflicting. Some say they got enough supplies to start a war. Others say they been gettin' low on supplies the last few years. Anyway, rumours don't matter. They live by a simple code now: anyone they don't recognise gets killed on the spot.'

Dylan hoped that wherever Mia was, she was nowhere near the Wolves' territory.

'Out east yeh got the Crows,' Martin said without enthusiasm. 'Bunch of lying, thieving, good-for-nothing scoundrels, the lot of 'em. And more evil than anything you could imagine. In the truest sense of the word.'

Dylan refrained from commenting on Martin's prior statement about liberating Silver Eagles' own supplies from time to time, deciding it best to play it neutral.

'Down south you got the Blades,' Martin said. 'Not many try to cross the river to get at them but sometimes things kick off there. The centre is where all the trouble's at, really. No one ever drew up an exact map of the territories, so it's all a bit confusing. Changes depending on who's in charge at any given time, for the most part. But the one thing they all want is control of the centre.'

'Why's that?' Dylan said.

'Because the one who owns the centre owns the connections with all the others. That one is likely gonna be able to create allegiances with ease. They'd have an advantage that the others wouldn't. And that would probably lead to the destruction of one of the other crews. Once one goes down, it'll be a free-for-all to expand territories. They're all fighting to take control over the whole city.'

Emptying his trolley of its rubble, Dylan turned to Martin as they began their return journey. 'And where do you fit in?'

'Me?' Martin said. 'I got no agenda. I only been trying to keep a few folks alive as best I can.'

'So why not leave? Surely you could find somewhere better to live outside the city?'

'It's not that easy,' Martin said. 'Everybody has their reasons. I got mine.'

Figuring that was all the personal information he was going to get from Martin, he changed tack. 'So where are you based?' He saw Jake nearby incline his head, his brother's silent fury losing out to curiosity as the conversation continued.

Martin looked at Dylan for a long while as he walked, seemingly assessing something in his mind. 'You sure you're not from one of the other crews?'

'I'm sure.'

'Still, they decide to torture you and you'll be bleating like a newborn lamb in spring. Let's just say my lot live in the tunnels. Everyone else has suspected it for years but they never been able to find us.'

'The tunnels?' Dylan recalled his mother's stories about her life before the Blackout. She'd told them how she and his father, Matt, had been forced into the tunnels, where'd they joined a rebel group known as the Disconnected. That's where she'd met Maxime, Jake's father, whom she'd fled with after Matt had sacrificed himself against some evil force. He'd always had trouble imagining that. Claire hadn't been so good at explaining it all. Most of the time it seemed like she hadn't wanted to. But she'd definitely said they had lived in the old disused tunnel system, which had been out of use since long before Blackout.

He decided to try his luck. 'Our mother used to live in the tunnels,' he said.

'Fuck off.'

'I mean it. She told us she was part of a group down there, a long time ago. Long before I was born. Even longer before Jake was around.'

'Oh yeah?'

'Hey, it's her story, not mine,' Dylan said. 'I've never been here. You don't need to believe me. I can't imagine anyone wanting to live in underground tunnels when they could have free run of the wilderness.'

'Your mother,' Martin said, 'what's her name?'

'Claire,' Dylan said. 'Claire Jones.'

Martin gasped, stopping in his tracks for a moment as he ran his hands through his bushy hair. The guards behind grunted something and he picked up his pace again, although his jaw seemed planted to the floor. 'Well, I'll be. You're Matt's kid.'

'How do you know that?'

'I knew your folks, kid. We ran together for a short while there, before everything went arse up.'

'No shit.'

'It was a long time ago, mind. Feels like a whole other lifetime now,' Martin said. He picked at the handle of his trolley as they walked on in silence, struggling with something as Dylan waited for him to get it out. Eventually, Martin sighed. 'I don't suppose your mother brought anyone with her when she left? You didn't know anyone else from her old days?'

'Just my dad,' Jake said, chipping in for the first time.

'And who would that be?' Martin said.

'Maxime.'

'Maxime is your dad?'

'Was,' Jake said.

'Ah, shit. I'm sorry to hear that. That there was a good man.' Like a child, Martin continued to pick at the trolley handle as he tried to hold back his next question. 'And there was nobody else that left with her? Not one?'

'Not that we know of,' Dylan said. 'Mum told us a few stories about her time in a rebel group called the Disconnected, living in the disused old Underground tunnels of London, but she never spoke of the people much. She didn't really mention names.'

Martin cleared his throat with a cough and picked up his speed as he pushed his empty trolley back towards the airport wall for the next load of rubble.

'Everything okay?' Dylan said.

'I'm fine, kid. Everything's good.' He sniffed and ran his forearm across his face. After they'd loaded up their next journey and left the airport walls once more, Martin brought the conversation up again. 'The Disconnected still exists. Not as your mother would have known it. I'm one of the only faces left from her days, but I've kept the base going all these years. Been growing the numbers again slowly but surely. Anybody on their own in the city who looked like they might be in trouble with one of the other factions, I tried to help. We were getting to be a pretty strong force again until the attack on Silver Eagles. The bastards took most of us out. I need to get back to our base and see who made it out. If we get there, we'll be able to pick up weapons and bring more numbers with us to look for your Mia.'

'You'd really get your people to help us look for her?' Dylan said.

'I owe it to your mother,' Martin said. 'She was good to me and I ... well, I let her down.'

'Why is everybody so obsessed with the past?' Dylan said. 'It's all anybody who didn't grow up in the Blackout ever wants to talk about.'

Martin chuckled to himself as he tugged on his beard.

Then, just as quickly as it had appeared, the smile was gone. 'Because, kid, when you get to my age, there ain't much looking forward to be done. So we look back. We turn our minds to times we understood, to memories of when we could still hope for more than a peaceful and painless death, to times when those we loved were still alive and our futures with them were still filled with possibility. It's a hell of a lot easier to talk of hope than regret. And I'm about done with regret, if you ask me.' He let out a long sigh. 'Word of advice, kid, try to live like you won't regret a thing. If you aren't working your way towards something, you're only ever looking back at what once was, and that ain't as pretty a sight as some like to make out. Mostly it's just hurt, and lots of it.' Looking over his shoulder to check the guards were still out of earshot, Martin lowered his voice. 'If you two can put aside this petty squabble of yours, we can get out tonight. I know how.'

'How's that?' Dylan said.

Martin smiled. 'The tunnels, of course. There's one under this airport. It was put out of use a long time ago, but if we can get down there, they won't ever find us. It's how we came here to attack them. I know where we need to go. The only problem is getting out of our cells. There's a lot of ground to cover and every one of the guards will be carrying a weapon. You boys ever taken a life?'

Both nodded.

'Okay. But I'm not having Claire's two kids trying to kill each other the moment we're out. You ready to put your differences aside for this?'

Dylan turned to Jake, hoping that the conversation with Martin had had as much of an effect on him, too. This man had known their parents. He was a friend and he was willing to put his people in danger to help them. Surely Jake could put aside his animosity, like Martin had said, and live without looking back in anger. 'What do you say, Jake? Truce? For Mia?'

After an eternal moment his little brother looked up at him, the rage on his face replaced with a more sombre expression. 'Truce.'

14

When the day shift ended, Dylan and the others returned to their cells. They'd each pulled some large nails from the rubble and hidden one on their person. At Martin's suggestion, Dylan had hidden his nail, which was as long as his hand, in his boxer briefs, making him rather uncomfortable for the last hour or so of his work. Every step had been taken tentatively, so much so that he was sure a guard would pick up on his rigid movements. But none did, and so they made it back to their cells with a weapon each. Nails weren't going to be much use against guns and melee weapons like bats and metal pipes, but it was something. A nail could be driven through a neck with relative ease. If they were smart about it, they just might be able to do it. After all, they weren't trying to take down the whole Silver Eagles crew. They only needed to get the cell keys off the guard on duty that night and then make it into the old Underground tunnel beneath the airport that Martin had mentioned. According to him, most guards would be positioned on the fence, looking out at the city in case anybody tried to attack again. Nobody would expect them to head into the terminal, especially with it in such disrepair.

There would be nobody in there that night. Once they had the keys, they would need to cover the ground across the tarmac to the terminal. That would be the riskiest part of the escape. They would be sitting ducks, with only the cover of night to protect them.

But that was thinking too far ahead. First they needed the keys off the guard. Dylan had his reservations about how they might pull it off but Martin had insisted there was no other way.

They waited in silence until late in the night, hoping that most of the Silver Eagles' crew would be asleep, save for those on duty. Then Martin started his coughing fit.

The guard on duty outside the fuselage yelled for them to shut up.

Martin continued his coughing.

The guard banged on the door. 'That's the last warning. If I have to come in there, you'll wish I hadn't.'

Martin's coughs grew more impressive. So much so that Dylan found himself a little concerned about whether Martin was okay. He had to remind himself it was all a ruse.

'Right, I warned you,' the guard said. He opened up the door and stepped in, crowbar in hand. When he saw it was Martin doing all the coughing, he hesitated for a moment. Dylan wondered whether that was because he wasn't sure just how dangerous the man-mountain was, or because he knew *exactly* how dangerous he was, having presumably fought against him in the original attack. He rattled the crowbar against a couple of other cells, including Dylan's, telling everybody to keep it down. Eventually he made it over to Martin's cell. 'You're making a hell of a fuss, mate.'

'Water,' Martin said in a hoarse voice. 'Please.' He lifted a pleading hand to the cell door before doubling over again as he coughed violently enough to expel a lung.

Dylan inspected the guard from the distance of his cell. The keys were clipped to his belt. Not some fancy clip. The belt had been threaded through the keyring, meaning it wasn't coming off without an exceptionally hard tug, or the belt itself coming off. There was no way they could get the keys off without the guard noticing. He tapped his cell twice, as agreed hours earlier. One tap would have indicated an opportunity to steal the keys silently if Martin could keep the theatrics up. Two taps meant they had to opt for the more lethal option.

Martin moved with the speed of a young buck, springing to his feet, his hand closing around the guard's neck before the poor sod knew what was happening.

Dylan watched Martin's fingers close around the man's windpipe. 'I guess we didn't need the nails,' he said as Martin crushed the man's throat before letting the body drop to the floor. He never even had a chance to scream.

Ignoring Dylan's comment, Martin pulled the corpse towards him and undid the guy's belt, liberating the keys. He proceeded to let the other prisoners out, all of whom hugged and thanked him for his efforts.

Dylan had not paid them much attention since he'd joined. They didn't look up to a fight. They were malnourished and injured men and women. Certainly not a force to speak of. If anything, they would be a hindrance in the escape. He knew better than to argue against Martin freeing his own people, though. Regardless of what happened next, it had been Martin who'd put himself on the line, taking the killing of the guard into his own hands. 'Thank you,' he said as Martin opened his cell door.

'Save it, lad. We're not out yet.'

After Martin left his cell, Dylan looted the guard's corpse. He had a shotgun slung over his back, a pistol in his belt, and the crowbar he'd been carrying. Dylan handed the shotgun and spare rounds from the belt to Martin, the crowbar to Jake, and kept the pistol for himself. It was a pretty standard nine-millimetre handgun. One he'd come across before. He knew before inspecting that it had a fifteen-round magazine. The guard had a couple of spare magazines in his trousers, which lifted Dylan's spirits immensely. It was better than they could have hoped for. Two guns and a crowbar. That was three half-decent weapons where before they'd had only nails. He and Jake handed the nails to a few of the others, instructing them to keep them just in case.

Once everybody was ready, they peered out of the fuselage windows. It was pitch black outside. From their vantage point, they could only see a couple of guards up on the nearby fence, both of whom seemed completely engaged in the fire they had going in a barrel up on their lookout point. They were facing away from the fuselage. It was now or never.

'You first,' Martin said to Dylan.

'You sure?'

'They see my shape, they'll know it's not their buddy. You're the closest to his physique. Go on, out you go.'

He had a point. Dylan stepped out into the night and looked around. Nothing. No guards nearby. Just the two up on the wall lookout post a short way away. They were still engrossed in some conversation while they stared into their fire. Stepping as lightly as he could so as not to make a sound, Dylan walked down the steps to the tarmac below, and gave the immediate vicinity another check. Still nothing. Nobody under the plane. Looking towards the terminal, he could see a fire in a barrel on an upper level, in the small section still intact. That's where the rest of the Silver Eagles' faction were presumably getting their heads down. Probably one or two on guard up there. They clearly hadn't seen the movement below, though. At least, they hadn't made any noise about it. The rest of the destroyed structure looked empty. Not wanting to hang about, he crossed the ground to the terminal entrance and, when the coast was clear, turned and signalled to the others that it was safe to proceed.

The others started to cross in short bursts, one at a time. It was achingly slow progress. With each crossing, Dylan's heart beat faster. His ears seemed to amplify every sound in the night so that each footstep sounded like a loud thud. He was certain that someone would hear them. To his surprise, and great relief, everybody made it across without any hassle, including Martin, who went last. As Martin's hulking shape crossed the open ground, Dylan held his breath, his grip firmly on the pistol, ready to open fire if everything went to shit.

'You good?' he said as Martin arrived.

'So far.'

'How many in Silver Eagles if this all kicks off?'

'Not sure, mate. Since we've been imprisoned, we haven't seen anybody but the few guarding us each day as they put us to work. I've no idea how many we actually got in the attack. But they had more than fifty when we attacked. Based on what I witnessed, I'm guessing we halved that number. There or thereabouts, anyway. Probably why they didn't want to speak to us just yet. I figure they've been trying to regather themselves to figure out what they can do next.'

'Okay,' Dylan said. He did some mental arithmetic on his ammo count versus the opposition. Three magazines at fifteen rounds each was more than enough for a bullet each, if it came to it. Problem was the likelihood of successfully one-shotting any attackers was damned near nil, especially in the dark. And they'd all be firing back the second he opened fire. 'Slow and steady, then,' he whispered. 'No noise whatsoever. Keep a few apart at all times. Martin, lead the way.'

'On it.' The great hulking figure moved ahead into the darkness, stepping slowly through the charred remains of the terminal.

A lot of the rubble near the entrance had been cleared by now, so getting into the building was relatively easy. However, once a little further in, it became harder to navigate. Broken glass lay scattered across the floor, along with burnt chairs and kiosks aplenty. Much of the floor above had collapsed in the fire, too, leaving large piles of rubble to navigate around. It was slow going. A crunch of glass echoed through the dark, bringing everyone to a halt. Dylan raised his pistol, pointing it in the direction of the noise ahead.

'My bad,' Martin whispered. 'Careful of the glass. It's fucking everywhere.'

Letting out a deep sigh, Dylan nudged his way forwards once more. If a bullet didn't take him in the night, he was pretty sure a heart attack would. To calm himself, he ran over the plan in his head. As Martin had explained it to him, there was a tunnel underneath the airport which had been put out of use years before the Blackout, when the city had decided to close the antiquated Underground system in favour of a more modern shuttle system above ground which better fit the layout of the city and allowed for improved transport across it for all its inhabitants. As a result, all of the Underground entrances had been bricked over and forgotten about. It was how the Disconnected had survived, living where nobody thought to look, in a system of tunnels beneath the city that allowed for movement without trace. According to Martin, this tunnel had been blocked off by a wall. During the attack, his people had created a small entry point, just big enough to fit one through at a time. He reckoned it would have been covered back up during the retreat, otherwise he'd have been interrogated about it by now. According to him, the Silver Eagles thought the invaders had scaled the walls without being seen. He'd not said anything to dissuade them of that notion.

Keeping an eye on Jake just ahead of him, Dylan kept moving. Their fragile truce still had him worried but there was nothing he could do about it right now. At least he had a pistol against Jake's crowbar if it came to it.

As they dropped down a set of stairs, a shot sounded behind them. Then a lot of shouting. Footsteps rang out like a stampede. *Fuck!* Dylan spun. They'd been caught. It was too late. They were outnumbered. In front of him a body flopped to the ground. One of the prisoners from the fuselage. She'd taken a bullet to the back of the head. All around her a pool of blood began to flow, the distant moonlight reflecting off the fast-flowing liquid.

Martin shoved his way past Dylan, shotgun in hand. 'Jenny!'

Obviously someone he was fond of. *Had* been fond of. Not anymore. Dylan looked up in the direction of the shooter. The two guards who'd been on watch at the wall stood just outside, looking in. Smoke snaked up from the barrel of one of the guys' rifles, which he now swung towards his next target. Above them all, Dylan could hear the pounding of feet as the others got in on the action. They'd be down soon enough. 'Take cover!' He ducked behind the charred remains of an old kiosk. It wasn't much more than a lump, providing just enough cover for himself. Beside him he could hear the sounds of others sliding into cover.

Not Martin, though. The big man was on his feet, walking straight towards the two guards, giving them everything the shotgun had.

Dylan watched as they ducked and scurried to the side to escape the buckshot. This was his moment to help. To have some effect on the outcome. Readying the pistol, he held his breath and took aim. One of the guards had run into the building towards cover rather than away across the open tarmac. He couldn't have been more than twenty or so feet from Dylan. Still, twenty feet was a long shot with a pistol. Add to that the lack of light and Dylan's beating chest and it may as well have been a shot from a field away. Nevertheless, he recalled his mother's training. Cool, calm and simple. Steady hands, steady breath, steady shot.

He squeezed the trigger. Heard the body drop.

One down.

Martin turned and nodded his approval to Dylan, who reciprocated the gesture. There was no going into the tunnel now, Dylan knew. Not until the battle had reached an end. No way they were putting themselves in a sealed passageway where their enemy need only point and shoot to seal the deal. Better to die trying to push back a little. Perhaps if they took a few out, Mia might be able to wander back this way and escape the city without any further hassle. That, at least, would be something.

Silhouettes filled Dylan's vision as he looked out from cover. Martin had been right. It was too dark to count, and too much was happening too fast, but twenty or so sounded about right. They really were fucked.

Except Martin didn't seem to see it that way. Dylan watched as two of Martin's shots sent a couple of bodies sprawling backwards in the night, while others took cover. Knowing their defence wouldn't last long, he scurried across the floor to Jake's position behind a pile of rubble. 'You with me?'

'Like hunting back home?'

'Precisely. Let's flank the bastards. They're all panicking about Martin and his shotty. We don't have long.'

'Let's do it.'

'Take some of the others with you,' Dylan said, before grabbing his brother's arm. 'And be safe.' Jake nodded back and moved off without another word. Dylan moved over to the right, keeping to the shadows. In the moonlight, it would be harder for the others to see in than it was for him to see out. They'd all just be looking into a black hole. He, meanwhile, could at least make out the silhouettes moving in panic across the tarmac. Most had come downstairs from above but had regrouped with their crew outside, presumably so as not to get caught in the crossfire. Noticing three lads setting their rifles up on an overturned table, Dylan took aim. It was quick. The first two were down before they knew what happened. The third turned to face Dylan in his panic, making the shot easier.

When the body hit the ground, Dylan ran out and picked up one of the rifles. It was a semi-automatic. Ten-round magazine. One squeeze of the trigger for each bullet fired. He turned to see Martin almost entirely surrounded and opened fire on the others. From a short distance away, where he'd flanked out from, he could hear the screams of those caught in a melee. Not everybody had guns.

Then, almost as quick as it had started, it was over. A last bullet rang out and a body dropped with a thud. Silence.

'You all right there, mucker?' Martin said from across the way.

'I'm good,' Dylan said. 'You hurt?'

'My ears are ringing but I'm good.'

'Mine too. Jake?'

No response.

'Jake!'

'Over here.'

Dylan saw his brother climbing out from under a body. The three met at the entrance.

'This might not have been the whole lot,' Martin said. 'Some of 'em might have been out on patrol. If they heard the commotion, they'll be on their way back. We best get a move on.'

'I'm so sorry,' Dylan said as he looked around at the fallen, 'about your people.'

'Let's make sure they didn't die for nothing. Come on.'

Taking Martin's lead, the trio left the battlefield and descended into the tunnel below.

15

The further into the city Mia walked, the more her doubt grew. It wasn't like she'd made it that far in. It still felt very much like the outskirts. The buildings were low and relatively spread out. What was left of them, anyway. Up ahead in the far distance she could see the tall high-rises, shattered glass and steel structures, long since overgrown with foliage. Either that or the glass was just dirty as all hell. That concentration was presumably the real city, not this dishevelled area.

Her doubt continued to gnaw away at her, like some rat sneaking into a supply stash at night, taking bit by bit until all that was left was a hollow shell. What if Dylan had been captured? Shouldn't she go back to check on him? What if she needed to help him? What if he'd been killed? What was her purpose then? Hoping that wasn't the case, she stopped to sit and think about it for a moment. Indecision was a luxury she could ill afford right now. Every step counted. Every second counted. Any wrong move might lead to something that affected her or Dylan down the line.

If he had been captured, the markings she'd made on the walls were of no use. Something deep within told her to return. But if she went back, she was opening herself up to the chances of running into the gang that had attacked them. Then again, heading inwards was just as likely to bring her into contact with others. There was no winning. And there was nothing without Dylan. She couldn't leave him. Not now, not ever.

Turning back in the direction she'd come, Mia decided it was best to try and find her way back to the point of the road attack and attempt to understand the scene. She knew the risks of returning to the area where the gang might be awaiting her return, but it didn't matter. If there was any chance that Dylan was still in the area, she had to go back. There might be tracks leading away that she could follow. Dylan had shown her how to track deer and small animals during their short adventure together. Perhaps she could apply the same techniques to tracking the man she loved.

The realisation blindsided her. Like walking smack into a wall in the dark. She loved him. It was so obvious now. It was more than some infatuation. In truth, she'd felt drawn to him since the moment she'd met him. To her it had not even felt like a choice. It simply was. Like some kind of force of nature. Stronger than will, stronger than desire. A magnetism she could not fight. One she did not wish to fight. She wanted nothing more than to be with him, to say it over and over and hear him say it back. What bliss it would be to spend her days counting the number of times they might declare their love for one another. It would certainly be a far cry from the realities of this world that only seemed to get more cruel by the day. Had she never met Dylan, she wouldn't have known this feeling. She would have been ignorant of the ache in her heart. And now, not only did she have to suffer the cruelties of everyday life, but also go on like this, without him? It was too much to ask.

I have to find him. I can't wait for him to find me. Keeping the image of her declaring her love to him in mind, she picked up her pace. If she really got a move on, she might get back to the point of the attack before the day was out. After all, much of her movement since had been erratic. Running in different directions. Crossing the water. Panicking. Hiding from others. Provided she kept her wits about her, she figured she could do it.

It was easy going for a while. She returned to the river crossing she'd made previously and followed the roads she had originally come down, noting the marks on the houses she'd made, impressed that she had done as suggested. Seeing them reaffirmed to her that if Dylan had got away from the attackers, he would have found her eventually—which, of course, he hadn't. Unfortunately, that meant he was almost certainly dead or captured. *Please be the latter. I'll find you. I'll break you out. We will be together again.*

The confusion started late in the afternoon when she got to the point at which she'd first started carving marks on house walls. The space between that first marked house and the point of the attack was unknown. It had all been a blur. She'd run for an age and not paid any attention to her surroundings. Now she had to figure out how to go about retracing her steps without any clues to guide her. Keeping her eyes peeled for old road signs, she kept going. She was looking for a big road, that much she knew. Eventually, one of these roads would point in that direction. She only hoped she wouldn't get lost before then.

As she sat considering her options she spotted a hare in

the grass. Her stomach gurgled at the sight of it, so powerfully she almost keeled over in agony, such was her hunger. Not wanting to spook it, she sat and watched. If she only had her bow, or a gun. At this point she didn't care if she alerted others. It would be worth it if she got to have one more meal. But she only had her knife. Life, as ever, was playing some cruel trick on her. Dangling hope and then taking it away. Growing up, she'd been told stories about different gods that people had worshipped before the Blackout. Some still did. But mostly it was just something people spoke of in her town. She couldn't understand how something like that could even exist. Surely there was no being out there that would inflict such pain and suffering on those who'd done nothing wrong. *Man still has choice*, she was always told when she spoke to these people. They implied that any failings in life were a result of choices made by people and that it was not their god's responsibility to step in. The gift was that freedom of choice. But Mia could not understand how one could watch over such cruelties and do nothing.

Shaking the thought from her mind, she trained her eyes on the hare. It was much like the many others she and Dylan had come across on their travels. He'd taught her their habits and how to set traps for them. They were fairly docile creatures but extremely jumpy when threatened. And a jumpy hare was a nightmare to track. Their hearing and vision were far superior to her own, and so she figured it had already spotted her. Stalking it would likely end in failure. She hadn't a chance of getting close enough to do any damage with a knife.

In the end, she gave up on the hope of eating meat that day. To set a trap, she'd have to consider staying overnight, and time was of the essence. She settled for picking blackberries from a nearby thicket. It wasn't much but, after a few handfuls, she started to feel a little better. The dull headache she'd had for most of the last day began to fade.

As she pulled the blackberries from the bush, staining her fingers in the process, she heard a couple of voices. A man and a woman. Definitely not the group she'd heard previously but perhaps part of the same community. Given how close she was to the original site of the attack, she figured they might well be part of the faction she and Dylan had been attacked by. This time there could be no running away. No slipping into the river in the dark and disappearing. She needed to find them and follow them. If she was lucky, they might lead her all the way back to Dylan. She could only hope. Ducking down into the thicket of bushes, she closed her eyes and listened again for the voices.

'I'm sick and tired of these patrols,' the female voice said. 'Why is Angus insisting on so many? Didn't we get most of the Disconnected in the fire?'

They were close. Extremely so. Mia could hear their footsteps coming down the road in her direction.

'You've just got to go with him, Prisha,' the man said. 'After everyone we lost, we can't afford another battle like that. If they come back or another faction finds out about our depleted numbers, we're in big trouble. He's just doing his job as leader.'

'Dev, he's completely lost the plot. His paranoia is off the charts. The only reason I volunteered for patrol duty was to get away from the poisonous feeling in camp. Besides, the way they're treating the prisoners isn't right. I saw Joe use a cricket bat on one of them the other day. Is that the kind of community we want to be? What if that was one of us who'd been captured?'

Prisoners. Mia's heart leapt. Perhaps Dylan was with them.

'If one of us had been captured by another gang, we'd be lucky to get a cricket bat,' Dev said. 'Let's just be grateful that we're still part of a community, however few in numbers we are now. It's better than being on our own. Imagine trying to survive in this city alone? We'd be dead before the day was out.'

'Fair enough,' Prisha said. 'Let's head back.'

'Agreed. I'm starving.'

Prisoners and food. With her mouth salivating at the prospect of a meal, Mia stalked after Prisha and Dev, hoping they would lead her to the man she loved. Failing that, hoping they'd lead her to food. Maybe even to weapons she might be able to steal. It took all her strength not to attack them right then and there, to take their weapons and any supplies they might have had on them. Better to wait, she figured. The rewards might be significantly greater.

'What do you think Angus will do with the prisoners?' Prisha said to Dev.

'After what they did to us, I don't suspect it'll be anything nice.'

'You reckon that's why we're not allowed to speak to them?'

'Probably has a lot to do with it, yeah. The less people know of them, the less concerned they'll be when Angus gets Joe to dispose of them.'

'Dispose of them? Is that really what it's come to? Are we really thinking of others as something to dispose of? Like unwanted trash?'

'I was just trying to find a way to say what we were both thinking without actually saying it.'

'I know,' Prisha said. 'I'm sorry. It's just such a nightmare. Part of me hates them for what they did to us. For everyone they killed. But I can't reconcile the idea of killing them for it.'

'They'd have done the same to us.'

'That doesn't make it right. Why is that always the response? Is it all just a race to the bottom? To align ourselves with the lowest common denominator?'

'Prisha, please. You're worse than—' Dev stopped himself from saying the next word, like it was something too punishing to say.

What could be so unbearable to mention? A name. Mia looked at the stiff awkwardness between the couple as they walked on ahead. *Yes, a child's name.* She knew the feeling well. Not of saying a child's name but of saying anyone's name who had passed. Especially when that someone was most important to the person you were talking to. Or had been. Mentioning those who were gone in such trivial conversations always seemed to do a disservice to their lives. It was like an insult to their memory. And so it was easier simply to avoid bringing them up. There were too many people she had stopped mentioning in conversations, she realised, feeling a deep sense of empathy for Prisha and Dev. But they were still the enemy, in theory. If Dylan was their captive, she would not think twice about what needed to be done to get him back. He would not become an Unmentionable. *Never.*

Up ahead, Mia saw a sign pointing to a HEATHROW AIRPORT. That was where she and Dylan were headed before they'd been attacked. Her heart leapt, just a little. They were going in the right direction.

She'd never seen an airport before. Of course, there was so much she'd never seen before. On their trip, Dylan had been the one to explain to her everything that was new to her. Almost everything. There were a few things on their journey that had been new to him, too. But not anymore. He wasn't around to explain anything now. Hopefully he was inside, alive and well. As well as could be expected. She hoped Dylan had learned from his treatment by Frank to be a more well-behaved prisoner if indeed he had been captured. His last imprisonment had almost been the death of him. Had he really been captured, she knew he would not have been able to sit still. Not for long, anyway. He'd have spent his time scheming, trying to figure a way out so he could get back to her. That was just the kind of man he was. As foolish as he was brave.

'Something doesn't feel right,' Prisha said up ahead.

Dev stopped and pulled the gun from his shoulder. 'What do you mean?'

Worrying that she was much too close, Mia took cover behind the stump of a tree. Whatever was up, she wasn't letting them out of her sight. Not for a single second. If anything was going to kick off, she needed the element of surprise. The weapons they carried were her best chance of survival. She needed to keep them close enough to take down without getting drawn into a brawl. That she would almost certainly not survive. Not the way they carried their weapons, anyway. She watched the way Dev held his weapon, his index finger resting outstretched above the trigger. The gun seemed an extension of his arms, swaying with him gently as he moved, always pointed in the direction he was looking. He and the weapon were one. Prisha, too, for that matter. They were not to be messed with. Mia had no intention of being drawn into a fight with them. Not unless it became absolutely necessary.

They came upon a large makeshift wall. More of a fence than a wall, but still sturdy. Much like the wall Mia had known in her own town. It had all the signature makings of a structure built over many years, added to and strengthened as better resources were found. Most of it appeared to have been made from metal poles liberated presumably from discarded buildings and street lamps. Between the poles were corrugated iron sheets, wooden slats and barbed wire. Not exactly enough to stop anybody who really wanted in, but enough to slow them down if they tried. At least nobody from outside could see in.

Prisha and Dev came to a stop outside the wall. Mia waited for them to do something. If this had been her own home, a guard, or somebody else, would have appeared over the wall by now to let them in. It seemed to her that the couple was waiting for just such a person. Butterflies took wing in Mia's stomach as the silence drew on. Listening to the beat of her heart, she counted the seconds away. Five. Ten. Fifteen. At twenty, she knew nobody was coming. Something was wrong. Dev apparently was of the same disposition. Getting Prisha to give him a boost up, he then instructed her to step back from the wall, before he pulled himself up and over.

Silence.

Mia's heart beat louder.

'Fuck me,' Dev said, invisible from the other side of the fence.

'What?' Prisha said. 'What is it?'

The gate creaked open a moment later as Dev stepped out and sat on the ground. Prisha went to him and put her arms around him.

Mia couldn't hear what Prisha said. Her eyes were trained on the view through the slit of the open gate. Bodies lay strewn across a wide expanse of tarmac. Up ahead, outside a burnt building, lay even more. It was a massacre. She felt the blood drain from her face as she blinked her dizziness away. Wiping the sweat from her palms, she gripped her knife tighter, circling Prisha and Dev, who were both in tears. She walked along the fence until she came to another gate, and let herself in as quietly as she could, knowing there was nobody on the other side. Nobody alive, at least. She had to know, though.

Stepping tentatively through, she assessed the fly-covered corpses, hoping the dread in the pit of her stomach was not a precursor to something she did not want to find. The smell was horrific. By the looks of them, the bodies had been out there for most of the day, if not more. She looked at every single body before moving into the charred building. There were more bodies within, but still no Dylan.

Stepping over one of the corpses, she heard a low croak from nearby. One of them was alive, only just. She rushed over the floor to the woman lying face up on the ground, her head covered in dried blood. She had been shot three times, judging by the pools of blood on her shoulder, stomach and thigh. Her skin was a ghostly pale grey. Mia scooped the woman's head up in her lap as she knelt beside her, and poured a few drops of water in the woman's mouth.

'You're not one of them,' the woman said, her voice barely audible.

'I'm looking for a man,' Mia said, her eyes filling with tears. She didn't want to say his name for fear of the woman confirming what had likely happened to him. After a deep breath, she continued. 'His name was Dylan.'

'Dylan ... he was here.'

'Was here?' Mia said. 'Is he still here? Did he get out?' She got no response. The woman's head lolled to the side as she gave out a last, hoarse breath. Mia got to her feet, looking at the bodies on the floor. The light was terrible inside. She'd have to drag every single body out into the light to know for sure. She heard the scuff of feet on the tarmac nearby.

'Who the fuck are you?' Dev said from somewhere behind.

Mia froze, every nerve in her body twitching. Run or fight? She didn't have long to choose.

16

'You need to slow down, Claire,' Tatenda said. 'Now is not the time to be reckless.'

Ignoring her friend's advice, Claire marched on. For the best part of a week since they had left Harry and the rest of his companions at Stonehenge, they had moved at Claire's pace. She'd pushed as hard as her own body would allow, finding depths of strength and determination within that even she was surprised to find. If anybody had a good understanding of their limits by now, it should have been her. But with her sons out there, she somehow managed to dig deeper every day. They were getting close now; she could see it as much as feel it. The old motorway leading into London. Some familiar buildings from a lifetime ago. She was being drawn back into a place she thought she'd never return to. The city had come to a standstill the day she left, it seemed. The only thing different about the skyline now was nature's indefatigable war with the old world. The result wasn't up for debate. Mankind had lost severely. *We didn't deserve to win.*

'Do you have any idea how you want to enter the city?'

Chipo said. 'Dylan and Mia could have entered it in any direction.'

'We take the most logical path,' Claire said.

'And which one is that?'

'We'll know it when we see it. If they've turned off at any point, it should be apparent why. Otherwise, we assume they've continued on ahead.'

'Okay,' Tatenda said, 'but first we eat. This might be our last chance for a quiet lunch before Chipo has to start pointing that crossbow at someone in anger.'

He had a point. Once they got to the outskirts, there was no telling who or what they'd find. A final rest was a good idea. It might give her a chance to get her head straight, too. Settle some nerves, perhaps.

Claire led them off the overgrown motorway to the shade of a tree, where she opened her rucksack and took out the remains of the deer they'd caught a couple of days before. 'This is the last of it,' she said as she pulled the last strips of leg from her bag. She'd wrapped it in a number of plastic bags to keep it from spoiling. Removing the bags, she shook her head. 'Do you remember before?'

'Before what?' Chipo said.

'The Blackout. We always had so many plastic bags lying about. Never thought that when everything else disappeared, they'd be the one thing we still had plenty of.'

'Besides the guns, you mean?' Tatenda said.

'Ah, yes.' Claire smiled. 'We really did save the best of ourselves, didn't we?'

'We make do with what we've got,' Chipo said, not quite tolerating Claire's trip down memory lane, if her tone was anything to go by.

Appreciating her friend's ability to know when not to indulge her, Claire set to work cutting strips of meat off the leg for the three of them. The last thing she'd done when she left London twenty years before was sit up on a hill in Richmond Park with Maxime and eat a deer as they watched the world end. Aircraft falling out of the sky. The city burning. Riots in the streets. Humanoid robots gunning the rioters down. It was all coming back to her as if it were yesterday. A nightmare long-buried, resurfacing in the blink of an eye. How fitting it was that the last thing she did now before returning to the city was finish her deer before heading in, as determined to enter the city as she once had been to leave it. Twenty years before she'd been terrified and alone, with only a relatively new friend in Maxime to look after her as her pregnancy caused her to slow down on their outward journey. At least this time she was returning with two good friends in Chipo and Tatenda, even if she was still terrified. The little bump she'd carried back then was now a man all his own, and he was in danger. Her fears about the world her little bump might have to grow up in had only since been confirmed. She never thought he might be hunted by his own kin, though. Part of her wondered why she hadn't foreseen something like this. After all, she'd witnessed the two men she'd loved die before her, one a willing sacrifice and the other cruelly taken in a moment of madness. Should she really have dared to hope for better for her boys?

The pang of loss cut her like a freshly dressed wound being torn once more as she was overcome with grief for both of the men she'd loved. Matt and Maxime. Both fine men whom she'd fallen for. She had never imagined herself without Matt. He had been her first. The one she'd planned her life with. Having lost him so suddenly, she hadn't expected to ever love again. But everything about Maxime was a surprise. A surprising delight in a world devoid of surprise delights. Perhaps because of this, she had fallen even harder for him. He had been everything to her. For twenty years they had built a life together against impossible odds, raising two boys. How quickly it had all gone to shit. Just like the godforsaken landscape before her. She looked ahead at the city. *What a disaster.* Had she not known her boys were somewhere up ahead, she'd have turned and run as far as she could without ever looking back. And she'd have been glad of it. There was nothing there for her. Nobody she knew. Only memories too painful to endure again.

'You okay?' Chipo said, shifting up beside Claire.

'Fine, thanks. Just gathering my strength. It's been a while since I was last here.'

'Bet it looked a bit different then.'

She nodded. 'That it did.'

'Shall we be off, then?'

'Yes, let's.'

THE MOTORWAY'S width unsettled Claire as they walked on towards the city. She didn't like walking down big old roads at the best of times. To her they were nothing more than death traps, allowing attackers to spring from roadside bushes unseen until it was too late. But now, as the countryside trees gave way to the concrete and metal husks of yesteryear, her skin began to prickle, her nerves getting the better of her. The buildings were so tall. Taller than she'd remembered. In two decades she'd become quite used to the smaller remnants of countryside buildings. Now she found herself looking up at these old buildings with trepidation.

'It's not safe,' she said.

'What's not safe?' Tatenda said.

'Up ahead.' She pointed her khukuri knife towards the monstrous structures in the distance.

'Did you see something?' Chipo said, taking aim with her crossbow.

'No,' Claire said. 'But I don't like it. We should leave the motorway as soon as we can. It's what Dylan would have done.'

'How could you know that?' Chipo said.

'Because I raised him not to be a fool. This is a dangerous road. He'd have wanted to move onto something smaller, I know it.'

'You're sure of it?' Chipo said.

'As sure as anyone can be of anything in this world,' she said, knowing that in her case, there was a fine balance between absolute surety and complete and utter uncertainty. Such was her confidence these days. 'Up ahead,' she said, pointing now to the rusted sign beside the road.

'Heathrow Airport?' Chipo said.

'Yes, let's take that road. It'll get us off this open space, at least.'

'All roads will be open, Claire. We're getting to the city now. We're not going to be able to escape the buildings. We're just going to have to change the way we move through it. The dangers will come from different directions. We'll have to watch out for what's above as much as for what's beside us.'

'Even so, something tells me he'd have left the motorway at this point.'

'Then what are we waiting for?' Tatenda said, a gentle smile forming across his face.

Buoyed by his calming presence, Claire returned his smile and switched her mind to a more alert state, if that were possible. It had been a long time since she had been in any city, let alone one as big as this. Chipo was right about its dangers. They would be different to what she was used to. There was no telling what lay in store for them. Her only hope was that her boys were both still alive and well. This couldn't all be for nothing. She wouldn't let it be.

The next road they took was big, too. Everything seemed bigger than Claire remembered. Twenty years living in a secluded forest dwelling with nothing but her loved ones had altered her perception of scale. The city she had once thought of as home now took on something more sinister in her mind. It was menacing. She felt an evil lurking beneath its remains. In the countryside, small towns had been overgrown almost to the point of disappearance. At least, towns whose populations had disappeared. But here the clash between man and nature was a much more gruesome battle. A battlefield bathed in green. She walked on with Chipo and Tatenda, only their footsteps providing any sound in the light breeze. They moved slowly, listening out for signs of life. The roads, thankfully, were littered with the carcasses of old vehicles, which provided a little cover for them to move between. But Claire figured if anybody was watching, they'd know about it soon enough. And she didn't reckon a rusted old frame would provide much in the way of protection.

Stepping around the remains of one old vehicle, Claire came to a stop. A blinding light flashed in her eye. At first she thought it might just be a shattered piece of glass, a remnant from when the car had been broken into years, if not decades, before. But upon inspection she noticed a brass shell casing on its side upon the tarmac. Chipo and Tatenda closed up behind her. Claire pointed to the shell casing. Without another word they spread out. It would be almost impossible to tell how long the shell casing had been there but if anyone could, Claire figured it would be Chipo. There wasn't a tracker out there even on a par with her, except perhaps her brother Tatenda.

A few minutes later they had collected more casings. Chipo pointed out some torn clothing on the vehicle's rusted frame where somebody had presumably hunched right up against it for cover. There was no telling what the clothing was nor who it might belong to, though. It was far too small to be of much use. Just some torn cotton threads.

'A shirt, perhaps,' Chipo said.

Claire said nothing. They checked the vicinity. A short way back down the road they saw some stray arrows lying on the road. 'Two groups,' Claire said. Telling herself Dylan and Jake weren't the only people in the world who'd likely learned to make arrows, Claire tried to push the thought of her sons being caught in this fight from her mind.

'A standoff, by the looks of it,' Chipo said.

'Like somebody had walked into another's territory?'

'Could be. But there's no real telling who that somebody was.'

'Is there anything you can tell?' Claire said.

Chipo looked at the tarmac for a moment. 'It was recent,' she said eventually.

'How recent?'

'A few days, perhaps. Not much more, I reckon.'

'Why's that?'

'Because any rains would have shifted that shirt. It wasn't really stuck in there. Even a light breeze might have blown it away. The shell casings, too. They haven't really got much dirt on them. Give it a couple of weeks and you'll see dust on top of each. The undersides would be cleaner where they would be protected from the elements.' Beside Chipo her brother nodded his approval of her assessment. 'Whatever happened here, it wasn't that long ago.'

Claire didn't know whether to be hopeful or worried. It could be her two sons had had it out right here where she stood, and ended each other. It could be one of them had been captured. Could also be that one of them had been killed here. Or it could be that this site had nothing to do with her sons at all and she was standing in the midst of some old turf war. 'Why aren't there any bodies?' she said, eventually. 'I've never seen this much evidence of a fight lying around without a body or two nearby.'

'My thoughts exactly,' Tatenda said.

'Two possible reasons, as far as I see it,' Chipo said. Claire waited for the summary. 'First, the one or ones attacked survived and hid the bodies of those they killed somewhere nearby. Out of sight so as not to draw attention to the killing.'

'You reckon that's possible?' Claire said.

'We can check the surroundings either side of the road but I wouldn't bet my house on it.'

'Why's that?'

'Because this many gunshots probably would have caught the attention of others. I don't reckon there's anywhere in the world right now where bullets aren't a valuable commodity. Anybody willing to fire a few off in anger was probably fighting for their life. Which meant they weren't thinking about being stealthy. If there was such a shootout, and somebody killed a bunch of their attackers, they'd have disappeared as fast as they could in any direction to put some distance between them and this site. Then there's the arrows. If I was the one who'd survived the fight, I certainly wouldn't be leaving perfectly good arrows lying around.'

'So what's your other theory?'

'Well, no bodies means nobody died, so my best guess is that whatever happened here, it ended up with somebody being captured and taken away.'

'Captured?'

'Indeed. It's a good thing, Claire. It means there's probably a base nearby. Could be that one or both of your boys is there. If not, it means they probably gave this place a wide berth. Either way, it'll tell us something about this part of town. We just need to do a little more investigating.'

'What are we looking for?'

'Somewhere you'd consider a good place to set up camp. A good strong structure, preferably isolated from others, with views to see anybody coming or going.'

Claire remembered the road sign at the turn-off. 'Like an airport?'

'Precisely like an airport,' Chipo said. 'Clear runways to see attackers from a distance. Terminals to build a base in. Yes, I reckon an airport would be a fine place to use as a fort.'

'Okay,' Tatenda said. 'We could be wrong, though, so let's keep our eyes peeled.'

CLAIRE CARRIED one of the arrows in her hand as she walked. The other she'd added to her collection in her quiver. Turning it over, she inspected its every detail. Its design was simple enough. A straight shaft, with a well-made stone tip. Fletchings made from chicken feathers, by the looks of it, and a small well-cut nock. This was no amateur job. The more she looked at it, the more she believed it was made by one of her sons. Both were experienced survivalists. It was basically all they did know. And both could be deadly with a bow and arrow. But more than their proficiency with the weapon, both were good craftsmen by nature. In a world devoid of professions, her sons had excelled at everything she and Maxime had taught them. Sure, there was a chance that this arrow could well have been made by somebody else, but there was a big difference between good quality and exceptional quality. Often, when she found the handmade weapons of others, she chose to destroy them rather than keep them, such were the standards she held. Life in the post-Blackout world did not allow for mediocrity when it came to protecting one's life. *Yes, this is almost certainly one of the boys' arrows.*

Up ahead, Heathrow Airport came into view. The old glass structure she had passed through so many times was a lot different to her memories, even from a distance. A makeshift fence surrounded the airport, much like the one back in Taunton, made up from a collection of rubble presumably put together over years. Chipo's guess had been spot on. Somebody had used the airport as a base, or was still using it as such. The fence looked to be intact from where she stood. Although, the building itself looked badly damaged within. Claire saw that much of the glass was shattered, and what was there was stained black from smoke. The building had been burned down, at least partially. She wondered how long ago it might have happened. There was no smoke billowing out from the building, and no signs of life from where they were. No guards atop the fence. Nobody patrolling the perimeter. 'Think it's abandoned?' she said.

'Only one way to find out,' Chipo said.

They approached slowly. The flat terrain didn't allow for anybody to take the high ground and watch for others, as Claire would have preferred. Instead they spread out, Claire moving slightly ahead as Chipo and Tatenda each took a flank, keeping fifty yards back. Claire kept low, crouching as she moved through the long grass, her bow out with an arrow at the ready. Not quite drawn taut, but not far from it.

When she reached the fence, or wall, depending on how one looked at it, she stopped, listening for signs of life on the other side. A good minute or so she stayed, looking only at her feet as she cocked an ear towards the base. She could hear a couple of crows squawking but that was it. Then, as a light breeze drifted over her from the base, the smell hit her. It was unmistakable. Rotting flesh had a distinct smell, in her experience. There was nothing else quite like it. Her nose twitched as it fought off the offensive odour.

She moved up and peered through the fence, taking a moment to register what her eyes were picking up. Before her lay strewn corpses, mostly up towards the building itself. It was clear some fight had taken place inside. The corpses didn't look to be too old, either. She'd stumbled across her fair share of human remains in twenty years and these couldn't be more than a day or so, if that. Whatever had happened here, she figured anybody alive had moved on. Raising her hand to give the all clear, she signalled Chipo and Tatenda over.

'What is it?' Tatenda said.

'All clear,' Claire said.

'There's nobody in there?' Chipo said.

'There are bodies in there, for sure, but none of them is alive. Take a look for yourself.' She waited for Chipo and Tatenda to both look through the gap in the fence. 'Some kind of battle, I reckon. Not long ago.'

'I see weapons on the ground. We should go in,' Tatenda said.

It had been a big battle. Claire stopped counting the

corpses when she got to twenty. They found more inside the destroyed building. With every corpse she inspected, she held her breath momentarily, waiting for one to be a familiar face, but thankfully her sons were not among them. Neither was Mia for that matter. What she did find was a trail of blood leading down a walled-off section of the terminal that had been broken through. 'We're going in.'

'Down there?' Tatenda said, pointing to the small hole in the wall. 'Why the hell would we do that?'

'This airport once had a connection to the Underground. My guess is that the source of this trail of blood knew of this tunnel. Probably they were the one who busted through this wall in the first place. Judging by the fact that most of the battle seems to have taken place in the building, I'm guessing they either burst out through this wall or fled back through it on their way out. They probably used it to travel through the city without having to move above ground.'

'There's no guarantee that your boys were part of this, though. How are we going to find your sons if we're always below ground?' Chipo said.

Pulling the arrow from her quiver once more, Claire turned it over in her hand. 'I think there's as good a chance as any that at least one of my boys was here. It's a hunch but it's all I have to go on. We can use the tunnel to our advantage. We'll pop up every chance we get, scout the area, assuming it's safe enough to do so, and then move again beneath the city's surface. It's how we used to move about when I was a part of the Disconnected. The tunnels kept us out of trouble.'

'And what if there are other people down in those tunnels now?' Tatenda said. 'On the basis of what you've just said, we could find ourselves face to face with another group also trying to keep out of the way of those on the surface. At the very least, it looks like we're likely to run into at least one injured person, who is probably not going to take kindly to strangers.'

'If that happens, at least nobody will have the high ground. I like my chances better in a one-on-one fight better than I like them walking through a city filled with tall buildings where people more familiar with the surroundings can sneak up on me. And if I'm right about my hunch and one of my boys has passed this way, then going into the tunnels will have been the right decision.'

Tatenda nodded. 'Fair point.'

Beyond the hole in the wall, the tunnel was utterly dark, without even a chink of light. Claire entered first, hoping she wasn't about to lead her two friends to their deaths.

17

Everything had happened so fast. Jake wasn't quite sure how he'd got to be walking down a dark and dreary tunnel with a relative stranger and his brother, whom he'd just fought beside after weeks of trying to hunt him down. He knew why, of course, but that didn't sit any easier with him, either. *Mia.* She was in trouble. All alone out there in an area she knew nothing about. She hadn't had the kind of upbringing Jake had had. She hadn't had an older brother to learn new skills alongside. To kill alongside. People, like blades, needed constant sharpening. Mia, despite her many qualities, was not what Jake considered sharp in terms of combat skills. She needed help. And like it or not, he knew Dylan would do everything in his power to rescue her. It was in his nature. Always the hero. But cities were dangerous places. Dylan would need a hand. And who better to help out than the little brother who'd grown up beside him, learning how to hunt together, to track and kill and defend together. And who knew Mia.

Dylan, of course, had known every string to pluck. He always did. If there was one person who could cut to the core of Jake's being with only a few words, it was his brother. Of course, there was more to it than that. The big man, Martin, had made it pretty clear that there was to be no more fighting, not if they wanted to make it out alive. A truce had been the only option. For now, at least. The only certainties in the world were that tomorrow the sun would still rise and more people would die. Jake knew that deep down, he did not wish for Mia to die. Even if she had chosen his brother over him. That was just something he had to live with. Just another pursuit in which Dylan had bested him. He wondered if his brother was even aware of the trail of despair he left behind him. *Unlikely.* Still, Jake had given his big brother a good thumping, at least. He couldn't recall a single occasion when he'd done so before. Many attempts but never a victory. The result of the fight certainly didn't heal any wounds but it helped all the same. There had been some catharsis in it, some sense of satisfaction. Like picking a scab and feeling the faint tingle of a burn. His hunger for revenge was somewhat satiated by having delivered a few blows. Until Martin had dragged him off his brother, that was. Dylan, of course, would claim that Jake had caught him unaware. Blindsided him. Or some other piss-poor excuse like that. But when Jake had tried those excuses as a kid, Dylan had pushed back, claiming he should have had his guard up at all times. *If only he could take his own advice.*

Martin's words had played on his mind, too. The advice about making a mistake he couldn't take back. The more Jake thought about it, the more he realised he could never bring himself to kill his brother. The desire had been a result of the rage he carried within. A dangerous mixture of shame and anger, wrapped up in a mind that had been twisted by Frank, a charming and convincing man. But

Martin had been right. Jake did not want to make a mistake he could not take back.

What he truly wanted, if he was honest with himself, was to be a part of his family once more. Not to be the one ostracised. He wanted back in, more than anything. Holding on to anger had got him nowhere good. It was time to let it go.

Breaking out of the Silver Eagles' base had felt good, too. Fighting alongside his brother again had been as natural as the change of seasons. Slipping from one state of life into another. Just like that. He wasn't about to admit it out loud but there had been some enjoyment there, for sure. Like putting an old pair of boots on again.

These tunnels, though, they could get fucked. Jake didn't like them one bit. Cold and wet, with air so dense it was difficult to breathe. All the while it felt like the walls were closing in on him. The only sound he heard besides the trudging of their feet was a constant slow drip of water, echoing loudly in the relative silence. He wanted very much to be back in his forest home, sitting around the fire, listening to his mother and father as they prepared a meal from the day's hunt. *It wasn't even that long ago.* Life wasn't for moping, though. It was time to set things right.

'Christ, it's frosty down here,' Martin said, as he led the way a few paces ahead.

Dylan mumbled some sort of agreement from just in front of Jake.

'Yeah,' Jake said. 'The sooner we get back above ground the better.'

'I'm not on about the temperature, lad. You two need to work your shit out.'

'We're good,' Jake said, not wanting to be drawn into a discussion on the state of his feelings.

Martin stopped and turned to face them as Jake and Dylan came to a halt. 'This isn't a game. I mean it. No fucking fighting. That means no silent festering and no plotting against one another. A truce is a truce. That's the only way you're getting my help. Whatever your past squabbles, it's time to bury it, all right?'

'Agreed,' Dylan said, not quite looking Jake in the eye. 'For Mia.'

Eventually, Jake nodded back. 'For Mia.'

'That's a start.' Martin turned and continued on his way. Jake and Dylan settled in behind. 'Now we've got a ways to go, mind. Most of the tunnels are still dry, even if the river did break its banks and flood the city a while back.'

'How's that?' Dylan said.

'The river? Ah, there were some old tidal barrages from long ago what used to keep it so the city didn't get flooded whenever it should have been. But after the world went to shite, so did everything that was keeping the city the way everybody wanted it.'

'No, I meant the tunnels still being dry,' Dylan said.

'The tunnels were closed off decades before the Blackout. Transport down here was too slow. Too antiquated. Most people from before the Blackout wouldn't even remember ever having used the old Underground. The entrances were bricked off before their time. I'd hate to think what else is buried beneath this city, lost to time. Anyway, we'll have to pop up soon and move above ground for a bit, but it won't be for long.'

'Why's that?' Jake said.

'Some of the tunnels didn't run completely underground, so where the old tracks went overground, they were built over. I know the way, though. You just keep doing as I say and we'll be good.'

'All right then,' Jake said.

Going back above ground felt to Jake like it used to when he'd venture out of the safety of his family's forest territory. He felt naked and exposed, like he was being watched. Above him tall buildings towered. Much taller than anything he'd come across before in his life. They stretched up out of the ground like fingers reaching for the sun. Like some greedy fool after another bite of food. Their shadows didn't move over him like plants did when bending in the wind. Instead they just smothered him. He wondered what it must have felt like to have lived so high up off the ground like that. So disconnected from the earth. So far from nature. His legs became unsteady as the craning of his neck into such an unnatural position made him dizzy.

'You all right there, mucker?' Martin said.

'All good,' Jake said, doubling over to rest his hands on his knees while he blinked his vision back to normality. 'Those things are huge.'

'Hmm?'

'The buildings.'

'Ah, yeah, 'spose they are. Novelty wears off after a while, mind. You'll get used to 'em.'

'People actually lived in those?'

'Lived, sure. Worked. Studied. Went to war with keyboard and screen. They did everything up there. By the end, most of 'em never came down.'

'You make it sound like a prison,' Dylan said.

'To some it was,' Martin said. 'To others, it was everything they ever wanted. And the rest, well, they probably just didn't know there were other options out there. Most just drifted along, not quite sure what life had in store for them. Life back then had a way of pulling you along without you noticing. You could have lived a whole life in one of those buildings before you'd fully grasped how much time had passed.'

Jake couldn't imagine wanting to spend a single day up there, let alone never wanting to come back down. He stepped in behind Martin, who'd moved off again, seemingly not wanting to stay above ground for any longer than was necessary.

Martin led them into a quiet path between two buildings and gestured to a circular steel plate in the ground. 'Give me a hand with the manhole cover,' he said to Dylan.

Jake stepped back, leaving the two more physically capable men to handle the task. Mentally cursing his brother, as always, for having been gifted with everything that was necessary to succeed in life, Jake bit his tongue. Saying it out loud would get him nowhere, he'd learned that long ago. It didn't make it any easier, though. Every time he deferred to his brother was another small humiliation inflicted. Another scar to bear. Perhaps Dylan didn't care. Perhaps Dylan didn't keep count. Not like he did.

A shaft opened up below them and they descended once more into the darkness. They walked on with purpose this time. Martin seemed much happier to be down in the tunnels again, his shoulders slouching a little as he relaxed, which put Jake more at ease than he felt he would be if he were traversing the claustrophobic paths of darkness on his own.

It was slow going in the dark. Jake struggled to grasp the passage of time. With no sun to track as it arched across the sky, no growing or diminishing natural light and no wildlife performing habitual rituals, he had no way of knowing how long it was taking. It felt like an age. They changed direction often, shifting from one tunnel to another, passing old platforms that looked like they rarely received visitors. The walls were caked in dust or mould, depending on how dry each one was. Jake had long ago lost his sense of direction and no longer knew which way he was pointed. His brother, too, seemed a little out of his depth, if his relative silence was anything to go by. Dylan could usually be relied upon to talk when talking wasn't necessary, such was his general confidence. But not now. Even he had apparently been made to feel insignificant down here. That was the thing about fear. Nobody was immune to it forever. Even the great Dylan was susceptible to it.

Martin pulled up behind an overturned shopping trolley. Jake and Dylan took cover on either side of him, awaiting their burly companion's next move. Martin let out a long whistle which echoed down the tunnel.

A moment later Jake heard another in reply. 'Who goes there?' some young lad said.

'It's me, Martin.'

'Martin!'

Jake heard the pounding of feet as a couple of people ran out from cover somewhere in the distance. He, Martin and Dylan stood up. Two young boys appeared, one holding a lit torch. Jake, grateful for the light, watched the flame for a moment before he saw the terror in the boys' eyes.

'You've been gone for so long,' one said to Martin. 'Where are the others?'

Martin let out a deep sigh. 'Better go get Marie, lads. Better get everyone, in fact. It'll be easier to tell them all at once.'

AFTER ONE OF the boys had darted off, while the other took

up his lookout position once more, Martin led Jake and Dylan through a makeshift wall, much like the ones around the various bases Jake had come across above ground. It was made up of old fencing, corrugated iron roofing, barbed wire and plenty of other materials presumably gathered over time. 'Welcome to Liverpool Street, home of the Disconnected,' Martin said.

'This is your home?' Dylan said.

'For longer than I care to remember, yes.'

The Underground station was bigger than most of the others they had passed through, with more platforms than Jake could count. Wooden torches burned in place along the walls, offering patches of light but not quite enough to illuminate the whole place. Jake suspected the fact that there weren't more torches had something to do with the amount of smoke being given off by each one. Presumably they had figured out over time what the balance was between acceptable lighting conditions and acceptable breathing conditions.

The platforms were filled with furniture. Most of it was used for sleeping on, by the looks of it, although Jake noted tables and benches for eating, weapons stashes, what looked like a fairly poor attempt at medical supplies, and other spaces to sit and congregate. It was a fairly sizable base, all things considered. Probably not quite the numbers New Britain had had when he and Dylan had arrived but probably not far short, either.

Hanging back while Martin addressed the others, Jake and Dylan kept to themselves. Jake listened as Martin recounted the story of his group's attack on the Silver Eagles. How they had successfully broken in through the tunnels. How the element of surprise had worked, if only for a moment. Martin spoke of Silver Eagles' overwhelming numbers, of their preparedness and weapons arsenal. It was a sad tale of a mission gone horribly wrong. Martin's voice dripped with regret. Only then did Jake begin to fully comprehend the losses Martin had suffered. He saw in the faces of the Disconnected the very same pain he carried every day. That of losing one of his own. Witnessing their pain as they learned their loved ones would not be returning brought to mind the memories of New Britain's attack on his own home and the death of his father. Perhaps Frank had not been the leader Jake had thought him to be. Somewhere along the way Frank had seduced him, he realised. It hadn't been real. *This* was real. What these people were going through, much like he had when Frank had killed his own father. He watched as family members huddled together and wept, seeking solace in each other's arms while Martin struggled to find the appropriate words. Jake stepped closer to Dylan, wanting to say he was sorry. For everything. For allowing the world to come between them. For ever doubting his brother's intentions. For allowing someone else to blind him to the world. He felt a well of shame open up within him like a chasm parting the earth. His brother seemed to understand, and placed a hand on Jake's shoulder. It was done. Whatever bitterness Jake had felt melted away, and he was profoundly grateful to be standing beside his brother again.

'And these two,' Martin said as he wiped a tear from his cheek, 'they helped me escape. Brave bastards, the both of 'em. They fought alongside me. Without them, I wouldn't have made it back. But then they come from good stock. As it happens, their folks used to belong to this very group. Most of you have joined us in the years since the Blackout, but Dylan and Jake here, their folks were a part of the

Disconnected back when we first rose up against Connected Industries.'

A woman stepped forward to look more closely at Jake and Dylan.

'Marie, they're Claire's kids,' Martin said.

A look of shock registered on the woman's face. Her mouth opened and closed silently.

'It's a pleasure to meet you,' Dylan said, stepping forward to take her outstretched hand. 'Thank you for allowing us into your home.'

Still Marie appeared at a loss for words. Her eyes filled to the brim as she stood holding Dylan's hand. Jake couldn't make out what it was that had her so consumed with emotion at the sight of him and his brother.

Marie turned to Martin. 'The others?' she said.

'I'm afraid not,' he said, his head bowed low.

'Eoin?' she said.

'No,' Martin said.

Jake had not heard Martin's voice break like that in the short time he'd known him. It was an awful thing to see a man so broken. Whatever it was they were looking for from him and Dylan, they had not found it. He felt compelled to apologise for having let them down, although, not quite knowing what for, he kept his mouth shut.

Marie's lip trembled. She took a deep breath. 'Jonathan?'

'No, Marie. I'm sorry,' Martin said. He walked over to her and embraced her tightly, his giant form consuming her. Somewhere beneath all the brawn, a gentle whimper could be heard.

Martin turned back to Jake and his brother. 'Marie's husband Jonathan knew your mother. Knew both your fathers, too.'

'What happened to him?' Jake said, unsure of how else to respond.

'Last we heard, he was with your mother as they mounted an attack on our enemy. My partner Eoin, too. Then the world went dark. That was two decades ago.'

Before Jake could even think of how to go about responding to a statement like that, a young girl came running up to them all. Another youngster. Jake wondered if she too was a scout, like the two boys who'd been stationed outside the Disconnected's base. She placed her hands on her head and arched her back, taking in deep breaths as sweat dripped down her face. If Jake were to guess, he figured she'd been running for minutes at full speed. Even longer, perhaps.

'What is it?' Marie said to the girl, regaining her composure.

The little girl looked up at Jake and his brother, clearly unhappy at seeing two strange faces in her home. Then she returned her gaze to Marie. 'They're coming,' she said.

'Who? Who's coming?'

'All of them. They must have heard about our attempt on Silver Eagles. The other factions have all been sighted on the move, all carrying weapons. They're moving quickly, too. I think there's going to be a battle.'

18

Claire led the way through the tunnels as Chipo and Tatenda followed. With every step she took, memories came flooding back of her old life. The city, even on its deathbed, would not let her go. It drew her back in like an unseen current. She was powerless to resist it, she realised. Two decades and still she felt its pull. No matter how much she'd told herself that home was her old forest dwelling, or the new town in which she'd recently taken over, there was only one true home. She felt it now. It was a place she knew almost as well as she knew herself. Even in darkness, she knew where she was going. Each time the tunnel opened up to the platform of some other old Underground station, she stopped to get her bearings. Just to check that her memory had not failed her. But every time it was the station she had expected to find. The familiarity resurfaced like the feeling of riding a bike, although that too was something from the old world. Like the feeling of drawing her bow, then. Whatever it was, it was instinctual. She knew London like she knew no other place.

Before long she found it.

Liverpool Street.

The familiar old makeshift fence was still in place, although it had been added to in recent years, she could tell. *People still live here.*

'Stop right there,' a young voice said.

It reminded Claire of one of her boys when they had been much younger. The brave little face appeared from behind a bollard, torch held high in one hand, pistol in the other. *Is there no innocence left at all?* 'Hello,' Claire said, holding both her hands up in surrender.

'Who are you?'

'My name's Claire. I used to live here.'

The boy paused for a second. Claire wondered what was going on in his little mind as he mulled over her words. 'I've never seen you before,' he said.

'It was a long time ago. Before you were born.'

'Will anyone here know you from before?'

'That's what I've come to find out. Who is your leader?'

At this the boy seemed to realise he'd spoken too much. He put his torch into a placement beside him, picked up a brass bell and began to ring it. The sound echoed through the tunnel, alarmingly loud. Claire could almost feel the walls of the tunnel vibrating around her with each clang. All the while the boy kept his pistol trained on Claire and her two companions.

'Should we be concerned?' Chipo said.

Claire didn't have an honest answer for that. 'Let's see how it plays out.' It had taken some convincing to get Chipo and Tatenda to agree that checking her old base might be worth a shot. They had thought it best to keep exiting the tunnels to check for signs of her sons above ground, but the more time Claire had spent down in the tunnels, the more she'd felt herself pulled towards her old home. Towards the place in which she and the rest of the Disconnected had once holed up before making their last stand. She couldn't come back to London and not check what was left. Who was left. She had to know. The city willed it so.

Tremors moved down the tunnel as pounding footsteps echoed from within the boy's base. A cloud of dust loosed itself from the ceiling, blurring Claire's vision momentarily. She braced herself for what was to come, keeping her arms up in surrender and checking back over her shoulder to ensure the Chipo and Tatenda were doing likewise. As the pounding grew louder, Claire heard panicked voices. The bell, she figured, was not something to be used lightly. When she had been a part of the Disconnected, sightings of others down in the tunnels were slim to none. Assuming most of the city's old Underground entrances were still bricked off, it would likely still be the case today. All the more reason for alarm.

Bodies poured out from behind the fence into the tunnel before Claire and came to a stop. Most carried weapons. Blades and bows mostly. Some torches. A couple of guns but not many. Claire strained her eyes to get a better view of the faces in the flickering light. They were hard, gaunt faces, etched with panic. But not ones she recognised. Most were much too young to have been around two decades before. Then the crowd parted as a large man made his way to the front. At first all Claire saw was a dark black shadow. But as the burly figure passed a torch Claire saw a fiery red beard. A beard she had once known well. The tunnel was silent, save for the sound of Claire's footsteps as she walked forwards. *It can't be.* 'Martin?'

'Claire?'

The accent was still the same, even if the voice was slightly more gravelly. She'd have recognised that rustic

West Country accent a mile off. He'd aged in twenty years. But that was no surprise. She saw now that his beard had a lot more grey than it had last time she'd seen him. Again, no surprise there. What did surprise her was seeing him standing. Memories flashed through her mind of Martin's betrayal the night she had gone on a mission with him, Maxime and Zaheera, the then leader of the Disconnected, to destroy a power-supply station that would bring the city to a standstill while they mounted an attack on their enemy. She saw again the flash of the muzzle followed by Zaheera's groan as Martin turned his gun on her, betraying the person he'd sworn his allegiance to. Martin had left Zaheera lying wounded in Claire's arms while he made off with a corrupted police android to attack other members of the Disconnected, including Matt, her fiancé.

She remembered Martin's excuse for his betrayal. How he claimed he was doing it for Eoin, his partner, despite Eoin being a member and fierce advocate of the resistance. Claire had managed to intercept Martin's attack on the others just in time, but they had decided not to kill him. Eoin had tied him up and left him for dead instead. Claire had assumed Martin had died in the destruction of the building they'd left him in.

'You're alive,' she said.

'For my sins, yeah.' He stopped a good few feet from her, his large frame curled inwards like some fearful child.

Claire was at a loss. She wanted to go and hug the man she'd once considered a friend. She wanted to beat him for his betrayal. She wanted to sit down and cry for all the loss she'd endured, all the memories and the hurts that the sight of him brought back. As she stood there, unsure of quite what to do, she heard more footsteps.

'Mum!'

Again, an unmistakable voice. Her heart leapt. 'Dylan!' He was alive. Her son ran to her and embraced her, providing the strength she needed to remain on her feet as she clutched him fiercely. Her eyes blurred as tears flooded her vision. 'My boy.' Then, as she wiped the tears away, she saw something else. Someone else. 'Jake?'

'Hi, Mum.'

Her younger son walked closer into her vision. Claire's heart beat so fiercely it threatened to burst. Her head swayed with dizziness as she tried to comprehend what she was seeing. Both sons. Alive and well. They had not killed one another. She'd made it in time. She'd found them. Until now she'd not put much thought into what she'd do or say when she found them. If she found them. Her only mission had been to try to catch up to them before what she feared most would happen. She wasn't sure what she'd expected if she came face to face with Jake again. Not after he'd attacked his brother. After Chipo had almost killed him. It seemed Jake too was at a loss with how to proceed. He stepped tentatively forward then stopped, keeping his distance. She let go of Dylan and embraced her youngest son, covering his head in kisses. 'I'm so sorry. For everything.'

'I'm sorry, too.' His voice broke a little as he said it, the boy still not quite a man.

'How did you find each other?' She didn't really care about the answer. She only wanted to hear their voices. To hug them over and over. Her life since the Blackout had involved enough pain. This was a moment to savour. Her relief was like a weight lifted from her shoulders. So heavy had it been that she felt she was standing correctly for the first time since the attack in which Jake had disappeared.

'We were captured,' Dylan said behind her. 'Separately.

But brought to the same place. That's where we met Martin. He helped us escape.'

'They helped me,' Martin said. 'Tough lads, your boys.'

It was only then Claire realised something was wrong. She stepped back from Jake's embrace and looked around, scanning the other faces. 'Where's Mia?'

'THANKS,' Claire said as she accepted a mug with a generous pour of Scotch from Martin. The others had been taken to rest up and be fed but Claire, safe in the knowledge that her boys were alive, wanted to catch up with Martin. Two decades was a long time and she had questions to ask. Likely he had plenty of his own, too. She gripped the mug, hoping it would help steady her shaking hands. The emotional rollercoaster of the day had rattled her to her core. The Scotch helped, though. A rare treat in which she'd not been able to indulge in some time. She sipped it slowly, savouring every moment as her throat took flame. 'Good to see supplies in London haven't completely run out.'

'Indeed,' Martin said. 'But they will soon enough. The gangs who've taken over various parts of the city are always at each other's throats—thieving, killing, destroying. It's a wonder anything or anyone in this city is left standing.'

'So, nothing's changed there, then?'

Martin smiled. Claire felt some of the tension in the room dissipate and was grateful for it. It was good to see her old friend smile, even if he had betrayed her a long time ago. She struggled to hold on to such ancient anger. So much had happened since then. Much worse and much better things. Right now, a familiar face was something. In a world that mostly took things from her, it was nice to have something, or someone, given back. And he'd helped with the boys. 'Thank you,' she said.

'For what?'

'For keeping my sons alive.'

He dismissed her thanks with a wave. 'Like I say, it was them who helped me. I'd never have broken out of that fort without them.'

'How were they when you met them?'

'Jake was caught first. He didn't say much for a while. Kept mostly to himself. There's a lot of anger in that one. He carries the weight of the world on his shoulders.'

'You're telling me,' Claire said.

'Then Dylan got caught. That really set things off. I didn't realise they were brothers at first, what with their different complexions an' all. But I sensed something was up between them soon enough. There was something sour there. Left a bad taste in my mouth, you know?' Claire did. She nodded but said nothing. 'The faction that caught us, the Silver Eagles, had us doing work to repair the terminal my lot had destroyed in our attack on them. Jake kicked off something feral. He went after Dylan the first chance he got. Pounced on him and let fly with everything he had. He's got a lot of fight for such a little mucker. I thought Dylan wasn't long for the world, so I did my best to drag them apart.'

'I'll be forever grateful for that.'

'Don't worry about it. If I may ask, though, what makes a couple of brothers turn on each other like that?'

At a loss for quite how to respond, Claire looked up at the tunnel ceiling to gather her thoughts. She sipped more of her Scotch. Let it warm her from the inside out. 'This world,' she said eventually. 'This awful fucking world that we created. Sometimes I wonder if we did the right thing bringing down Adam and the rest of Connected Industries.

But then you knew it would come to this, didn't you? You were the only one who saw what we'd all become.' Martin said nothing. Only looked her deep in her eyes. 'I remember what you said. You said we'd taken it too far, that you only wanted a quiet life with Eoin. You could see this all going to shit.'

'I saw nothing,' Martin said. 'I was a coward. I was selfish. All I wanted was for Eoin and me to get away from it all.'

'Well, you were right to want that,' Claire said. 'I wanted something similar. I tried to raise my boys away from the rest of the world. We holed up in a forest as far from London as we could get. But it didn't last. There was this gang—New Britain—' Claire turned her head away for a moment, the pain and disgust at everything she'd endured momentarily overwhelming her. 'Prick of a leader. He killed Maxime.'

'I'm sorry.'

Not wanting to relive Maxime's loss, Claire ploughed on as her vision blurred with tears. 'Then he took my boys. Left me tied to a tree to die as he set our forest on fire.'

'Christ.'

'Like I said, he was a prick. I managed to escape, though. Made some friends along the way.'

'The two you came with?'

'Chipo and Tatenda, yeah. They helped me attack New Britain's base. I managed to get Dylan out but Jake, he'd been turned by the leader, Frank. The bastard had corrupted his mind. I don't know how. From what Dylan's said since, it seems he preyed on Jake's impressionable nature. Convinced him that the way he was running things was the only way the world could be set right again. Anyway, we killed him. But Jake was caught in the crossfire. He didn't take too well to it. Maybe he thought I'd chosen to defend his brother over him. I don't know. Whatever it was, he disappeared after Frank died. I spent weeks looking for him. Every day I prayed I wouldn't find his corpse out there somewhere. Meanwhile Dylan had met himself a rather lovely young girl.'

'That this Mia he's so concerned about?'

'That's the one,' she said. 'They left the base we'd liberated to go on an adventure. They wanted to see the world.'

'And you let them?'

'I can't keep them cooped up forever,' Claire said. 'Maxime tried to get me to understand it for years but I wouldn't listen. I thought I could keep them in our little forest dwelling for always, safe from the rest of the world. But I had to come to terms with it. Dylan's his own man now. I couldn't have prevented it even if I wanted to. Anyway, the problem came when Chipo found tracks she thought were Jake's trailing after Dylan and Mia. It was then I knew Jake was set on revenge. Dylan said that during their imprisonment, Jake had really turned to Frank's way of thinking. He'd become rather enamoured with Mia, too. But she chose Dylan. I suspect that played a part.'

'I'd imagine it did,' Martin. 'In fact, if it weren't for her being in danger now, I'm not sure he'd have agreed to a truce with his brother.'

'Well, we better find her then,' Claire said.

'We'll help with that.'

'Thank you, Martin. I don't know what I've done to deserve your generosity.'

'Please, after what I did—' He seemed unable to find the appropriate words. His eyes, too, looked full to the brim with tears.

'I just can't believe I found you back here,' Claire said. 'After all these years. You never left?'

'I couldn't,' he said.

'Why?'

'Eoin.' He cleared his throat.

Claire felt her heart leap into her mouth. She wanted to be sick. *Of course.* He didn't know. He hadn't been there for the final attack. He knew nothing of what had happened. He'd been left to die, then the world went dark. The poor man was ignorant of what had happened to the rest of the Disconnected. 'You waited all these years for him?'

'I'd have waited until my dying day.'

'Martin, I'm so sorry.' Her eyes failed her. Tears streamed down her face.

'I'm not stupid,' he said, wiping his own tears away. 'I know how it sounds. But if there was any chance he survived, any at all, I couldn't give up on that. This is the place he knew. If he did survive, this is where he'd return to. So I stayed put. For him. He deserved that much.'

'Martin—'

'I know. Just tell me what happened. I need to know.'

Where to start? It was not a story she ever wanted to tell. Her kids hadn't been told the full details. Even she and Maxime, talking privately, hadn't revisited it in any particular depth. Ghosts were supposed to stay in the past. Buried. Fading memories that eventually blew away with the wind. But they hadn't. They'd stayed with her all these years, haunting her in her sleep, waiting to catch her off guard. The only difference now was she was finally turning to face them head on. Revisiting them so that she could move on from them once and for all. Perhaps facing them might even be cathartic. Anything was possible in this world.

She turned her mind back twenty years to the night in which the world had changed forever. 'After we left you to die, we returned here to the rest of the Disconnected, then we made our attack on Connected Industries. We were confident of taking Adam down. With the power to the city cut and his backup data centre destroyed, we knew that bastard artificial intelligence was running on only the resources available to him in his headquarters.'

'Can't have been easy, mind.'

'Not by a long shot,' Claire said. 'The city had already started its descent into anarchy. We could hear gunfire and looting. Adam had set the police bots on the populace. But we kept going. The Connected Industries building was easy enough to get into. Maxime and some others kept guard outside while we went in. Eoin was there. As were Matt, Zaheera and Jonathan. But that fucking robot had its own support. We were set upon by drones and other androids. Got dragged into an ugly fight. Jonathan was killed first.'

'You should tell Marie. It'll give her some closure.'

'I will,' she said. 'He fought well. She'd be proud.'

'I suspect she'd rather have him by her side.'

'Yes, well.'

'And Eoin?'

'He was unlike anything I've ever seen. One of the bravest men I ever laid eyes on.' She ignored Martin's watery eyes. Best to push on. At least the story would be over soon. 'You should have seen him. He was so quick.'

'But Adam was quicker?'

Claire couldn't look at him. Instead she looked at her feet while she gathered her strength. 'Yes. He shot Eoin out of a window.' She cleared her throat. 'I'm so sorry, Martin.'

'It's okay,' Martin said, tears streaming down his face. 'Now I know. Did the others survive?' Claire shook her head. 'How?'

'Zaheera went out grenade in hand, blowing Adam half to pieces in the process.'

'Good for her.'

'But Adam still had a trick up his sleeve. As it turned out, he'd put his kill switch in Matt's head when they'd installed the AI in him. It was Adam's final defence. Ensuring the AI he'd helped create in Matt would never turn on him for fear of his own life. But he never knew Matt. Not properly. Not like I did. Matt ...' She wiped a tear away. 'He turned his gun on himself.'

'Christ. I'm so sorry, Claire.'

'So am I. But it worked. The world went dark. I found Maxime afterwards. He helped me out. Said he'd stay with me to help me through my pregnancy. The world fell apart around us but we grew close. After Dylan was born, Maxime stuck around. We were a family by then. We kept heading west, getting as far from London and any other major population as we could. Then Jake came along. All of a sudden I had two boys to raise in a world I'd helped destroy.'

'Do you think they'll ever forgive us?'

'Who?'

'The young ones. The future generations. For what we did. The wrongs we committed. For the world we left them.'

'I don't know,' Claire said. 'Until recently, my only focus has been keeping Dylan and Jake alive. Thanks to you, that's still the case.'

'I'm glad to have done something,' Martin. 'I've spent twenty years trying to atone for my sins but I only seemed to get dragged deeper into murkier waters. Further from being the person I thought I was. Until I couldn't see clearly anymore. This world has a way of bringing out the worst in you if you let it, you know?'

'Only too well.'

'Well, I'm sick of it,' Martin said. 'The past is done. Nothing's bringing Eoin back. But I can continue to try and help. That's all I can do. Help rebuild, you know? Make something worth fighting for. Remind people we still got a little humanity in us, somewhere deep down. The kids deserve it. They didn't ask to be born into this. They just inherited our poor choices. We owe them a second chance.'

'You're a good man, Martin.'

'Nah, I'm just an old man who's tired of being a shite one.' He drained the last of his Scotch and stood up, pulling Claire to her feet in the process. 'Now, let's go help your lad find his girl.'

19

Mia accepted her slice of hare with a nod. 'Thanks.' Dev smiled back at her from across the fire in the dark, the flames giving his face a warm glow, while Prisha set about purifying some water. Mia was grateful to have run into the couple. Had it been anyone else in this world, she would likely have been killed on the spot. When Dev had first stumbled on her back at the old airport, she'd thought he had every intention of doing so. Thankfully, Mia's pleas had worked on Prisha. The carnage they'd stumbled upon had likely had some effect, too. Dev and Prisha had been part of that group. The bodies Mia had found strewn across the tarmac had been Dev and Prisha's people. The shock of finding them all dead likely took some of the vigour out of the couple's resolve. They too were all alone now. They too had to weigh up their options. Gone was the safety they had had in numbers. From what Mia had overheard as she'd trailed them to the Silver Eagles' base, it seemed like the couple had not been entirely convinced of their group's decisions of late. Prisha, especially, had voiced concern about some guy called Angus, whom Mia presumed had been their leader.

Mia knew all too well what it was like to live somewhere and not agree entirely with the decisions of the leadership. For years she had lived under Frank's rule, under New Britain's rule, choosing to ignore some of the less savoury aspects of life within the group so long as the collective kept her safe. And they had. They'd kept her alive. Had given her a life that she'd been relatively happy with, until she'd met Dylan and realised just how much was missing from it. At least Dev and Prisha still had each other. Everything else was gone. Everyone else. But they were still together. That was something. More than she had, at least.

She thought of the woman she'd found on the ground at the airport, breathing her final breaths, who'd confirmed that Dylan had been there. He had been taken prisoner by this group. But she'd not found his body anywhere amongst the corpses. Initially, it was a relief, but then her mind tortured her with the possibilities. He could easily have been injured. Perhaps he had been killed not far from the airport. He could have been taken prisoner again, by some other group. Whoever had been involved in the battle, they'd killed the entire Silver Eagles faction. Although, she, Dev and Prisha had not been able to find any evidence of an attack from outside. It seemed, if anything, that the prisoners had staged an escape. None of the outer fences or walls had been damaged. There had been no tracks found outside the perimeter. And all the bodies were found somewhat central to the base, as if drawn in towards people who had been within the grounds when the fighting had kicked off. Dev was confident it had been a prisoner revolt. Prisha agreed. Mia, too, when she really thought about it. 'What will you both do?'

she said, hoping to take her mind off thoughts of Dylan's safety.

'I don't know,' Dev said, poking the embers of the fire. 'The city is a dangerous place. We only stayed because of the safety provided by the group. Now that that's gone, I'm not sure of our chances. The other factions are unlikely to want to take us in. People don't like strangers here. They only trust the faces they know.'

'It's the same everywhere,' Mia said.

'That's what I'm afraid of. Moving out of the city is likely just as dangerous as moving further in. Nowhere is safe.'

'You could join us,' Mia said. 'Once we find Dylan, you're welcome to stay with us until you've figured out your plans.'

'That's kind of you, thanks,' Prisha said.

'Please, you could have killed me the moment you saw me. Now you're helping me find Dylan. If anyone has shown kindness, it's you.'

'It's a rare thing these days. Someone has to,' Prisha said.

Mia nodded back. 'I'm glad you think so.'

'What were the two of you doing before you got separated?' Dev said.

'You don't know?'

'No. We were a big group. Angus wasn't exactly the most forthcoming of leaders. Most people only found things out on a need-to-know basis. Prisha and I worked patrols, mostly. We never spoke to prisoners. Wasn't our responsibility, so it wasn't something we ever got insight into. That's just how it was with our faction recently. Life inside our base had grown a little twitchy, what with winter on its way and supplies running low,' he said.

Mia weighed Dev's words, not quite sure whether this was a ploy to draw out more information which he could then use against her. Had she not stalked the couple before witnessing them stumble upon their own dead, she might have thought they were sizing her up. Trying to find out whether she had any others with her. Whether she was worth keeping alive as some kind of bargaining chip, or whether to rob her and leave her for dead.

But she knew it was mostly her own insecurities at play. Her own inability to trust anybody who hadn't yet earned that right. In fairness to them, Dev and Prisha had shown her nothing to cause suspicion since the initial hostility. If she couldn't take a chance on a couple as down on their luck as these two, there was likely nobody she could take a chance on. 'We were exploring,' she said after a while.

'Exploring?'

'Yes. Both of us grew up in very sheltered existences. We met by chance.'

'How so?'

'Dylan's family was attacked by my own group. They captured him and his brother. I met him when he was brought to our town.'

'And you just walked out of your town hand in hand with a prisoner?'

'Not quite. His mother came back for her sons. Brought some others with her. They took over the town, killing our own leader in the process.'

'I'm sorry to hear that,' Prisha said.

'Don't be. He wasn't a very good one. I told myself his rule was necessary. That he had kept his people safe for years. I believed that I could learn to live with the unease I felt within, telling me that something wasn't right. If I was safe, nothing else mattered. We had food, shelter, a system of order. What did it matter if that order was a little oppressive? I figured it'd be the same elsewhere.' She watched as Dev and Prisha shared a look. It seemed her words had had some effect on them. Perhaps they understood her. Then again, perhaps not.

'Anyway, after the town was liberated, Dylan and I decided we would go out and see a bit of the world for ourselves. All my life I've listened to the old ones talk about their lives from before the Blackout. They talk about travelling the world, meeting other people, studying other histories. Yet all I've experienced is fear. Fear that tomorrow will be the day that something gets me. A trap, perhaps. Or a blade. Or a bullet. If not that, then the cold. Or some disease. Dylan and I decided to stop living in fear. We decided life was worth living. To its fullest. So we left.'

Dev cocked his head at her. 'You left a perfectly safe town to head out into danger, holding nothing but another guy's hand in your own, to go "exploring"?'

Mia nodded.

'I really hope I get to meet this Dylan.'

'Why's that?'

'It's not often you meet people who still live on hope.'

'Someone has to. It's a rare thing these days,' she said.

'Where is this town of yours?' Prisha said.

Mia pointed to the west, over her shoulder. 'A few weeks that way. You should go there. Dylan's mother is rebuilding. She has visions of communities living in harmony, trading supplies, coming and going in peace. I've never seen anything quite like it.'

'That sounds nice,' Prisha said, taking hold of Dev's hand and looking deep into his eyes.

Mia felt like she might even excuse herself to give them their moment. As it was, she gazed into the glowing embers. Just as she was staring most intently, the embers burst apart in a cloud of sparks. There, in the fire pit, an arrow quivered.

Instinctively, Mia rolled to her side. Turning around to

face her enemy would only be to offer herself up as a target. Another arrow struck the ground where her head had been only moments before. She rolled until she was behind a bush before stopping to take in her surroundings. Dev was on his feet already, gun in hand and firing into the darkness. Prisha had scurried across to a nearby mound and was fumbling over her weapon, without any success, to ready the thing for a fight. Mia heard the *whoosh* of an arrow sailing overhead. This would all be over in a heartbeat if she didn't get a grip.

Taking a deep breath to calm her nerves, she reached behind her back and pulled the pistol from her belt. There had been a plethora of weapons lying on the ground in Heathrow, some simple and blunt, others more deadly, although not all had had any ammo left. The pistol had. From her last count she knew she had seven rounds left in the magazine. Another in the chamber. Eight rounds with a short-distance weapon against unknown numbers of enemies in the dark. She didn't like her odds. Another arrow whipped by.

'Go!' Dev shouted. 'Now!' He took a knee and reloaded. In the blink of an eye he was on his feet again, firing into the darkness.

Mia looked over the bush she'd taken cover behind. She saw two bodies on the ground nearby in the darkness. No idea whether they were dead or alive. There wasn't any point wasting two shots unless absolutely necessary, though. From behind a tree not more than twenty yards away, another arrow flew towards her, missing her by a hand's span at most.

'Now!' Dev said.

Mia crouched and ran over to Prisha. 'We have to move back. We're in the open out here.'

'Where to?'

Mia scanned the darkness. She could barely see a thing. Only the nearby embers provided much in the way of something to look at. But she knew the park they'd settled in was relatively small. If they could make it to the edge, they could disappear down a road and lose their attackers. 'To the exit,' she said.

'Okay.'

They stood, facing the same direction as Dev, guns out and moving backwards. Prisha either had more ammo or was less concerned about it running out than Mia. She fired sporadically as they moved backwards. Dev, still ten yards or so in front of them, looked over his shoulder and acknowledged their movement with a nod. He started to inch back. His eyes were locked on Prisha's when the arrow cut through his neck. Prisha let out an awful scream and ran to him. 'Prisha, wait!' But Mia was too late. Prisha was struck twice in quick succession. She pirouetted in front of Mia before landing in a slump on top of her dead lover.

Mia, giving up all hope, turned and ran. She never saw the arrow that hit her. Never even heard it over the pounding of her footsteps and her heavy breathing. It pierced her shoulder, sending her sprawling to the ground. As she lay there, waiting for her attackers to catch up with her, she didn't think of her dead acquaintances. She thought of Dylan. She thought of the conversations they'd had as they'd adventured out across these unknown lands. She thought of their talks about their futures and what lay in store for them. It wasn't meant to end like this. It wasn't fair. *So much for hope.*

20

Jake sat silently across from his brother, who was talking to Chipo and Tatenda. His mother was still with Martin. Jake couldn't quite comprehend how much they had to catch up on. A lifetime, literally. They had known each other before he was even born. It made his own life feel insignificant by comparison. Then again, if they could find each other after all these years, perhaps there was still hope for Mia. Even if she had chosen his brother, she deserved to live. That, ultimately, had been the thought that had swayed him. Whatever his opinions regarding his standing within his family, Mia didn't deserve to die. He had been wrong to wish her harm, he saw that now.

Watching his brother converse with Chipo and Tatenda, Jake felt the old sense of safety he'd felt as a kid whenever Dylan was nearby. As if his presence meant Jake was going to be okay, no matter what. They may as well have been back in their old forest dwelling, Jake quietly going about his own business, safe in the knowledge the Dylan was nearby, ensuring his little brother was kept safe. There was so much Jake wanted to say. So much to apologise for. But where to start when all there was to talk about was the wrongs committed against one another? Instead, he simply watched his brother converse with these other people he didn't know.

They were discussing the state of Taunton since its liberation. Chipo and Tatenda, by the sounds of it, had helped liberate the town from New Britain's rule. Chipo's face Jake knew all too well. She was the one who had burst through the door with Claire when everybody had turned on him and Frank. When his own mother had been unable to pull the trigger, Chipo had been the one to fire her crossbow, killing Frank and taking Jake with him out a window and onto the roof below. Had it not been for the roof, Chipo's shot could well have killed him, too. But he felt no enmity towards her. No anger. It was simply the way of the world. She had acted in accordance with her friend, Claire. They were a team. And here they still were. That counted for something. If anything, it was he who stood out amongst these people. It was he who had once been the enemy. He had a long way to go to make amends, he knew.

Despite being related to two of the group, Jake felt like the odd one out.

Although, it had always been this way. Even when it had just been him and his family. He had always been different. That much was clear to him. But this time, it was not because of personality. It was due to actions. Actions he had committed against these people. They all might not be saying it out of respect to Claire, but he could read it on their faces all the same. Chipo and Tatenda kept offering him polite, distancing smiles, as if they were waiting for him to make a move against them. Their hands never too far from their weapons when in his presence. Trust wasn't something the siblings doled out freely, it seemed.

Claire returned from her meeting with Martin. 'Got a minute?' she said to Jake and Dylan.

Grateful for the distraction, Jake let himself be led to a room without anyone else. Just his brother and mother. All the family he had left. An oil lamp sat burning on the table inside, giving the room a warm glow. His mother closed the door behind him and then gripped Jake and his brother in a hug so tight he found it difficult to breathe. Not that he had any issue with it. He still had his reservations but it felt good just to be the three of them again. Family. No one else.

'I'm so glad you're both alive,' his mother said.

Jake looked across at Dylan, the brother he'd tracked for weeks with the intent of killing, grateful it had not come to that. He nodded at his brother. 'As am I,' he said.

'I pray neither of you ever has children. From the moment you were born, I've never stopped worrying about either of you. But since the attack on our home, I don't think I've had a moment's rest. I think I've aged a decade in the last few weeks alone.'

'We're here now, and that's all that matters,' Dylan said.

Jake was grateful for his brother's statement. Although, he still couldn't tell how much of it was true. Dylan wanted to go save Mia, that much was clear. Whether there would be any repercussions afterwards, he didn't know. Whatever happened, Jake knew it was no longer within his control. He had accepted the truce. Martin had been right. They wouldn't have made it out of the Silver Eagles base alive without the truce. And now, they needed it to survive this terrifying city. But none of that mattered to Jake. All he wanted was for his brother and mother to understand how sorry he was. Words, unfortunately, just wouldn't suffice.

His mother seemed to sense this. She pulled the two of them in again in an even tighter embrace, if that were possible. 'Whatever happens, nobody ever comes between us again, okay?'

'Okay,' Jake said.

'Okay, Mum,' Dylan said.

They sat in silence for a few minutes, enjoying each other's company once more. Jake wanted very much to ask them both about the state of the town, but shame prevented him. Asking about it would only point out that he had not been there, that he had chosen a different path. He wanted to say how much he missed their original forest home, too, but that again was a conversation that would only bring sadness. Jake wondered whether he would ever be able to talk about his father without a lump forming in his throat. 'How was your catch-up with Martin?' he said eventually, hoping that would allow the three of them to talk without having to discuss his own failings as a member of the family.

'It was good,' his mother said, a smile forming on the face that so often showed concern. 'I had thought Martin dead long before either of you were born.'

'What happened to him?' Dylan said.

'He was a part of our group. In fact, he was one of its founding members, along with a woman called Zaheera. They formed the Disconnected long before I joined. Martin considered himself Zaheera's protector. They all lived down here for years before the Blackout. Then Matt and I joined after we realised what was happening in our society, how we'd all been duped.'

'By the robot?' Jake said, still unable to quite picture it.

'Yes, by the robot. Adam. Anyway, Martin was fiercely loyal. To Zaheera, to the Disconnected, and to his partner Eoin. None of us saw it coming.'

'Saw what coming?'

'His betrayal.'

'What do you mean by that?'

'When we decided to take out Adam, there were a number of things we had to do first. Taking the city's power out, destroying his backup data centre. There were a lot of steps in bringing everything down. We split up into groups. Martin turned on us during one of the missions. He shot Zaheera.'

'Why would he do that?'

Claire shook her head, much as she would when he had asked her difficult questions as a kid. 'He said he was doing it for Eoin. Said he wanted out of the life we were all living at the time. Somewhere along the line he'd lost his appetite for revenge. He just wanted a quiet life away from the danger. At the time we were shocked. When we regrouped, we left him to die in a building we blew up. I thought that was the end of him. But he got out in time. Seems like he's been living here ever since, trying to make amends for his transgressions. Seeing him again was almost as much of a shock as seeing you both still alive.'

'And you've managed to forgive him?' Jake asked, wondering whether his own family could ever forgive him.

Claire thought on it for a second as she stared back at him. 'I'm not sure it's a case of whether to forgive or not. We've all committed wrongs that we wish we could take back. I doubt anybody could have put Martin through the mental torture he's put himself through all these years, living down here, waiting to see if Eoin would come back to him, knowing he might never get a chance to put it right. He's had to live with himself every day, knowing what he did. I'm sure it was punishment enough. As for me, I gain nothing by holding onto bitterness. There's nothing I can change. I'm learning to let things go. I'm learning that life goes on. All I can do to honour those I've lost is to keep going on. There has to be something in that. We all have to move on. It's either that or give up entirely, and that I refuse to do. Not with you two still around. Besides, each mistake we make is a chance to learn. To improve. Look at Martin. When he found out you were my sons, he decided to help keep you alive. Whatever his reasons for that, whether he thought it a small chance to make things right, I am forever indebted to him. Everybody deserves the chance to make it right.'

Jake couldn't think of anything else to say. If she meant what she'd said, perhaps there was still hope for the three of them. Regardless, Dylan looked to be getting more twitchy with every passing second. Mia was still out there. Every second they spent gathering their strength down here was another she spent alone and in danger.

FEELING a little more at ease about the chances of making things right with his family, Jake returned with them to the rest of the Disconnected. Martin stood hunched over a table, along with a few others, including Marie and the young girl who'd turned up from her scouting duties to announce that the other London factions were on the move. Dylan rushed ahead and pushed his way into the huddle. Jake stood back, choosing instead to listen in. He wasn't the pushing and shoving type. Never had been. Besides, when it came to discussions about Mia, his was not the most important voice in the room. Better to hang back and help when needed, as he'd said he would. If they were going to have any hope of finding her, they'd need to work together. Jake knew he would need to fit whatever mould that took.

'What are we looking at?' Claire said to the group as she neared the table. A couple of them eased aside to let her into the huddle.

'Bit of a crude map of London,' Martin said. 'At least, London as it is now. We've updated it a little.'

'What's that?' Claire said, pointing at something Jake hadn't a hope of seeing.

'Blue means under water, or somewhat flooded,' Martin said. 'River burst its banks a while back in a fair few spots. You're better off traversing some parts of the city on a raft than you are on foot.'

Jake's curiosity got the better of him. He moved in closer, peering over the girl scout's shoulder to see the old map they were all staring at. None of it meant anything to him, but he assumed it meant something to his mother. She'd be able to understand some of what Martin was getting at.

'And the red lines?' Claire said.

'Territory boundaries for the four main factions within the city, besides ourselves, of course. Not that anybody ever had the sense to actually agree to dividing up the land. This 'ere's more of a guidance sheet for us lot so we know whose turf we're trespassing on when we go out for a supply run.'

'And what happens if you're caught trespassing?'

'No one who's ever been caught has made it back to tell us,' Martin said, his voice trailing off in the same way Claire's did when she spoke of regret.

Jake wondered how many of his people Martin had sent out on supply runs, never to return. He couldn't imagine the pain of living with such decisions. Already he was struggling with the consequences of his own actions and how they had affected his family. Seeing how they might damage a whole community only made the prospect of leading one less enticing. He tried to guess how Frank might have felt about such things as the leader of New Britain. The man had never spoken of guilt or regret. Everything to him had seemed so black and white. One or other. No room for confusion or indecision. But how could somebody make such decisions without struggling with the consequences of their choices? The more he thought about it, the more flaws he saw in Frank's supposedly steadfast thinking. And how wrong he had been to have become so swept up in the man's philosophy. Jake looked closer at the map, with its crude pencil drawings layered over the original design. He saw the four main factions Martin had mentioned: Silver Eagles to the west—Martin had put a cross through it—Wolves to the north, Crows to the east, Blades to the south. 'Where are these gangs now?' he said to the young scout.

She appeared alarmed by his question, turning to Martin for some kind of apparent approval.

'Go on, Fiona,' Martin said. 'Tell us.'

Fiona swallowed, her dust-covered face stricken with terror. 'They were heading west.'

'Who was?' Martin said.

'Wolves and Crows. I didn't go south to check on the Blades. I ran back here instead. I'm sorry.'

'Don't be sorry,' Martin said, putting an arm around the girl. 'You did a good thing. Without you, we wouldn't know the others were on the move. Seems like news has spread of what went down in Heathrow. Maybe via scouts. Maybe something else. Either way, the other factions are making a move. Whoever ends up with control of the west side will effectively double their territory. It'll give them control of the city.'

'What about Mia?' Dylan asked Fiona. 'Did you see a girl on her own, about my age? Short. Dark hair.'

Fiona shook her head.

'Nothing?' Dylan said.

'I'm sorry.'

'It's all right,' Martin said. 'Means nothing. We'll send scouts out through the tunnels. Chances are she's still somewhere west, or at least slightly west of centre. That's the way you came in. That's where we'll look first.'

'We should go now,' Dylan said, thumping his fist down on the table, 'before it's too late.'

'Easy there, lad,' Martin said. 'I get you're itching to be off but this city's a dangerous place. It requires planning to navigate. It'd be dangerous enough with the seasons changing, let alone the fact the others are moving because of what happened to the Silver Eagles.'

'What have the seasons changing got to do with it?' Jake said.

'I'm guessing the populations were pretty small for you growing up, kid. Just you and your family, I believe, until recently? You remember what it was like when one of you got sick? How it'd affect the whole family? I'm guessing it affected everything. Whether you were able to go out hunting or foraging. Whether you needed to isolate from the others to prevent unnecessary risks.'

Jake nodded. Martin's estimation was spot on. The family had developed a system of isolation whereby the sick family member would sleep in a different part of the log cabin to prevent the others from catching whatever it was they had. It almost never worked. Eventually everyone caught it. But it was usually enough to get a few more days of hunting in to prepare for the period of illness. Usually one of the parents, assuming at least one was free of illness, would head out to a nearby settlement to try and trade for supplies. Sometimes there were diseases spreading through the settlements, too. In such circumstances, the family simply kept their distance. Every winter was hard going. Jake could remember every single one as far back as his third or fourth birthday. He recalled the relief he and his family felt when they made it through to spring each year.

'Well,' Martin said, 'imagine that at scale. Imagine sickness and suffering spreading through an entire faction. Imagine the implications. Kids dying before they've had much of a chance to live. The elderly being taken too soon. Wounds getting infected, to the point where amputation becomes the safest option, even if that then brings other risks with it. Resources run out. Dangers increase due to an inability to properly scout your territory. Housing falls to pieces and repairs become impossible. Winter brings a black mood with it in this city. One so dark it consumes your soul. Hope and satisfaction become distant memories. Productivity comes to a halt. Then despair sets in. Despair begets grievances, and those beget violence. I've seen winters bring whole factions to their knees, this one included. And it won't be long until the next winter is upon us. I can feel it. We all can.' Heads nodded around him. 'What that means, lad, is that the streets would be dangerous anyway. People moving about to source the last supplies before hunkering down for winter. Raids taking place. Gangs moving about in areas they wouldn't normally go near. At this time of year, anything goes. Now there's word spreading through the city of the attack on the Silver Eagles. People know there's an entire territory to raid. A whole section of the city up for grabs. That means supplies, potentially. It also means control. More land. More space to spread a population. Think of how that would help during a winter. Think of how it might set up a faction for success in the summer. More land to grow crops. The possibility of linking two parts of the city under one banner. Everybody will make a play for it. Of that I have no doubt. There's going to be a lot more movement out there than we're used to. It means we've got to be careful. We've got to be smart about this. If we go charging out there in a rush, we've no hope of helping Mia. All we'll end up doing is putting ourselves in unnecessary danger.'

'What should we do?' Dylan said.

'We're going to be strategic about it. As I said, we'll send scouts out through the tunnels. They'll keep an eye on things. They can report back on the movements throughout the city.'

'And us?' Jake said.

'We're going to eat up and restock our weapons. Then we need to head west. Find somewhere to set up a small base. Can't keep traipsing all the way back here every time we need to scarper. There's a big park near the West End. Hyde Park. My guess is if Mia is feeling lost and alone, she's going to seek comfort in an area that looks less intimidating than some of the skyscrapers in this city. I reckon Hyde Park is as good a place as any to begin our search. If we set up base there, the scouts can bring word of their observations from the nearby areas.'

Claire stepped in, putting an arm around him and his brother. 'Okay, Martin. We'll take your lead. Let's get ourselves fed and restocked. Mia's out there somewhere, waiting for us. Let's not let her down.'

21

Dylan ate everything that was put in front of him. Most of it could hardly be identified. The stew was less a mix of meat cooked with veg as it was, he guessed, a collection of supplies well past their acceptable eating date, had they been left in their original form. It didn't matter. *As long as it gives me the energy I need to find Mia.* Besides, it wasn't a particularly offensive taste, more a bland one. Something indecipherable. But it filled his belly and for that he was grateful.

Thanks to Martin, the Disconnected were helping a great deal more than could be expected. Granted, he considered himself lucky that his mother had found an old friend. The Disconnected would likely not have been as keen to help had there not been some historical ties between them. Whatever the case, Dylan was simply appreciative that he had a team of people on his side to help find Mia. He had a full belly and a full arsenal of weapons. Rifle, pistol, bow. A healthy supply of relevant ammo for each. Knives too. It was more than he could have hoped for.

Having finished his food, he set about inspecting and

cleaning each weapon. There could be no mistakes. No room for error.

Claire walked over and took a seat on the bench beside him. 'You ready for this?'

'I just hope the others can keep up.'

'We'll find her, Dylan. I promise.'

'It's finding her alive that matters to me.' At that his mother was silent. She gave him a long look which he struggled to quite understand. Pity or concern, he didn't know. Empathy perhaps. After all, she'd lost people too. She knew exactly what he was going through. She'd been there before. More times than was perhaps fair for any one person to go through. 'You know this place we're going to?' he said, hoping to avoid pitying looks.

'Hyde Park? I did, once. I'm not sure I'd recognise it now, if what I've seen of the city is anything to go by.'

'What was it like back then?'

She looked up at the ceiling. Dylan thought for a moment that perhaps the conversation had come to an end but eventually her eyes returned to focus on his. 'It was beautiful. Although, I'm not sure I fully appreciated it at the time. Your father and I, if we could ever be dragged away from our jobs, would sometimes picnic in Hyde Park on summer afternoons. We'd take sandwiches and wine and books, and we'd rest up against one another, using the other as a pillow, and enjoy each other's company. Sometimes we'd lie there in silence for hours. Other times we'd read passages to each other that we enjoyed. And sometimes we'd just watch others go about their business, whether it was little children frolicking in the sun or friends and couples walking hand in hand. I always enjoyed that park.'

'Sounds nice.'

'Yes, it was.'

'Do you struggle with the world as it is? The world you speak of from before the Blackout always sounds so different, so carefree.'

Again she was silent for a while. 'It was different. And yes, I do struggle with it. But I struggled then, too. I didn't like the way it was going. We weren't so much carefree as we were ignorant of the forces around us. That change has been a good one, I guess. Every day I know where I stand now. My concerns are real. Nothing is taken for granted. But I do struggle with every day being a struggle for life and death. Especially with you and Jake. Knowing this is the only world you'll ever know makes me a little sad. I wish you could have seen humanity at its most hopeful. When we still aspired to goals beyond figuring out ways in which to kill each other. But then I look at how much we didn't know. How passive we were. How much we took it all for granted. I'm grateful for the time we had as a family. It's not that I wouldn't change it, but I guess I find it hard to think of having different memories. They are what they are. We've had some good times.'

'We have,' Dylan said.

'One day you'll create new memories of a family all your own. With Mia. You'll see what I mean then. I only hope we can build something better before then. Something safer. Bring a little humanity back to our way of life.'

'I only hope we find Mia before it's too late.'

'Yes, well, we better be off then. Gather your things. Go check on your brother.'

'Sure.'

She grabbed his shoulder gently as he made to leave. 'I don't need to worry anymore, do I? About the two of you?'

'No,' he said. 'I suspect he'll always hold something against me for Mia and I being together, but I can't really fault him for that. And neither can he fault me for her choosing me. It's just the way things happened. We're good.'

'I'm glad to hear it,' she said.

Dylan walked along the platform and found his brother. Jake was hunched over, putting a rifle back together, the gun oil on his hands reflecting a little of the nearby torchlight. Dylan took a seat beside him. 'You ready?'

'I'm ready,' Jake said.

'Jake, before we leave ... I'm not sure how to—'

'Don't worry about it. Let's go get her back.'

'Okay,' Dylan said, exhaling a sigh of relief as he saw the earnest expression on his brother's face.

THE TUNNELS MADE DYLAN UNEASY. There was no getting used to the darkness. It was so unnatural, the complete lack of light. The cold, stale air and the stench of mould. The quiet trickle of water somewhere nearby. He couldn't quite fathom how Martin and the rest of the Disconnected had lived down here for so long. But it did allow them to move about the city unnoticed, which was particularly useful. Dylan's only concern about underground travel was that they might pass Mia by unknowingly. The thought of missing her threatened to tear his mind in two. Martin had to be right. He knew the city far better than Dylan, so if he said that it was unlikely for her to have made it so far in then Dylan had to go with it.

Even if Martin was right and Mia was still somewhere near the West End, there was still no guarantee of finding her. She could well have been caught, as he had been. She could have been injured, left to die. His mind seemed intent on playing out the worst possible fantasies as they walked, so much so that he noticed Jake settle in beside him. His little brother had developed an impressive knack for knowing when Dylan needed company. Not conversation, just a silent presence to prove that he wasn't all alone. They walked in step behind Martin and Claire. Behind them Chipo and Tatenda walked side by side. And so it went, a long trail of Disconnected snaking their way through the tunnels unbeknownst to the rest of the city.

'Do you think it was a good idea, leaving some of the others behind?' Dylan said, trying to give his mind something else to concern itself with.

'What do you mean?' Jake said.

'Leaving Marie and the others back there. Surely every able body we have is another to help cover the ground, to help fight any enemies. We'd find Mia faster with more people.'

'Perhaps, but they've already fed us, given us weapons and ammunition, not to mention many of their own people. They still need a few to defend their own home. That's their right. We have to be grateful for the amount of help they've already provided.'

'I am,' Dylan said. 'It's just—'

'I know. We'll find her, I promise.'

Up ahead Martin came to a stop. The big man-mountain hunched down behind a rusted Underground train carriage, one arm held up signalling for the others to stop and do likewise. Dylan crouched low, his grip on the automatic rifle tight. Slowly, he inched forwards in the dark towards Martin's torch. Up ahead, through the broken windows of the train carriage, he could just make out a platform, although he couldn't read any signs at this distance. 'Where are we?' he whispered.

'Hyde Park Corner,' Martin said. The man-mountain signalled for some of the scouts to make their way over to him. Dylan shuffled back to allow them all to circle their leader. 'Right, muckers, you know your roles. Spread out and look for signs of a young woman on her own. You've had her description. You know who you're looking for. Keep an eye out for other factions, too. There's a good chance a girl on her own might have been taken prisoner if she crossed paths with the wrong lot. You see any other groups, you move in closer to check whether she's there with them. And be safe. As safe as possible, anyway. Don't stay above ground for any longer than is absolutely necessary, you hear?' Nods all around. 'Good. You're to check back here whenever you can. If it's not me back here, then leave word with whoever is. We want to find Mia before any of the other factions do. We also want to know what's happening with the other factions. If you see anybody moving in such a way as to put us in potential trouble, you let us know. Got it?' Again, nods from every scout. 'Off you go, then. We'll be setting up base in this station. Assuming it's safe enough to do so, we'll set up another base above ground in the park, too. If anything happens to block your route through the tunnels, you just peg it back to the park. Be safe.'

Dylan watched as the kids left in pairs. The routine of it all surprised him. They were well trained. Much like he and his brother had been back in their forest home. He recalled how he and Jake would monitor the perimeter of their territory every day, setting and fixing traps, checking for signs of intrusion. Taking action when necessary. These kids were no different. Only their methods and surroundings were.

Those who remained set about inspecting the Underground station, checking that it was indeed empty, that no entrance had been breached. Martin instructed some of the Disconnected to take watch in different sections of the tunnels so that the others could rest up on a platform and wait for nightfall. At Martin's instruction, Dylan and the rest who weren't taking watch settled down for a short sleep. There was no guarantee how long the night ahead would be, Martin said, so now was as good a time as any to get their heads down. Besides, attacks always worked best late at night, when darkness was an ally.

DYLAN'S EYES opened in the darkness to a gentle nudge. It was Chipo.

'Come on,' she said. 'We're moving out soon.'

He blinked away the stars in his eyes and looked down the platform. Tatenda was nudging Jake awake. Many of the others were already up, readying themselves in quiet determination. 'Thanks,' Dylan said. 'I'm up. Where's my mother?'

'With Martin. They went to check that the street entrance is clear. They just got back.'

'And?'

'And we're good. There's access to the street through a manhole cover that the scouts have used frequently when moving through this area in the past.'

'Hasn't anybody wondered what's below the streets? Wouldn't someone have tried their luck coming down a manhole by now?'

'I asked Martin the same thing when he went to check. He said they put makeshift locks on the manholes from beneath. That way anybody above ground who might wish to try their luck would assume the covers were welded or bolted in place. He's pretty confident that nobody has made it into the tunnels. If they had, he reckons they'd have heard about it by now.'

'Fair enough,' Dylan said. In the short time he'd known

the man, he had found Martin to be very matter-of-fact. The burly man-mountain wasn't one to make false claims—at least, it didn't seem like he was. If he was confident that the tunnels were safe from the other factions, that was good enough for Dylan.

Once they were above ground, though, their advantage was lost. There was no way that a group of twenty or so people could flee beneath the surface without being seen if it came to a fight. They'd have to stand their ground. He hoped it wouldn't come to that. His only concern was Mia. Finding her alive. That was all that mattered now. He took Chipo's proffered hand and let her pull him to his feet.

'Be careful out there,' she said. 'If we find her—'

'*When* we find her.'

'When we find her, no running off. No screaming or shouting. You need to be calm and controlled. For her sake. We don't know what we're heading out into. There might be others nearby. There might be traps. Imagine what you'd have done back home. Now imagine that in a city as big as this. We have to be ready for anything.'

'As long as we find her.'

'Okay,' she said.

'Okay,' Dylan said.

He went and found his mother, who was attending to Jake.

'All set?' she said.

'Indeed. Just received fair warning from Chipo about staying calm when we head out there.'

Claire smiled. 'She was the same with me when I first came for you two after New Britain had taken you. Besides, she's right. We need to be careful out here. The three of us don't know this place like we did our home. We don't have our traps to rely on and we don't know the terrain. Anybody out there is likely to have an advantage over us. Our best bet is sticking with Martin and the others. They'll be able to guide us appropriately.'

'Unless all hell breaks loose,' Jake said.

'Yes, well, in that event, it's every person for themselves.'

'Those are odds we can deal with,' Dylan said, his hand resting on the bow that covered his right shoulder.

Another grin crept across his mother's face. More sinister this time. 'Yes, they are.'

Having readied their weapons, they settled in with Chipo and Tatenda before following Martin up onto the backstreet in the darkness. Stars dotted the night sky, providing a natural light that Dylan and the others had been denied in the tunnels below. They reminded him just how vast everything was. His world down in the tunnels had become so focused, so constrained, as had his thoughts on the task at hand. *Find Mia.* Only now, as the sky opened up the world around him, the task seemed to grow, too. The realisation hit him that Mia really could be anywhere. There was no guarantee they were within miles of her. For all he knew she'd fled the city and was halfway back home by now. For a fleeting moment, a part of him hoped she had. At least that would mean she was alive. Alive and beyond the dangers of this city. In all likelihood, though, that just meant she'd be in danger in some other territory, which, he figured, would be even worse. The not knowing would kill him. He had to find her, if only to give his mind a rest from this torture.

One by one, they scurried across the street into the shadows of a nearby building. Martin was up front. Ahead, Dylan could see the long shadow of what looked to be a colossal stone arch with a single gateway beneath. It was situated on a roundabout between two grassy corners.

Something sat atop the arch but in the low light, Dylan could not guess what it was. Still, he felt somewhat humbled in its presence. The buildings in this city were all so different from the ones he'd grown up raiding as a child back home. The ones here were large, intimidating structures that made him uneasy. They were much more menacing than the ones back home. But this did something else. He was in awe of it. There was something beautiful about it, sitting beneath the moon. It was like stumbling across an oak that was hundreds of years old in a forest of slim, much younger trees. Everything around it paled by comparison. It seemed to command respect from him, or wonder. He could not quite tell. But it was one of the first times in his life that a structure such as this had provoked such a reaction from him, except for the stone circle he and Mia had come across a few weeks before. That had truly been something.

In the moment, he wondered whether perhaps there was in fact some beauty to the old world. Whether they had done a few things right. Looking up at it, he tried to imagine what it must have looked like back then, surrounded by other buildings still in good shape. Not the abandoned and dishevelled messes that now stood in the streets beside the park. Whether people would have stopped to admire its majesty, or whether it was just another structure in a world full of impressive structures. It was impossible to tell.

He was brought back to reality as Martin ordered them over the grass and into the park on the left. They moved low and fast, taking it one at a time to cover the open space. Thankfully, there was enough tree cover and tall grass to move without feeling too exposed.

Martin signalled them all into a circle around him, where he sat beside what would once have been a fountain.

Dylan had never seen one working before, but his mother had told him about them when they had stumbled across the odd one on their travels. He understood that water should have flowed in some form through the structure but he failed to see why. Claire had explained it to him, stating that there had been many decorative designs back then, but the concept still eluded him. It had been hard to appreciate the idea of an object which was useless, valued purely for its beauty. Having seen the stone circle and now the arch, he was starting to understand. While he still preferred to appreciate a well-laid trap, he could now see how he might appreciate a decorative structure for the feelings it brought out in him. Atop this particular fountain was a small statue: a figure holding a bow and arrow. *How fitting.*

While the others listened to Martin, Dylan's mind continued to drift. As did his eyes. It was then he saw something move in the distance. At first he didn't quite believe he'd seen it. Whatever it was had flashed past so quickly he hadn't had a moment to register it. Then he saw another. And another.

He signalled for the others to quieten down. Martin caught the instruction and did as he was bid. The group fell into a deathly silence, hunkering as low as they could. They all turned to face the direction Dylan was looking. Dylan's eyes focused on the gap between the trees where he'd seen the flashes. They had been too big to be foxes. Deer, perhaps, but he doubted it. The third flash confirmed it. People. A gang, of sorts. Could be one of the factions Martin had mentioned. Could be just a small group of raiders making their way through the city at night, hoping to gather supplies without running into trouble.

'We should follow them,' Dylan whispered to Martin. 'If

there are people in this area, they may have already found Mia. She could be their captive.'

'She could also have run a mile if she saw them. You could be wasting your time. She could be hiding up a tree or in some building, holding her breath until everybody has disappeared. There might be others in the area, too,' Martin said.

'We won't know unless we investigate. We have to go after them. If we find nothing, we can move on.'

Martin didn't seem too keen on the idea. His face scrunched up into a ball of beard and furrowed brows. 'They'll hear us if we all try to go. Either that or we'll be too slow and they'll get away. We also promised the scouts some would remain here and set up camp.'

'Plans change,' Dylan said.

'That they do, lad, but my word is my word. You go after them. Take a few with you. We'll stay behind and scout the area. If you find something that warrants us all being there, you send one back to call us in. Sound fair?'

'Sounds fair.' Dylan turned to go, unconcerned with who might go with him. He was happy to go on his own. It might even be easier that way. He felt a tug on his arm and saw his brother looking back at him.

'I'm coming with,' Jake said.

'Me too,' Claire said.

Chipo and Tatenda shifted up to him too. 'That's five,' Dylan said. 'Any more and we'll be more likely to get seen.'

'All right,' Martin said, putting a hand on Dylan's shoulder but looking directly at Claire. 'Stay safe. Keep your heads cool. Watch out for each other. We're right here. You come back here and get us if you need. Don't go doing anything stupid. You're smart enough to know a trap when you see one.'

Claire nodded back. They moved off without another word, crossing the road through the arch he had seen earlier and into the other park on the opposite side. 'You know where we are?'

'Green Park, if my memory is correct,' she said.

'You know where they might be headed?'

'I have an idea.'

'Okay, then.' Dylan took the lead. He pulled the bow off his shoulder and readied an arrow. Guns would be a last choice at night. Muzzle flash. Noise. No, his bow would do better. That or a blade. As they crossed into Green Park he saw the figures disappear into the darkness behind a tree. 'I count at least six.'

'Seven,' Tatenda said. 'Each with a gun in hand. Assuming we find nobody else, we're already outnumbered. No sudden decisions.'

'Agreed,' Dylan said. They spread out, like he and his family had done when hunting deer back home. He tore a fistful of grass and let it drop from his hands. The grass blew towards him. 'We're downwind.'

The tracking was slow going. In the moonlit surroundings, shadows danced between the trees. A gentle wind blew through the long grass. They followed the strangers, keeping to the trees where possible. On the other side of the road Dylan saw a low brick wall with black steel fencing running alongside. The road opened up and Dylan saw a large stone building, bigger than any he had ever seen before, within the grounds of the black fences. The strangers stopped their scurrying and crossed the road. Dylan saw them clearly now. Seven indeed. Tatenda had been right. They moved with the casual confidence of those returning to the safety of a hideout. Only this was more than a hideout. It was a fortress.

The strangers were met by others patrolling the grounds, torches in hand. The flickering flames cast wild, dancing shadows upon the walls of the giant building. 'What is that place?' Dylan said to his mother.

'That is Buckingham Palace.'

The name brought back memories of books his mother had found and gifted to him throughout his childhood, but still it rang hollow. It was just some made-up place from the pages of some book until now. Now he saw it for the stronghold it was. 'We should get the others.'

'Yes, yes we should,' Claire said.

22

Mia's eyes opened. Her eyelids felt heavy, as if weighed down by some invisible force. She heard them slick back over her eyes as she pushed them up again after a second attempt. Like lifting a fallen tree from across a path.

Almost instantly the pain in her left shoulder kicked in. It felt ripped through. The visions came back to her with force. The attack in the night. Dev and Prisha fleeing with her. The arrow piercing Dev's neck. Prisha turning back for her love. The arrows piercing her. It was a nightmare on repeat. She'd barely known the young couple, yet she was overcome with remorse. She recalled how Prisha's eyes had lit up when she'd told them both about her recently liberated home town. How it stood as a place for trade within a broader community. Allied communities. A place where all were welcome.

She knew what she'd seen in Prisha's eyes. Hope. She'd known the feeling once, too. It had been hope that had excited her so much about Dylan. Hope for the life they might have together. And yet it was already over. She should be dead, she knew. The arrow that had struck her had felt like the final blow among a hailstorm of blows. Mia had accepted her death, lying there on the ground, her new acquaintances dead nearby. They were gone. Dylan was gone. There was nothing left to hope for. When she'd closed her eyes, she had not expected to ever open them again.

And yet she did.

Only, she was not where she had been when they had closed. It was still dark. Whether the same night, the following one, or even many nights since, she did not know. All she could tell was that she was in some kind of courtyard. A quadrangle of sorts. Her hands and feet were tied to a nearby pole in the ground. Not much by way of a prison, but enough to prevent her from getting away for now. Her heart started to race. She tried to think back to the attack. Racked her mind to work out whether she'd seen the faces of her attackers. She drew a blank.

A young girl hobbled past in front of her and Mia called out to her. The girl stopped to look at her. She was carrying a burning torch. Mia saw the scars on the girl's face. Burns, no doubt. It looked like her skin had melted. How she could hold a burning torch, having lived through whatever had done that to her face, Mia didn't know. The poor thing couldn't be more than nine or ten at best. The torch was almost equal to her in height. 'What's your name?' she said.

The girl turned to face her properly, dragging one of her legs with effort. Mia noticed it then. It wasn't a leg. Not a real one. It was a stump. A wooden leg, crudely made. From what she could tell, it was off by an inch or two. Slightly too long when compared to her other leg. Mia wondered how uncomfortable it might be to walk with. She understood the look on the girl's face now. Hope had long since left her, too. Her eyes were dead. Close enough, anyway. No spark shone out from behind. No life. No joy. 'Crows,' the girl said.

'Your name is Crows?' Mia said.

'Not me. Us. We're the Crows. The faction.'

'Oh,' Mia said, not quite getting the significance. Another gang, presumably. Like Dev and Prisha's lot. 'Do you have a name?'

'Nine.'

'You have nine names?'

'No,' the girl said, her impatience evident on her burned face. 'It's my number.'

'You don't have a name?'

'What use do names have?'

Mia wasn't quite sure how to respond. She'd never met anyone without a name. Then again, she'd never met someone who had both lost a limb and been burned and survived to tell the tale. 'I'm Mia,' she said.

The girl showed no visible reaction to the introduction. Mia may as well have mumbled a random noise. 'You'll get your number soon, provided you don't do anything reckless,' she said.

Again, Mia didn't know quite how to respond to that. The girl was so cold. So matter-of-fact. Presumably getting a number meant they weren't planning on killing her, at least. 'What happened to your leg, if you don't mind me asking?'

'Wound got infected. Maxed out my medicine limit. Had to go.'

Mia tried to comprehend the gravity of what the girl was saying. Tried to relate it to her own experiences growing up. Frank had imposed many rules within New Britain but even he had not resorted to denying someone medicine if they needed it. Even he had not amputated someone's limb to save supplies. Not even when they were being punished. She recalled the lashing Frank had given Dylan after he'd tried to escape. Mia had been instructed to nurse him back to health. To keep him alive. Even then she had not been given a limit on how much of the medical supplies she was allowed to use. Yet this nameless girl appeared not to care. Either that or she simply knew no different. The injustice of it was not apparent to her. *Every tribe is different.* Still, she wondered how harsh life had to be if amputation was routine. 'I'm sorry to hear that,' she said, eventually, not knowing what else to say.

'Why?'

'I ... I don't know. I'm just sorry you lost your leg.'

'Don't be. It wasn't your leg. I work as good as you. Better even. You see if that shoulder starts to rot. That's right near your heart. I'll be impressed if you last the week. We thought you weren't going to make it when we got the arrow out.'

So defensive. So angry. What was it about this group that made people so hard? She looked about and saw others at work. Not talking. Just getting on with it. Methodical. Efficient. Lifeless. Her concern for her own safety began to grow. 'What's going to happen to me?'

'You talk too much,' Nine said. 'One will deal with you. You tell him where your faction stashed their supplies and you'll be fine. You try to hold out and you'll only make it worse for yourself.'

'My faction?' Mia said. 'I'm not from here.' Her panic grew. 'Please, you must explain it to the others. I'm not from this city. I don't know anything about what you're looking for,

I promise.'

'We'll find out whether that's true soon enough. Everybody speaks the truth in the end.' With that, she turned and hobbled off towards a pair going into the large building on one side of the courtyard.

Mia was left wondering who this One was. The leader, presumably.

She didn't have to wait long to find out.

From a set of stairs beside four pairs of stone pillars came a bald man followed by two of his guards, both carrying melee weapons: one a bat and the other a blade. The bald man approached Mia. His clothing was dark, and in better condition than she'd seen on the others. He showed no evidence of scars, or of dismemberment, like Nine had. Only his eyes told a similar story. A lifeless one, devoid of spark. They looked numb to the world. 'How do you like the digs?' he said, the words spilling out of his mouth as if he had not been taught how to separate each one. They came out, ''Owdyu-lark-e-digz?'

Mia had never heard an accent quite like it. It took her a moment to process what he'd said. She looked around the white stone walls surrounding the courtyard, lit up beneath the moonlight by torches placed along each wall, and took in the sheer size of the place. 'I've never seen anything like it.'

'Too right. Bet the old owners are tossing and turning in their graves knowing it belongs to the likes of us now. It's the people's palace now.' He circled Mia before coming to a stop in front of her. 'What were you doing with the other two before you got caught?'

'I wasn't with the other two, really. I was—'

'That's not what I heard. I heard you'd been traipsing

further into the city when you were caught. My lot had been tailing you for a little while. So, come off it. Which lot are you with? You Wolves or Silver Eagles? No way you're one of the Blades. One of us would have recognised you by now.'

The names meant nothing to Mia. Except Silver Eagles. That was where she'd found the bodies. She'd seen the sign spray-painted on the building in Heathrow. That was Prisha and Dev's faction. Judging by this guy's animosity, it wouldn't do to be a member of any faction. Honesty was her best shot. 'I'm not from here. My boyfriend and I, we were passing through. Only, he got caught.'

'He got offed, did he?'

'I don't know. I was looking for him.'

'Best give up on that one, love. He's probably long gone by now.'

'He's alive, I know it.'

'Sounds like shit to me,' he said. 'Sounds like a nice tidy little cover story. Same as we train our lot to say if they ever get caught. You making shit up so you don't have to tell us where your stash is, that it?'

'No, please.'

He knelt down in front of her. Twisted his head to the side, presumably to get a better look. Either that or to convey the seriousness of his tone. 'See these two lads behind me? See the blood already on their weapons? You want to add yours to that?'

'No.'

'Then out with the information. You're not Wolves, are you? Not from where you were found. You're one of the Silver Eagles. Are there any others of you still alive? I heard you suffered a few losses. Maybe too many.'

'I'm not one of the Silver Eagles,' Mia said, her voice becoming more exasperated with every rebuttal. Her honesty wasn't working. He was taking her words as lies. She had to try and make him see the truth. If not, he was going to have her killed then and there; she could sense it in his frustration. He had that same anger she'd seen in Frank. The kind that snapped from *calm* to *kill* in a heartbeat. 'I used to be New Britain,' she said. 'You know them?'

'Who the hell is New Britain?'

'New Britain was my faction. It doesn't exist anymore. Our leader was taken out. The group no longer exists. Those who remained are a free people now.'

'And you left?'

'With my boyfriend, yes. We were spreading word of our liberated town so that others could come and seek shelter or trade as needed. It was a chance to go out and see some of the world.'

'Getting a good view?'

'I've seen better.'

One of the guards stepped forward and whispered into the bald guy's ear. 'That's a good point, Twelve.' He turned back to face Mia. 'If you are from out of town, how come you were partnered up with folks from Silver Eagles? The other two we've seen before. Perimeter scouts. They used to patrol the outskirts. Why would perimeter scouts be working with someone from another faction?'

'Because their faction was attacked,' Mia said. 'I saw it.'

'You saw the attack?'

'No, I saw what remained. Afterwards. I saw the bodies. I found Dev and Prisha. They were on their own. They were helping me find Dylan.'

'So if we go marching over to the Silver Eagles base in Heathrow tomorrow, we're not going to run into an ambush? You weren't sent out here as bait?'

'You have my word,' she said.

'We'll find out when we visit the base tomorrow. That's the only reason you're still alive. If I find out you're not telling me everything, if you're lying, you're going to have a very painful day ahead of you. I promise you that.' He left with his guards in tow.

Alone with her thoughts, Mia felt the warm slip of a rogue tear streak down her cheek. *What would Dylan do in this scenario?* He'd try to figure out a way. Just as he had when he'd been captured by New Britain. He'd found the weakness within the system. Her. She needed to do something similar. Before it was too late. Her shoulder would take an age to heal, and it would likely get worse before it got better. Therefore, she was better off acting quickly. Tomorrow they'd be on the move again. She wondered if that wasn't in fact a good thing. Being taken back to Heathrow. No. She'd already tried that. Dylan wasn't there. He'd moved further into the city. She couldn't go back. Not without him. If she tried to run while they were on the move, she'd be killed. Better to escape at night, if she could manage it.

She started to look around the camp with fresh eyes. Counting the number of Crows. Assessing the strength of their weapons. She counted more than twenty. It was hard to keep an exact number. There were some who moved about on the roof above, and some who came and went through the courtyard archway. Presumably there were more outside. That made their numbers somewhere between thirty and forty, she figured. A lot of people with a lot of weapons. Not impossible to slip past but not easy. What was impossible, at least at first glance, was getting out of this quadrangle without being seen. There were no plants to hide behind. No grass to disappear into. Only a few tufts had broken through the quadrangle's surface over the years. There was no way, even if she were to break free of her binds, that she could make a dash through the archway and out into the night. She needed to make it into the building. From there she might be able to disappear into a room and then out through an open window. Even then, with guards patrolling outside and the roof above, it would not be easy. She'd need a weapon.

Hearing the distinct step and knock of Nine's artificial limb, Mia signalled for the young girl to come over.

'Yes?' she said.

'I need a little privacy,' Mia said. 'From the men. Could you take me? Is the plumbing in working condition inside?'

'We checked when we took the place over. Some of it still works.'

'Could I please make use of it?'

The girl considered her for a moment before eventually untying her. 'How fast are you?'

'Not fast enough, I suspect,' Mia said.

'No, not fast enough. So don't try anything stupid.'

'You have my word.'

'Means nothing to me. Move.'

Balling her hands into fists, Mia felt some of her blood return to her fingers as they prickled with heat.

Nine stayed a few paces behind her. A smart kid, by all accounts. 'Through there, on the left,' Nine said.

Mia did as she was told.

'Did you get your number yet?' Nine said.

'Not yet, no.'

'That could be bad for you. You should hope that you didn't anger One.'

'I tried not to. He's a hard man to please.'

Nine was silent at that for a moment. 'Yes, he is. Well, if you do get a number, I reckon it'll be Twenty.'

'Why's that?'

'Because it just became available again.'

'What happened to the old Twenty?'

'One saw no more need for him.'

23

Claire sat with the boys while they waited for Chipo and Tatenda to return with the others. She could sense Dylan's tension as he fussed over his weapon, pretending to clean it one moment, looking off into the darkness the next. He wanted to get to Mia.

She knew the feeling. When Dylan and Jake had been taken by New Britain, she had not been able to stop for a moment. Had it not been for Chipo, she'd have likely done something foolish and reckless. The difference was that she had seen her sons taken by New Britain. She'd known that they were somewhere within New Britain's base when she'd found it. There was no telling where Mia was, though. She hadn't the heart to tell her son that they might never find her. Or that they might only find her corpse. The world had taught her not to get her hopes up.

But it did not feel right passing on such pessimism to her children. She wanted them to have more. To want more. To believe in more. And that meant putting her own concerns aside in favour of support for the two people she loved most, one of whom was desperate to find his partner.

She checked over each son's weapons, knowing she no longer needed to do so. In reality, she hadn't needed to do so for years. They were accomplished fighters by now. Not something she was particularly proud of, but it allowed her to sleep a little easier. At least, now that they weren't going after one another. She appreciated that both let her check their weapons over without complaining, knowing it was more for her benefit than theirs. They were older than their years. Again, something she wasn't entirely happy about. Thinking of the childhoods they had been denied because of the actions of herself and the rest of the original Disconnected almost brought a tear to her eye, but she knew there was no point in wondering what might have been. If things had been different, she might never have had her time with Maxime. Jake might never have existed. And that thought was worse than anything else. So whatever it was they had been denied by way of a childhood, she was at least glad that she had raised two fine young men, both of whom were putting their lives on the line to save another. That was something.

She heard the rustle of bodies moving through the grass nearby and turned to see Martin's considerable form attempting to keep low in the grass. He wasn't doing a very good job of it—he'd have had to go prone for that—but at least the darkness helped prevent him from being seen.

'All right, muckers?' Martin said, his jovial tone painfully at odds with the severity of the situation, although Claire appreciated his constant efforts to maintain high spirits. He was still the man she remembered from before. She waited for the others to come in closer. 'You see where they got to?' Martin said.

'We did,' Claire said.

'And where'd that be, then?'

'The palace.'

'Good choice,' Martin said, scratching his beard. 'Fences still in place around the perimeter. Open ground between the fences and the building itself. High walls. I'd have picked the same spot if I wanted to take this part of the city. It'll be a nightmare for anybody to attack.'

'But not impossible,' Claire said.

'No, not impossible. We have the darkness on our side. That's something, I guess.'

'There's no guarantee that Mia's in there,' Claire said. 'If she's not, we could still slip away into the night.'

'We could, but that might also create a problem for later. If anybody is going to make an attempt on the west side of the city, we need to make sure it's a faction we actually have a chance of making peace with. I'd rather it not be the Crows.'

'Why's that?'

'Rumours, mostly. Some things our scouts have seen.'

'What rumours?' Dylan said.

Martin looked at his own people, as if he were about to spill some nasty family secret. Claire wondered whether he had lost any of his own to the Crows over the years. Or whether some had been lost in battle. Her friend did not look too comfortable.

'Each faction has their own system of governance,' he said. 'To be honest, I'm not particularly inclined to any of them. That's why we keep to ourselves, below ground, away from them all. Wolves do a lot of hunting. They grow some of their own stuff, for sure, but they do a hell of a lot of raiding. If it's them in the castle, we could be in for an ugly fight. I'd not want to face off against any of them on the best of days. Blades, too, have their own nasty streak, but I'm not sure how much would just be down to defence. When evil waits at your borders, it's hard not to think in kind. I'm sure many would say something similar about us. But the Crows, there's something truly horrific about them. They've been aggressively building in recent years. We've seen the fires from miles off. We sent scouts in to check the area around their Stratford base.' He paused for a moment. 'Some never made it back. Those who did reported stories of a nameless culture, where everybody is given a number. They spend their days doing hard manual labour, even the little ones, for a leader who is trying to re-engineer some of the old technologies. The way one scout reported it, it sounds like they've been working on a large wood-burning generator to give them power again. So far, it hasn't worked. Not well, at least. I'm not sure why. Maybe they're missing parts they need. Maybe they're heading west to look for those parts. Either way, all of us who've been anywhere near them have seen some horrors. They withhold medicine from their own, choosing instead to amputate limbs instead of wasting supplies. It's the same for clothing and food, from what we've gathered. They're hard people, with little room left for happiness. They've a brutal justice system, too. On our scouting trips to their part of town we often find beheaded corpses, with no other signs of struggle. Given we've never seen that when coming up against other gangs, we can only assume it's something they do to their own.'

'So why stay?' Claire said. 'If you know you've got factions like that on your doorstep, why not just leave the city entirely? Head out and find your own land to call home.'

'Now that you've confirmed what I'd long feared regarding Eoin, that may now be an option. Previously I couldn't leave. Marie couldn't either. Not when there was a chance Jonathan might turn up one day. Now that we know, it makes the idea of leaving a little easier.'

'You don't have to do this,' Claire said. 'You've done more than enough for us already. We can take it from here. You should take your people and leave. Get out of the city before it descends into war. If what you've told us about the various factions is true, nothing good will come from this fight for control of the city. Not without all of them being willing to lay down their weapons.'

'That'll never happen. No one side will lay down their weapons for fear of the others refusing to do so. And I can't see a situation in which all sides ever willingly put their weapons down as one. People have a hard time trusting one another. It's always been that way.'

'Then you should go. Go now, please. Head west. We can give you the directions to meet up with our people back home. You'll be welcomed there. You can start anew.'

Martin weighed Claire's words for a while. He looked at each of his people in turn before returning his gaze to her. 'Not yet. When we find Mia, we may well take you up on your offer. Might be nice to head back to my part of the world again.'

Claire gave him a strong embrace, the kind she usually reserved for her kids. 'Thank you. All of you.'

'Let's get on with it, then,' Martin said.

'How do you propose we scope the area out?' Claire said.

'We spread out,' Martin said. 'Not too thin, mind. There aren't enough of us to encircle the grounds, but I'd rather not get drawn into a choke point.' He broke a small branch off a nearby tree and split it into twigs, which he then placed on the ground in a square shape, which Claire presumed was the castle itself, surrounded by more twigs, which she took for the fencing. 'We can take this side of the building from where we are in Green Park. At best we might have enough to keep an eye on the other side from the palace garden. If it turns into a fight, coming from two sides might be enough to make them believe our numbers are more impressive than they really are. Might scare 'em off without having to get drawn into anything too ugly.'

'And if we do get drawn in?'

'Then better we stay together. By remaining on two sides, we can still fight as one if needed.'

His theory was sound enough, but Claire still didn't like it. She never liked approaching other bases. No good ever came from it. If she wasn't already certain that Dylan would just return anyway, with Jake likely following simply to make up for his transgressions to his brother, she'd leave now and let the search for Mia end without success. As it was, she knew better than to try and convince either of her sons to turn their attention elsewhere. At least Martin and the Disconnected were staying. That much was something. They had a fighting chance, whatever or whomever they ran into.

With that thought in mind, she moved forwards with the others to the edge of the park. Only the road lay between them and the castle.

'Look,' Chipo said, pointing to its roof. 'Guards on top.'

'And on the ground,' Tatenda said.

Claire surveyed the grounds. She'd seen the palace plenty of times during her years before the Blackout. She'd seen the king and his family paraded to and fro, but she'd never really stopped to appreciate the building. Martin's crude layout with the twigs had been fairly accurate. It was a mostly square building. The entrance was an archway which led into a sort of quadrangle. Assuming they made it over the fence in one piece, going through the archway would be suicide. 'There's no way we're slipping past all of the guards twice. If we're going in to take a look, we're doing so by taking some guards out. I can't see a safe way to extract without getting ourselves into more danger.'

'Agreed,' Martin said.

'The ones on the roof need taking out as soon as possible. If they get sight of us, even now, we're in trouble. There's no way we're getting a single clean shot off from here, let alone multiple. I assume the faction is relatively low in number. Most will likely be in the quadrangle, standing round a fire or something. Any others, I assume, will be in the main part of the building to the rear. I doubt they've got people in every room along the side facing us. If we can cover the ground between the fence and the building without being seen, we can climb up into the building through one of the windows and then make our way to the roof from there. Once we've taken the guards on the roof out, we can signal for the rest to come in. Or we can do a recce of the area and, assuming no sign of Mia, make our way back here.'

Martin pulled a knife from his belt. 'Well, you're not going in without me. Let's take two small groups. That way, if one runs into trouble, the others can step in.'

'Okay,' Claire said. 'Dylan and Jake with me. And Martin, I guess. Chipo and Tatenda, you take a few others in the other group.' Both her friends nodded.

'Luca, Dan, you go with Chipo and Tatenda,' Martin said, pointing to two of his people. Both shifted over to the siblings without another word. They were tall, lean men. Dan was a little taller, with fair hair, while Luca's features were darker. Their eyes gave nothing away. Claire could see instantly why Martin turned to them. They looked capable and reliable. 'The rest of you stay here,' Martin said. 'Keep your eyes on the roof. When you see the signal, spread out and make your way into the building. If you see us running from the building back in this direction, be prepared to defend us with everything you've got.'

Nods all round.

With her heart beating against her chest, Claire crossed the road to the fence. She loosed her khukuri knife from its scabbard on her belt and waited for the guard nearest her to pass by. She watched him closely, taking his pacing into account. Watching how often he turned his head. She compared his movements to that of the nearest guard atop the roof. He was almost too high up for her to make an accurate assessment. He seemed to be pacing in a circle, of sorts. Every few seconds he disappeared from view. Every time he reappeared her heart beat faster still. She took a deep breath, counted herself in and hopped the fence, moving low and fast. She made it to one of the guards patrolling the grounds without him noticing, ran her blade across his throat, and pulled him into the shadows.

One down.

She took a moment to steady her nerves and looked across for signs of the other team. She saw Tatenda take another guard out.

So far, so good.

The palace windows were mostly damaged, which she was thankful for. Martin gave her a boost up and she climbed to the first ledge. She peered in. *Clear.* Lifting a foot to the ledge, she pushed herself into the room and turned to help the others in. Martin boosted her two sons up, who then turned to lift him in. What had taken a matter of seconds felt to Claire like an eternity, each minute sound echoing in her head like clanging bells. She was sure someone had heard them. However, the silence put her paranoia into perspective. 'Everyone all right?' she said.

'We're good,' Dylan said. 'Let's see if there is anybody in the next room. If we can look in on the quadrangle, we might be able to tell whether a trip to the roof is even necessary.'

'Good idea.' Claire led the way, holding her blade tightly. Each step was torture, the way their feet padded in the quiet. Even their breathing was loud to Claire, so much so that she found it easier to hold hers. Making it across, she saw a flickering light out the window. There was a fire somewhere below. She looked across the quadrangle and saw nobody in her direct eyeline, so she crept up to the window ledge and peered over. The others followed.

Claire could hardly make out the dark figures moving below. There were too many of them. Easily more than the numbers her own group amounted to.

Beside her, Martin gasped.

'What is it?' she said.

Her friend brought his hand to his mouth. He looked like he'd been struck by a dagger. 'Eloise,' he said.

'Who?'

'What have they done to you?' Martin said, his voice dripping with pain.

'Is there a member of the Disconnected down there?'

'The little girl, down there on the left,' Martin said. 'She's hobbling around. They've cut her bloody leg off, the bastards. We thought she'd been killed. She was one of our scouts. Went missing about a year ago. Maybe less. We've got to get her out.'

Claire looked down at the girl. Took in the way she moved about. Easing between the others. No animosity towards her from any of them. She seemed quite at home.

Claire put her hand on Martin's shoulder and tried to steady the shaking giant. 'You've already done so much for my family and me. We'll gladly go in for her if you say that's her, but—and I'm only saying this because someone has to—are you sure she wants saving? She doesn't appear to be in any trouble.'

'I don't care,' Martin said. 'I have to get her out. She's family.'

'I understand. Let's get to the roof. We need to take out the guards, then we can signal the others.'

24

Dylan wiped a bead of sweat from his brow. His nerves were on edge as they ascended through the building. He'd not seen Mia down there but that didn't mean she wasn't somewhere below. However, one of Martin's people was and that was all that mattered right now. Just as Martin had put himself on the line for him, he and his family needed to do so for Martin and his people. He'd help Martin save Eloise. It was the least he could do.

Each staircase they reached only increased his sense of anxiety. It was nothing like hunting deer. Hunting wolves, perhaps. Besides defending his own family territory, the only real attack on another population he'd ever been a part of was the final attack on New Britain, and that had almost killed him. He still had the scars to show from that one.

Thankfully, they made it to the roof without coming across anyone else. It gave him a small sense of hope. Perhaps this gang's numbers weren't too high. They hadn't filled the entire building, which meant perhaps those they'd seen in the quadrangle were the majority.

Once on the roof they moved fast. The guards were

either looking out towards London or they were peering down at their own lot in the quadrangle. Not one of them was ready for an attack from their own position. Dylan watched his mother take one out from behind, the man disappearing into the shadows in a soundless heartbeat, guided by her dangerous yet gentle hands. Chipo, Tatenda and the others had also made it up. Had he not been looking for them, he wouldn't have seen them. They were moving low and slow. The guards near to them were oblivious.

Dylan turned his attention to the last guard, a few feet in front of him. The man was about his height, carrying a long-range rifle with a scope, something Dylan had not seen in a long time. He thought of how useful the weapon might be for hunting. How he and Jake might use it together, like they had as kids. Becoming proficient. What might be if they all made it out. He hadn't given a moment's thought to anything beyond getting Mia back to safety.

The guard's gentle whistling brought Dylan's thoughts back to the present. He didn't recognise the tune. Then again, the old people had more to draw on from before the Blackout. All he had were the songs he'd heard his family sing. His mother had once gifted him some strange device which had the sole purpose of playing music, and had vowed to search for a way to power the thing, but it had never come to fruition. Apparently, if he ever got the thing to work, he'd be treated to something special that Claire always said she missed about the old world. One of its better achievements, according to her.

He slowed his breathing, counting the guard's steps. *One, two. One, two.* He bolted like a hare across the space between them, knife in hand.

The whistling stopped.

Dylan was almost upon the guard when the guy turned to face him. It was too late. The guard barely had a moment to register his attacker before the knife plunged into his neck. The force with which Dylan hit the guy took them both down together. For a moment Dylan thought the guard was still alive, and so he pulled the knife from the guy's neck and plunged it into his ribs, but it was unnecessary. The guard's body was limp.

Dylan saw Martin's hand appear and accepted the big man's help in getting to his feet.

'Thought you'd almost ballsed that up,' Martin said.

'So did I for a moment.' He hunched over, resting his hands on his knees, and drew in a couple of deep breaths. His face was warm with the guard's blood. Wiping a slick of it away from his eyes with his sleeve, he looked down at the corpse. 'You know who they are?'

Martin spat on the ground. 'Crows. No doubt about it.'

'How'd you know that?'

'What they did to Eloise. Nobody else in their right mind would ever think to do that to a child.'

'Does that change our plans at all?'

'It changes nothing. We go in and we get Eloise out. We check if Mia's there too. If she is, we get her out as well.'

'And the rest of the faction down there?'

Martin looked at Dylan, his expression as lifeless as the nearby corpse. 'They decided their own fate when they took one of ours.'

'I'm glad we're with you, Martin. I wouldn't want to be going up against you, that's for sure.'

Martin's face showed no reaction to Dylan's statement. 'Let's get the others.' He tore a stretch of shirt from the deceased guard and walked away.

Dylan followed him over to the side of the building

facing Green Park, where the rest of the Disconnected were hiding in the grass. To their credit, he couldn't see them. They had darkness on their side, but still, it helped to settle his nerves a little. The rest of the Crows were still ignorant of their arrival. Martin waved the piece of shirt he'd taken from the guard's corpse. He did so for a good ten to fifteen seconds, by Dylan's count. Eventually, Dylan saw a response from down in the grass. Somebody stood up and walked forward, waving their hands. Dylan couldn't tell who it was from this distance. The shadow moving through the grass was soon joined by many more as the Disconnected moved from their position. Like an army of ants, the shadows filled his vision, crossing the road and then rushing the palace itself. They'd seen where the two teams had made it in and were following suit. The attack had begun in earnest.

Without another word Dylan and the others descended the building to meet with the rest of the approaching Disconnected.

ONCE THEY'D RECONVENED, Martin split everybody up into small teams to flank the quadrangle through the two sides of the palace they'd come in. Dylan, Jake, Claire and Martin continued as one team. Although to Dylan, the presence of the others receded, and he felt as if he was on his own. The light had started to shift in the sky above. Most would not have noticed it. To the average person it would still be pitch black. Even those who spent a lifetime outside, away from city factions or smaller urban groups, would not have noticed the slight shift towards the dawn of a new day, he knew. Only true hunters. The ones who rose in the dark. Whose killing was done long before the first ray of sunshine warmed the morning dew. The real predators. His mind slipped into its natural state. To Dylan, it was just him and his prey. Gone was any anxiety. Any trepidation. Only anticipation remained. In a hunt, this was his favourite moment. The moment before the kill, before everything went right or wrong, before the glory or the defeat, when all he had to go on was his own conviction.

Their instructions were simple: retrieve Eloise and look for Mia. No mercy. This was, as Martin had put it, a chance to right wrongs. To level the odds. One faction down was an opportunity for all the other factions to fight for control of the newly available space within the city, but two factions down would mean fewer factions fighting over a lot more space. Fighting between the rest might even be avoided if terms could be agreed, although Martin had been careful to caution against anyone getting their hopes up on that. It didn't matter to Dylan. Only Mia mattered. Getting her back safely and helping his new friend retrieve one of his own.

Most of the Crows were asleep on the ground floor. Claire had suggested the early morning attack based on experience. It had been the same tactic she'd employed when attacking New Britain, which had worked well. Dylan could vouch for that. The attack had freed him. Now he moved with her and the others through the rooms of unsuspecting sleepers. It wasn't so much an attack as it was a massacre. Some of the Disconnected had stationed themselves a couple of floors up so that they retained the high ground in the event of a brawl, but Dylan did not think they would be necessary.

Their killing was swift and relentless. Unforgiving. Final. He gave no thought to those who met his blade. Most were dead before they knew what was happening. Those who didn't die instantly were dead shortly after.

Dylan was mid-kill when he heard the scream from a

nearby room. Thankfully, the voice was not Mia's, but it changed everything. In the blink of an eye, the quiet executions gave way to screaming and shouting. To weapons firing. Dylan could hear feet pounding in every direction. Chaos erupted around them. And they had not yet found Eloise or Mia.

All around, darkness gave way to light as dawn signalled the coming sunrise, the grey tapestry stifling the golden rays for a little longer just as Dylan suffocated the life from another member of the Crows out in the quadrangle. This was not a morning for bright rays of light, anyway. When they did eventually come, they would only shine on the dead.

Dylan looked for his brother and mother in the madness. Claire looked well protected by Martin as the big man used his superior strength to bludgeon some poor soul who had badly miscalculated the odds of his success. His mother's blade soon ended the lives of three others nearby, all of whom had made even worse miscalculations, assuming her to be the easier target. Out of the corner of his eye Dylan saw Chipo and Tatenda, back to back, cutting elegantly through the furore as if in some private dance only they knew.

The bat came from nowhere. It thumped Dylan in the back, taking his breath with it as it sent him face first into the dirt. He turned over onto his side just in time to miss the second blow. The bat connected with the ground where his head had been only moments before. Above him he saw the feral expression of a man almost twice his own size. It was no wonder the blow had taken his breath from him. Dylan didn't think he could survive a second open blow to the body from his attacker. The man looked like he could take on Martin and still have energy left over.

Sensing the next blow, he rolled to his right this time, evading the bat by no more than a hand's span, but it gave him the time he needed. He kicked out with his right foot as hard as he could, connecting with the man's ankle.

Even with all the carnage around, the snap of bone sent a shiver down Dylan's spine. For a fleeting moment, he almost felt sorry for the man, but the moment passed. The man let out a feral howl. Dylan kicked up, this time connecting with his attacker's groin. The man flopped onto his back, screaming in agony. Dylan was about to get to his feet when he felt a whoosh of air over his head. Jake's arm came into view as his little brother sent a dagger deep into the man's chest.

Jake turned to face Dylan. 'You all right?'

'All thanks to you, yeah.'

'Any sign of Mia?'

'Not so far.'

'What about Eloise?'

'No sign of her, either,' Dylan said. 'Let's go.' They weaved through the crowd and back into the building towards its rear, where they had yet to check. Dylan kicked an old door in and burst into the room. Nothing. Completely empty. His frustration grew as he sheathed his blade and took the automatic rifle off his back. Every second that they didn't find Eloise was a second closer to something tragic happening, he knew. And if Mia was anywhere here, the odds of finding her alive were diminishing. He started to call out for her. 'Mia!' No response. *'Mia!'*

'You sure shouting is the best option?' Jake said, moving his aim around the room.

'I think they've noticed we're here. The element of surprise is long gone. I need to know if she's here.' He walked through the door to the next room, calling out even louder. 'Mia!'

The distant reply came faintly. 'Dylan?'

Dylan and Jake both spun round at the same time.

'Did you hear that?' Jake said.

Dylan was glad his brother had spoken first. Otherwise, he might have thought his mind was playing tricks on him. 'It's Mia—she's here.'

'It sounded like it came from outside.'

Dylan threw caution to the wind and headed for the doors back to the quadrangle, not stopping to check for danger as he passed through. Jake followed. The battlefield was awash with blood and corpses. The numbers had dwindled significantly. As Dylan made his way through the doors, he saw the Crows beating a retreat towards the archway.

Above him, a few floors up, came the sound of two gunshots in quick succession. Dylan turned to look up. It was one of the Disconnected.

'They're coming!' the voice said.

Dylan saw Martin look up at that moment. 'Who?'

'The others.'

'Which others?'

'Wolves and Blades. We better get out of here, now.'

Dylan turned to look at the surviving Crows fleeing through the archway. He saw the little girl, Eloise, moving with them and then, as his eyes went from head to head, he saw her. 'Mia!' Her arms were tied behind her back and she was being shoved forwards by a guard holding a gun. She turned at the sound of his voice but was pushed through the archway before Dylan could hear what she'd said.

Martin, breathing hard and spattered with blood, ran up. 'Eloise!' he shouted.

The little girl came to a halt beneath the archway, turning on her one good leg. She looked back. Dylan couldn't make out her expression from where he was, although the morning light afforded him a better look at her silhouette.

'Eloise, please, it's me,' Martin called.

'Nine, move!' came the instruction from a member of Crows beside her.

The girl wavered for a moment, before turning once more and heading out through the archway.

Martin dropped to his knees, slamming the dirt with a fist. 'Bastards!'

Claire appeared through a door below the lookout who'd flagged the arrival of the other factions. 'We need to go. The other two gangs are almost upon us. If we don't all want to die here and now, we better get out of here.'

'They've got Mia,' Dylan said, rushing up to her. 'We need to go after them, now.'

25

Claire could sense the urgency within the whole group. Martin was itching to get after Eloise. Dylan had all but bolted after Mia. Jake was raring to go after the both of them. And the rest of the Disconnected looked like they either wanted to give chase or run as far from possible from the other two approaching factions. Claire certainly didn't want to get caught between them all. They'd already taken a number of losses. The one thing she knew was that they couldn't stay in the palace. They didn't have the time to block the entrance, and they didn't have the numbers to cover all the low entry points where others could climb through broken windows like she had. The building was simply too big.

The safest option, as far as she saw it, was to go after the Crows. 'It looks like they've headed towards St James's Park. Do you think they're headed there with any purpose or simply fleeing, Martin?'

'Might be going for the river,' Martin said. 'Maybe they think they can lose us all if they make it to the other side. Westminster Bridge isn't too far from here.'

'Well, let's make sure we get to them before then. The Wolves and the Blades will be on us in a matter of minutes. Let's get out of here.'

'Right,' Martin said, 'everybody stick together. Anybody who can't fight, stay here until we've left. Then, when it's safe to do so, head for the station. We'll come back for you if we can. Hopefully these new people will follow us out instead of coming in here. If we can get Mia and Eloise back, we can try to disappear into the Underground. When we're able to, we'll come back here and get the injured. Everybody okay with that?'

Claire watched as everybody nodded in unison. Her appreciation for Martin's leadership was growing by the second. Not only had he performed admirably in battle, he'd shown a particular loyalty to his own that she guessed was in some part making up for the lack thereof twenty years before, and was proving himself to be as quick a thinker as he was a fighter. 'Okay, let's move.'

Leaving the few injured members behind, they headed through the archway towards St James's Park. Claire took a second to analyse her surroundings. The other factions were closer than she'd thought. Ahead of her the Crows were heading for the bridge which crossed the small lake in the centre of the park. Martin had been correct. It did look like they were making a run for the river, although they were moving much too slow. On the other side of the park, towards the treeline, another faction stood waiting for them. 'Who's that?' she said.

'Wolves,' Martin said.

She looked over her shoulder to the third group approaching from beside the palace. 'That'd make them the Blades.'

'It would.'

'We don't have enough ammunition to fight them all.'

'Neither does anyone else. There aren't enough supplies in the entire city for a fight this size between all of the factions.'

'You think any of us can survive this?'

'Not a clue,' he said. He pointed to a few of the Disconnected who were still holding on to guns. 'You stay here,' he said, pointing towards the monument between the palace and the road. 'You're the line between the rest of us and the Blades. You take out as many as you can. Don't let them get through to us. We don't want to have to fight while looking over our shoulders. Everybody else, you're with me. We're going to get Eloise and Mia.'

Claire looked at her two sons. 'You stay close to me at all times. We all look out for each other, all right?'

'Yes, Mum,' Jake said.

Dylan simply nodded his head.

He was the one Claire was worried about. With Mia in the mix, she couldn't be sure of his ability to keep his head during the fight. She made a mental note to keep a close eye on him. As much as was possible, anyway. Time was against them. The longer the fight drew on, the more likely it was that somebody would get caught in the crossfire. Mia's odds weren't looking great. Her hands had been tied when Claire had seen her and she was being shoved around. Even if she broke free from her captors, she'd have to cover ground with bound hands and no weapon. If she did something that reckless, Dylan would likely try to intervene, a dangerous move. The calculations and worries threatened to send Claire's head into a spin. She didn't like the idea of having to split the group, but Martin was right, they needed the line of defence to prevent them from heading into one fight with nobody covering their backs.

All too soon the morning birdsong was drowned out by gunfire. Up ahead the Crows clashed with the Wolves, both taking up positions on either side of the bridge crossing the lake. Claire moved forwards behind Martin, darting between trees for cover. The others followed behind, Dylan and Jake right on her tail. Martin set a slow pace. Not wanting to arrive while the others still had ammunition in their chambers, no doubt.

They made it to within a hundred yards or so before some Crows noticed their approach and opened fire. Claire rushed to the nearest tree and crouched behind. Dylan and Jake took cover nearby. One of the others wasn't quick enough. Two quick bursts of fire put him on his back, gasping for air as the blood pooled around him. There was nothing anyone could do for him.

She popped her head round the trunk and returned fire before ducking back. All around her bullets lit up the gloom, kicking up dust and chipping bark off the trees. She counted herself in, stepping out from the tree every few seconds to fire another short burst of fire, but at this distance she was struggling to get a clear shot. 'We need to get closer,' she said.

Martin had come to the same conclusion. He pointed to two trees a short distance ahead, perhaps twenty yards or so.

In the midst of the gunfire, the distance seemed much greater to Claire. She bolted before her mind could convince her it was a bad idea. Every step of open ground covered felt like a mile. The long grass stretched out before her as she zigzagged across the terrain. Left. Two steps. Right. Three steps. Breathe. Left. Two steps. Right. Four steps. Trying all the while to alternate her rhythm so as not to look too predictable to any nearby shooters who might be counting her movements to line up a shot accordingly. A bullet whistled over her shoulder just as she changed direction once more. Had she taken another step in that direction before changing course, she'd have likely taken one to the chest.

Thankfully, sheer will carried her all the way. Two more clouds of dust were kicked up in front of her as she reached the tree and ducked down behind it to catch her breath. She checked the magazine in her automatic rifle. Empty. The pistol, too, was empty. *Fuck.* She'd been right. They didn't have enough ammunition.

Just as she was starting to panic, the shooting came to an end. Claire knew she was out but when she looked around she saw that every one of the Disconnected was out, too. It wasn't just a lull. Peering round the tree, she saw that it was the same for both factions on either side of the bridge. Everybody had been reduced to melee weapons or bows and arrows. As she watched, what remained of the Crows advanced over the bridge towards the Wolves, causing the Wolves to retreat. At the same time she heard a roar from behind and turned to see the Blades advancing towards her. The line of defence had been overrun.

Glancing across at the tree beside her, she saw that Martin had sat himself down and was clutching at his shoulder, his face pale and sweat-drenched. *Shit.* 'Martin!'

'I'm all right,' he said, breathing deeply. 'Just a scratch. Looks like the line didn't hold.'

'Looks like it, yeah.'

'Best fuck off then, eh?'

'Yes, let's,' Claire said. 'We've almost caught up with Crows. They've just crossed the bridge. If we move now we might still be able to get Mia and Eloise back.' Safe from gunfire now that everybody was out of ammo, she walked over and proffered her hand, which Martin accepted with his good arm. She pulled the big man to his feet. 'You good?'

'Better than ever,' he said between clenched jaws. 'Come on.'

This time Claire took the lead. Gripping her khukuri knife tightly, she ran for the lake with the others in tow.

She never heard anyone loose the arrows. Only saw the sky darken above her as she started to cross the bridge. She stopped in her tracks, looking up at them as they arched towards her, knowing it was too late to save herself. All she could do was try to prevent anyone else from being caught in their path. She turned and screamed for everyone to halt. Martin was hurtling towards her, his face etched with fierce determination. The man-mountain covered the distance between them in a heartbeat, crashing into her and slamming her to the ground beneath him.

She lay face down, paralysed by his weight as the arrows struck. Each blow to her friend was a knife to her heart. She felt him tense above her, refusing to cry out in pain as he was struck. Once, twice, three times. After the third strike, he coughed up a mouthful of blood onto her and let out a deep groan.

'You good?' he said, his voice a hoarse whisper.

'Martin! What the hell were you thinking?' With a huge effort, she rolled him off her onto his side and crouched beside him. 'You absolute fool.'

'Atoning for a mistake I made twenty years ago.'

'You reckless idiot.' She turned to the others. 'Boys! I need your help.'

Dylan and Jake came running over and helped Martin to his feet, propping him up beneath each shoulder.

Claire could see the three arrows were all lodged in the top half of his back. Pulling them out was not an option. At least not on the battlefield. They would tear through him and cause him to bleed out then and there. By the sounds of his voice and the fact that he'd coughed up a mouthful of blood, she figured that one of the arrows had pierced a lung. 'We need to get out of the park, now.'

'What's that?' Chipo said, pointing to a building in the distance.

'Westminster Abbey,' Martin said, blood drooling from his lip onto his chest, his head lolling forwards.

'We can recover there,' Claire said. 'Mia and Eloise aren't getting far. We'll go after them soon enough. We just need to regroup.'

'Better make it quick,' Tatenda said, pointing back towards the approaching Blades crossing the park.

Claire turned to Martin, who was weighing down her two boys beneath his shoulders as his legs began to give out. 'Can you make it?'

He nodded his head and groaned, more blood spilling from his mouth.

'Come on.' She led them from the park, across the road and into the buildings behind, hoping that they would be quick enough to lose anybody who might be coming after them. If they could make it to the abbey, they might just be able to set up a defensive strategy and save her friend who had risked his life for her.

They moved as fast as they could. As fast as they could get Martin to move, anyway. Claire sent Chipo and Tatenda ahead to check that nobody had already taken the abbey. It was impossible to tell where the others had got to. All she could hear was the sound of the Blades charging across the park. She kept walking, setting a pace that she knew was excruciating for Martin. It was for his own good, though. They slipped down backstreets and changed direction several times. Thankfully, the abbey came into view as they rounded a corner. Chipo and Tatenda were standing outside the entrance, facing away from each other as they kept an eye out for anybody else. Tatenda gave the thumbs up. Claire advanced across the road with the others in tow.

'The building's clear,' Tatenda said as Claire reached him.

'Good. Let's get inside before the others see us. Close the doors and set up guards. I need to see to Martin.'

'Of course,' he said.

Ignoring the worried look on Tatenda's face, Claire guided her sons into the abbey, where they laid Martin down on his side. He had gone silent. His skin was ghostly white. She cut his shirt along the side and saw the horror that lay beneath. The arrows were buried to the midpoint of each shaft. She wanted to be sick. There was nothing she could do. Pushing them through would only pierce other organs and kill him in the process. Ripping them out would be just as damaging. Leaving them in there would do nothing except guarantee continued bleeding and eventually infection.

'Claire,' Martin said, his voice almost a whisper.

She walked round to his front and knelt beside her dying friend, taking his hand in hers. His grip was slight. 'Martin, I'm so sorry.'

'It's all right. This has been a long time coming. I've been waiting.' He coughed up another mouthful of blood, his eyes rolling up towards his forehead as he did so.

Claire shuffled forwards and rested his head on her lap.

'I'm glad we found each other again,' he said.

'Me too,' she said, making a hopeless attempt to wipe the tears streaming down her cheeks with her one free arm.

'Thank you for saving me. For saving my sons. For everything. You've been a true friend. I'm so sorry I can't save you.'

'Don't be,' he said, his voice growing more faint. 'I'm going to see Eoin again, finally.'

Not knowing what else to say, Claire sat stroking Martin's head gently as he passed away.

26

Dylan knelt down beside his mother and put his arm around her, holding her as she sobbed. Her whole body shook against him. Everyone in the abbey was silent, the mood sombre. 'He was a good man,' he said. 'None of us would have made it here without him.'

Dylan didn't want to hurry her but he knew the other factions were nearby, either coming for them or disappearing into the distance. Neither was acceptable. He couldn't lose Mia now. Not after coming this far. Not after the cost paid by Martin and the others. And they couldn't just sit around and do nothing while others were advancing on them. 'Let's make sure that wasn't in vain,' he said, and gestured for his brother to come over. 'Help Mum lay Martin to rest somewhere in here. We need to figure out what we're going to do.'

'Of course,' Jake said, stepping in to take his place.

Dylan called a couple of others over. 'Help Jake move Martin's body. Keep him somewhere central, away from doors and windows.' The two men nodded. Dylan walked over to Chipo and Tatenda, who were talking to a couple of others he'd met underground. Dan and Luca, Martin had introduced them as.

'What do you want us to do?' Chipo said.

'I don't know. Mum isn't ready to move. Not yet. She needs a moment to pull herself together. We all do. How are we on numbers?' He looked around, counting the heads. It didn't take long. Twelve, including himself. Chipo and Tatenda said nothing. They didn't need to. 'Does everyone at least have a weapon?' A few of those still standing raised the weapons they were holding. It wasn't much. Pitiful, in fact. A few with bows and arrows, although those would be almost useless if fighting switched to close range, and the arrows would run out soon enough. The rest had blunt melee weapons and blades. Bits of metal. Pipes. Sticks and bats.

Worse than the lack of weapons was the looks on their faces. They looked distraught. Defeated. Their leader was dead. So too were most of their friends. They'd fought through the night. Most looked dead on their feet; dark bags beneath their eyes, dirt and scratches all over their bodies. Some were carrying injuries that required attention. Others' wounds were more emotional. Dylan's own muscles ached all over. A combination of exhaustion and pain.

'It can't end like this,' he said, loud enough for all in the abbey to turn towards him. 'It won't. I refuse to let it. For most of my life, I grew up hiding from the rest of the world. It was just my family and me. We didn't trust the outside world. My brother and I were brought up to believe that communities created risk. Too many variables when you put people together. Disease. Danger, from within and without. Struggles to feed everybody. As a rule, we kept to ourselves. It was only recently that I came to truly understand what it meant to be part of something bigger. I've seen what it's like to foster a sense of being. To care for others, like Martin did with all of you. He saved my life. He saved all of our lives. He kept you all alive for years. And he refused to give up on anybody. Until his dying breath, he was trying to help us get Mia back, and Eloise. We can still do that.' He pointed to the doors. 'Somewhere out there, the other factions are also trying to regroup. They all suffered losses too. It wasn't just us. They're weak. They're hurting. And they're worried that we could come bursting through the door any minute now. This doesn't have to be the end of us. If we're smart, we can still take advantage of the situation. We can get Mia and Eloise back and then we can disappear, or better yet, we can stay and take control. We can make this a day to remember. Not just the day we lost many of our friends and loved ones, but the day we won the city back, too. Perhaps after today you won't need to live underground anymore. If we make it through, we can decide what the future of this city is. We just can't give up. Not yet. Not until we're done. For Martin.'

'For Martin,' Luca said.

Dylan felt his chest expand as he breathed in new hope. They weren't giving up. There was still a little fight left. The flame, however small, was still alight.

'What should we do?' Dan said.

Dylan looked around, taking in the true majesty of the abbey for the first time. He'd come across old churches plenty during his years, but none like this. The stone pillars seemed to stretch up to the sky, the ceiling so far up as to be a world away. Patches of the stained glass windows were still intact. Dylan felt miniature in such a great hall. Intricate carvings were etched into every part of the building. There wasn't a single section that was plain. Everything about it was exquisite in its nature. He couldn't quite comprehend how such a structure had ever been built. It had stood the test of time much better than many of the steel and glass structures he'd come across before.

But it still had weaknesses. There were too many places where others could break in. As a place to take up a defensive position, it was lacking. 'We need to fortify all the entry points. Make it so that there is only one main way in. If anybody tries to attack us here, we need to force them into an approach that gives us the advantage. By funnelling them through, we may be able to put the last of our bows and arrows to use. Reduce the numbers a little more. Failing that, the building can serve as a base for some to rest while the others go looking for Mia and Eloise. Split up into pairs. Block the doors with whatever you can. Leave those doors as is,' he said, pointing to the doors they had entered through. 'They'll serve as the beginning of our funnel.'

Quietly, everybody set to work. The abbey was filled with chairs and benches, as well as mattresses and other possessions that had been brought in over the years. Dylan figured people had been using the building as a home, rather than a place of worship, for some time.

Jake joined him as they set about piling benches against one set of doors.

'How's Mum?' Dylan said.

'Not great. I'm worried about her.'

'Me too. Just give her a little time to gather her thoughts.'

'What if somebody attacks right now?'

'Then we're all dead and none of it will have been for anything.'

'Don't say that.'

'Let's be quick about it, then,' Dylan said. He grabbed one end of a long wooden bench and gestured for Jake to take the other end. They lifted it off the ground and carried it over to the nearby door and stood the bench up against it. 'We need more.'

'How about you?' Jake said.

'How about me, what?'

'You all right?'

Dylan couldn't help but be touched by his brother's concern. Jake had always had a way of knowing when Dylan was struggling. Even now, as he put up his toughest guard for the benefit of the others, his little brother knew the turmoil he was going through. Part of him was relieved that their bond was back to its original strength. Before the family had been torn apart by New Britain. 'I'm worried about Mia,' he said, eventually.

'I know.'

'We need to go find her. I don't even know if she survived.'

'We'd have seen her body in the park if she hadn't,' Jake said. 'She's alive. And she's somewhere nearby. We'll get her back, I promise.'

Dylan knew his little brother was just trying to help him feel better. The words were empty in reality, though. There was no guarantee they would get her back. There was no guarantee they'd even find her. His attempt to rouse the others had been as much for his own benefit as for theirs. He had been trying to convince himself not to give up. 'I just don't know how we're going to do it.'

'We'll figure it out. The option will present itself when the time is right. Like when we used to hunt together. We'd lay the traps and we'd scour the perimeter. Eventually, something would happen. It'll be the same here. We just need to be smart. Stay sharp. We'll know the moment when we see it.'

'I hope so,' Dylan said, lowering his voice a little. He

picked up a chair and placed it on the stack covering the door. 'What about the others? You think they're up for this? You think they can make it count?'

'I believe so. They've fought well so far. They're hurting but they responded well to you. You can lead them through this. I should know. I spent enough time letting you drag me around.'

Dylan smiled. 'What I'd give to be back in our old forest hut, setting traps and doing perimeter checks every day, eh?'

'And jumping off waterfalls.'

'I thought you hated that.'

'I did, at first, but eventually I came round to your way of thinking. You were good at breaking me out of my shell at times. Without you I wouldn't have known I could push beyond my limits.'

Dylan smiled at that. 'Without you I wouldn't have learned there were limits. You kept me in check. You think we'll ever go back there? Back home, I mean.'

'Probably not. But that doesn't mean it's gone. It's still in here,' Jake said, tapping his chest with his fist, just over the heart. 'Besides, we can build something new. Something better.'

'I'd like that,' Dylan said.

'Well, let's get this place in order, then.'

'Yes, let's.' Having barricaded the door, Dylan went to check on the others. Dan and Luca were moving a large chest to the base of a mound of stacked chairs. 'Need a hand?'

'Thanks,' Luca said, shifting his grip so that Dylan could grab a corner of the chest. 'You think this'll hold?'

Dylan could see the concern in their eyes. Their confidence was shot even if their determination wasn't. 'I do,' he said. 'It doesn't need to hold forever. All we need is enough time to get a few arrows off. It'll give us the advantage. That'll be enough.'

'Okay, then.'

'I'm sorry about Martin.'

'Thanks,' Luca said. 'I'm sorry, too.'

'Stay strong. As he would have done.' He left them to it and went in search of Chipo and Tatenda. The abbey was huge. Far too big to cover every side with the numbers they had. Thankfully, it looked like Chipo and Tatenda had thought the same. The siblings had set down a series of obstacles that led away from the one entrance that hadn't been barricaded.

'To slow them down,' Chipo said, following Dylan's line of sight. 'It'll give me a little more time to put this to use.' She held her crossbow up. 'Enough to make the shots count, I hope.'

'They will. I've seen you use that thing enough times before. I'm glad you're here.'

'Us too,' Tatenda said.

'I think we're ready,' Dylan said as he surveyed the barricades. 'Let's get everyone into place.'

Chipo nodded. 'We'll take care of that. You go check on your mother.'

Claire was at the rear of the building, beneath the largest organ Dylan had ever seen. Martin's body lay on the floor, his eyes closed and a blanket covering him up to his neck. He looked almost peaceful. She must have broken the arrow shafts off so that she could lay him on his back. 'You okay?' he said, taking a seat beside her and looking at the body of the man he'd come to respect in such a short space of time.

She wiped a tear from her cheek. 'I will be.'

'I'm going to miss him.'

'As am I.'

'It doesn't seem fair that we always lose the good ones.'

'Sometimes I think it's punishment for everything we did. For the world we left you.'

Dylan let out a long sigh. 'It's not so bad. We're making progress. Look what we managed back home. You changed the world once. We can do it again.'

'I don't know. Every generation always thinks they can do it better than the one that came before. That's what we thought, anyway. You'd think one of the generations might actually have set the world to rights by now, considering all their bluster. Twenty years ago, we all thought we were so right to break the system. It was such a flawed and unfair one, and had we done nothing, it might well have been the end of us. Humanity was on a cliff edge. We thought it was more than our right to tear it all down; it was our duty. For the sake of our own survival and the future generations.'

'From what you've told us over the years, it sounds like you did the right thing.'

'Perhaps,' Claire said, 'but the cost has been too high. We've lost too many. The body count is getting hard to ignore.'

'They knew the risks. We all do. Still, we take them because we believe in something better. That belief, that hope, drives us. Things can come right again. Look at us. Our family is mending, getting stronger. We're growing. That's worth fighting for. At least, I think so. And I'm not going to stop. Mia's out there, somewhere, and we need to get her back. But we can't do it without you. This family needs you. I need you. So, you can't give up. You have to keep on fighting. For all of us.'

'You're right,' she said.

'Come on, Chipo and Tatenda have been readying the others.' Feeling buoyed by the fact that he'd managed to get his mother out of her momentary spiral, he walked with her back to the others, who were standing by the set of doors which had not been barricaded. Some were seeing to each other's wounds, patching up what they could with torn shirt strips. Dylan counted them all again and noticed the number was one short. 'Where's Jake?'

27

Jake slipped out of the abbey through a broken window. There was a small drop to the grass below which padded his landing. Nobody saw him leave. They were still busy fortifying the building against attack. Dylan had gone to talk to their mother. Jake knew this was his only chance to get away unnoticed.

With blade in hand, he moved away as quickly and quietly as he could, crossing the road towards the sandy-coloured stone building opposite the abbey on the river's edge. The building was as majestic as the one he'd just left. This one he recognised from a few of the books he had read growing up. The tall bell tower on the far side, with a clock face on each of its four sides, was its giveaway: the Palace of Westminster. Somewhere inside that tower, he knew, was Big Ben, a large bell which he'd laughed at as a child, wondering why people in the old world had taken to naming trivial objects and buildings. It didn't make sense to him then, but now, in the presence of such a structure, he understood why it deserved a name. It was the kind of structure that would stay in the mind long after having seen it. In all his life, Jake had only seen simple buildings, mostly made of brick, steel and glass, or what remained of it. Small buildings, without a single memorable feature. Nature had long ago reclaimed most of them, such that he had little appreciation for what they might have looked like in their prime. Yet in this city he'd seen buildings which he could only describe as beautiful, a word he did not often relate to the remains of the old world. *Why didn't they build them all like that?*

The clock tower stood high above the rest of the palace, as it did most buildings in the area. It hadn't yet been taken over by the moss and foliage plaguing the base of the palace, but it was damaged. It looked like there might have been some sort of small explosion up top. Bullet holes punctured the tower's sides while some of the stonework looked perilously loose. Still, it was standing. If he could get up to the top, or near enough to it, he would have a good vantage point from which to see what was happening nearby. He might even be able to spot one of the other factions. From up there, he might just be able to figure out where Mia was and what could be done to save her.

He thought of the conversation he'd had with his brother. How Dylan had indicated his pleasure at having Jake back in his life. How he'd even said he'd like to build something new with Jake. The idea of once again living with his brother, working together on something as they had before his estrangement, gave him hope. Something to look forward to. He thought too of how happy their mother was now that the family was back together again and on good terms. Externally, it seemed that they had forgiven him for his transgressions.

Yet it didn't sit right with him. He felt an ache in his belly that he could not quite define. Shame, perhaps, or something close to it. Guilt, even. He still felt a fool for having fallen for Frank's charm, and even more of a fool for letting that evolve into a rivalry that momentarily tore the family apart. He had disgraced his loved ones. When they most needed him and he them, he'd turned on them. If he hadn't done so, they might not all even be in this situation. Dylan and Mia might still be gallivanting through the countryside arm in arm, young lovers with a future ahead of them. His mother would be safe at home, as would Chipo and Tatenda. And the majority of the Disconnected, including Martin, whose bodies now lay strewn across the city, rotting in the sunshine, would have gone about their lives none the wiser. *It's all my fault.*

What would it take for them all to forgive him? To truly forgive. Not simply play nice because they were in the midst of a battle for their lives. He suspected that if he wanted their sincere forgiveness, he would have to earn it. And to do that he would need to do something worthy of greatness; something selfless, like go out on his own and find Mia and Eloise.

It was the smart move anyway. Had they all gone storming through the streets, they would likely have been spotted, or heard. But sending someone out on their own now was a suicide mission. Especially after the battle that had just taken place in the park. There was no guarantee of returning to the group. With the other factions out for blood, being on his own was almost certainly a death sentence. They had all suffered losses and they were all likely looking to end their fights with victory. However, if he could find out where the Crows had retreated to, where they were keeping Mia and Eloise, he could take that information back to the group and help lead a more strategic attack. One that could result in fewer deaths. One in which the group could all get out of this alive. That or go in and rescue Mia outright, if the opportunity presented itself. Perhaps then he could truly feel at peace, having done something actually worthy of forgiveness.

Then again, if he did anything foolish and got himself captured, he would only be putting the group more at risk. *Would they even come to rescue me again?* They no longer had the numbers, nor the weapons. All the more reason to find out where Mia was being kept and make the appropriate move.

He made his way round the palace to the riverbank, ensuring nobody from the road could see him. Going through the palace would be to risk coming across anybody inside. He would need to be smart if he was going to attempt that. Right now, he wanted only to get to the tower. His next move would become apparent once he had the lay of the land.

Looking across the great expanse of the water, he doubted that anybody on the other side would notice one person moving alongside the palace from that distance. Still, he kept low. The city was once again deadly silent. It was hard to imagine that a battle had just played out nearby. Only the gentle lapping of the water against the riverbank provided Jake with any noise to mask his footsteps. He wondered where the other factions were. Presumably the lack of shouting and charging meant that everybody had lost sight of one another. That or they were playing the waiting game, holding out until one of the others made a wrong move, like a spider waiting for an insect to cross its web. Then again, perhaps they were all as scared as the Disconnected. Perhaps their losses had been as bad, or worse. He could only hope so. Either way, there could be no wrong moves.

Moving through the palace grounds, he entered the tower. A narrow staircase wound its way up, which he followed to the top, past the clock faces and the large bell itself, as well as the four smaller bells. Then came another spiral staircase leading to a platform within the top of the tower, containing what appeared to be a large lamp. The top of the tower was indeed damaged, as he'd seen from below. Bits of rubble were everywhere. He started to wonder how sturdy the tower was. Whether any damage had been done to the core structure itself.

From up top Jake could see out over the city below. It was without a doubt the highest he'd ever been, so much so that he clung to the stonework as his legs lost all vigour. This was much, much higher than the waterfalls back home that Dylan had often encouraged him to jump off. Those jumps had been terrifying for Jake. They'd taken all of his bravery to even approach and all of his blind faith in his brother that everything would be all right. Dylan wasn't with him now, though.

Just as he had at the waterfalls, he closed his eyes for a moment and drew in a deep breath. *One step at a time.* Keeping a firm hold of the stonework with one hand, he stepped close enough to the edge to peer over and opened his eyes. The roof of the tower stuck out below him, such that he could not see the ground directly below, but he could see the road beside it. Again, his legs felt weak. Too long up here and he figured he might not be able to stand at all. He wanted to be back on solid ground, clinging to something rooted to the earth. However, he had a duty to his family. He'd left for a reason. Looking back towards the abbey, he couldn't make out any movement within. A good sign. If nobody had seen the Disconnected go in, there would be no way to tell there was a trap waiting within. Not without entering it. Just like he'd built his traps back home. By the time the victim knew what was happening, it was already too late.

Looking further afield, he saw for the first time the sheer scale of the city, which had been impossible to comprehend from ground level. It went on forever, as far as the eye could see. But he could not see any sign of life. Not on this side or the other side of the river. The streets were empty.

Jake's eye caught the flash of movement just as he was turning away to return to the staircase. He swung his head round, unsure whether his mind was playing tricks on him. He waited. There, again, another movement. There was no mistaking it.

A man's head poked out from behind a pillar in the building across the road. The man checked left and right, then swiftly crossed the road onto the grounds of the Palace of Westminster, where he disappeared from view somewhere below Jake. Then another person followed suit. Before he could guess to which faction the people belonged, he saw her, hands still tied behind her back, being pushed ahead by some ruffian. *Mia.* The little girl, Eloise, followed closely behind, hobbling across at a slower pace than the others. After her came another few heads. Jake counted five or six but couldn't be sure. It might have been more. Too many to take on by himself, for sure.

What do I do? Almost certainly, they wouldn't climb the tower. It wouldn't serve any purpose except that which he was currently using it for: to get a view of the rest of the city. If any of them were to come up here, it would probably only be one. Two at the most. And Jake would have the high ground. He might be able to get out of that situation alive if he was quick. If anything, then, Mia's captors were either seeking shelter in the palace or they were on the hunt, looking for Jake and his family, trying to end the battle. Perhaps that was the only reason that Mia was still alive. Something to bargain over. He had to get back and let everybody know, Dylan especially. He had to let his brother know that Mia was nearby, within grasp.

He moved as fast as his feet would carry him. Down the hundreds of steps, getting dizzier with every revolution of the winding staircase, until at the bottom his head was in as weak a state as his legs had been atop the tower. He heard the voices inside but didn't stick around to listen to their plans. It was more important that he informed the others before Mia got away. He bolted from the tower, crossing the road and heading back for the abbey as fast as his feet would carry him. The Crows were all inside the Palace of Westminster. None of them would see him running.

He realised his mistake as he started up the road. *The others.* Approaching the abbey, at the far end of the road, was one of the other factions. It was impossible for Jake to tell which one at this distance. He dived behind a tree, panting as he caught his breath, his chest heaving with every pronounced gasp. How stupid could he have been? How reckless? He counted to five, waiting for the shouts, but nothing came. Perhaps they hadn't seen him. He peered round the tree, slowly, just enough to see with one eye. The group were advancing as they had been. No shouting. No charging forwards. He must have just managed to get into hiding before they'd looked his way.

Changing direction, he took the alternate road towards the abbey. He moved slowly this time, sticking closely to building cover. There was no way in through the broken window through which he had left the abbey; it was too high. All he could do now was make a run for the doors which he knew to be free from barricades and hope the others would let him in without accidentally killing him. He waited for his moment to cross the road onto the grounds of the abbey, checking one direction then the other. Then again. *Shit.* Approaching along the alternate road was yet another group, the last of the factions. There were now two gangs approaching the abbey from different directions while another holed up in the Palace of Westminster. And he still had to cross the road.

Knowing he had no option, he counted himself in, closing his eyes and drawing a deep breath as if he were about to jump off a waterfall with his brother. He sprinted across the road towards the large wooden doors of the abbey. Down the road, the shouting began. He'd been spotted. There were seconds left to act, a minute or two at most before they descended on him. He banged the door with all his might. 'Let me in!'

28

'Open the door,' Dylan yelled. He stood back as Tatenda opened it just enough for Jake to squeeze through before slamming it shut once more. Jake rushed in, trying to speak while taking large gasps of air, his eyes darting in every direction as he gestured towards the door and then seemingly at other points within the abbey. 'Slow down,' Dylan said. 'What is it?'

'Mia—I've found her!'

'Where?'

'Nearby. Across the road.' Jake pointed to an invisible point over Dylan's shoulder. 'But we have a problem.' He drew in a deep breath.

'What problem?'

'The other two factions are both heading for the abbey, only neither knows of the other. And one's just spotted me. You need to go now.'

'What do you mean I need to go?'

'You all do. Go out the back, like I did. There's a broken window you can leave through. Slip out that way and head across to the Palace of Westminster. The big sandy-coloured building with the clock tower.'

'Like in the books?' Dylan said.

'That's the one. What remains of the Crows just entered it. I tried to count them. Fewer than ten, I think, but I'm not sure of an exact count. You can take them if you all go. Mia and Eloise are both with them. Both alive.'

'How much time do we have before the other two factions are upon us?' Dylan said.

'None. They're close.'

'We all need to go now. Come on.' Dylan turned to leave.

'No,' Jake said. 'I'm staying.'

Dylan stopped in his tracks and turned back to face his little brother. Somewhere behind him, the sound of his mother's gasp filled the abbey. 'What do you mean you're staying?'

'I have to. If we all go, they'll only follow us to the palace. There's no guarantee we can kill them all. You need to go now. Get Mia and Eloise and then get the hell out of here. Get back into the tunnels. I'll create a distraction. I'll draw the other two factions to the abbey. It'll buy you some time. Not much, but some.'

'I can't let you do that.'

'It's my decision,' Jake said. 'Now go, all of you.'

Dylan turned to Claire. 'Say something. We can't let him do this.' She looked frozen stiff, her face pale and her eyes watering. Dylan watched as she tried to protest but managed only to bring a shaking hand up to her mouth to stifle a cry. It was no use. His world was being torn apart again and he was powerless to do anything. His brother was right. If Mia really was nearby, they needed the distraction to improve their chances of besting what remained of the Crows. Each blade counted. The longer Jake could keep the other two factions near the abbey, the better their chances of successfully getting Mia and Eloise and disappearing to safety.

Only the odds of Jake making it out alive were almost nil. Two groups against one person. His brother was willingly walking into a trap of his own creation to ensure Dylan could get back to Mia. Claire had been right. The body count was getting too high to ignore, but he could not see another option.

'We don't have time,' Jake said. 'Go on, get out of here. I'll find you afterwards. Go get Mia.'

'I'm coming straight back here for you. Don't do anything fucking foolish.'

'I'll be fine. Go on, piss off.'

Dylan embraced his brother, holding him tightly. 'I won't forget this.' He stood back and watched as Jake rushed to their mother who, having lost all strength to stand, had collapsed upon the floor, shaking her head as if unable to comprehend what had been said.

Jake put his arm around her and gently patted her back. 'It's okay,' he said. 'I'll be right behind you.'

She began to cry. Dylan could see that she was trying to say something. Her hands gripped Jake's shirt above the shoulders and bunched it into a fierce grip between her two closed fists, protesting physically what she lacked the strength to do verbally. The room fell into an awful silence as everybody watched and waited.

Only Jake's quiet reassurances could be heard, Claire's crying turning to some silent internal torment that made Dylan feel sick. Jake helped her to her feet. 'Go, please. The longer this drags out, the more likely it is that we get backed into a corner and the fight turns against us. I'll find you soon, you'll see. Okay?'

She shook her head. 'You can't leave me. I came all this way for you. For you both. I'm not leaving without you.'

'You're not,' Jake said. 'I'm just hanging back for a moment. We'll all regroup as soon as this is over. This is the right move. The best move. It's the only way to have a chance of getting Mia back. You have to trust me. And I need you to look after my big oaf of a brother. Keep him from doing something foolish.'

'I want to stay.'

'You can't. It's decided. I'll come find you all as soon as this is over.' Jake gave her another hug before ushering her away. He turned to Dylan. 'There's no more time. You have to leave. Now.' He moved to the doors, his back to Dylan and the others.

It was done.

And they were out of time.

Dylan knew he wouldn't be able to leave if he tried to say something else. Reluctantly, he took his unwilling mother by the arm and ran for the rear of the abbey. The others followed. Behind him he could hear his mother's muffled sobs as she ran. He wanted to be sick. Jake had made his choice, though. Dylan could only react in kind. The best he could do was use the advantage his brother had gifted him and hope that Jake found a way to escape with his life.

He turned his focus to Mia, to the one outcome he might be able to affect.

They slipped out the broken back window, each climbing through as quietly as possible and dropping to the grass below. 'Keep low,' Dylan said. Out of guns and ammunition, he only had a bow, with few arrows, and a knife. It would have to be enough. He looked around for any sign of the other factions.

Nothing.

Across the road, directly ahead of him, was what looked like a main entrance to the Palace of Westminster, jutting out from the main building. To the left Dylan could see the famous clock tower he had read about. There was no time to appreciate it, though. He crossed the road first, darting to the porch covering the doors. He waited to hear if he had alerted anybody else. There was no sound. Not a single peep inside or outside. Not wanting to waste time, he signalled for the others to cross the road. Everybody huddled around him, awaiting further instruction. 'I'm guessing this isn't the only entrance. If we all go through this one, we might walk into a trap like the one we just laid in the abbey. We're going to split into three groups. One goes left, the other right, and the remaining few with me.' Beside him Claire nodded her approval of his plan. She still had not spoken a word since they'd left Jake behind. He suspected it was taking all she had to simply follow the plan and not break down entirely. 'Mum, Chipo and Tatenda with me. We'll draw the attention of the others as soon as we run into them. The rest of you, find your way through the building to us. I'm guessing you'll hear us when it all kicks off. You know what to do.'

They did. Luca took one group and headed down the left flank of the building. Dan took the rest and went right.

'Just us now,' Dylan said. 'Everybody ready?'

'We're ready,' Chipo said, moving to one side of the door, her crossbow up, ready to end anybody on the other side. Tatenda took the other, waiting with a steel pipe in hand. 'Stay behind me,' Dylan said to Claire.

He pushed the door open as gently as he could. It creaked slightly as it moved on its hinges. Not loud enough to be heard from the road, although he couldn't tell what the acoustics were like inside. He winced as it came to a stop. Nothing on the other side. Just another porch of sorts.

'Clear.' He moved in, placing each foot down gently so as not to make a sound. There was another door to the left. Again, they took up their positions. Same procedure.

Same result.

Just a long set of steps descending into a big empty hall. It reminded Dylan of the inside of a church, with its high walls and dark oak beams jutting out, supported by braces to create a sort of truss in support of the roof above. The hall was too big, too open. Even though he could see a door midway down, he decided against entering. If they got caught in a fight in this room there would be no cover. It would have made for a good trap, he figured, had he been the one defending. A big open space in which to draw would-be attackers to their deaths.

Instead, he walked on past the door to the hall and continued down a smaller corridor, towards what looked like a central, somewhat circular hall. From there he figured he'd get a better understanding of the internal makeup of the palace.

Dylan saw the head just before it disappeared from view. 'There! Up ahead.' He ran, but by the time he got to the central hall it was gone.

'What did you see?' Claire said.

'Somebody. A face. Only momentarily.' He looked around. The central hall was a large room, beautifully designed, with a patterned stone floor and intricate stone carvings upon the walls. Tall windows with stained glass dotted in amongst the pattern work ran from about a third of the way up the walls all the way to the top, where they arched into a gold-patterned ceiling, from which hung a large chandelier. Off the central hall in four directions, including the one from which they had just come, ran four corridors.

'Where did you see the face?' Chipo said.

'Down there,' Dylan said, pointing down the corridor to his left. 'It came from that direction,' he said, raising his voice intentionally so that it echoed down the corridors. He wanted them to know he was here. To know they were about to meet their ends. He wanted Mia to know that he had come for her. That everything was going to be okay. More than anything, he wanted to draw them out. To avoid being funnelled down any particular corridor of death.

He realised too late that choosing any particular corridor, rather than staying put, would have been the better option. It might have given him access to another part of the building. Instead, as he turned in a circle, he saw Crows coming out of doors in each corridor. They were approaching from every direction, like ghosts in the night. The funnel had pushed Dylan and the others inwards. The trap was the centre of the building. They were surrounded, with no way out other than to fight their way through. He couldn't see Mia or Eloise down any of the corridors. Presumably that meant they were being kept as prisoners somewhere further in, which meant even if they made it past these attackers, there were more waiting elsewhere.

Dylan liked his chances less and less. He backed slowly into the centre of the hall, beneath the chandelier, until he, Claire, Chipo and Tatenda were all back to back, facing each one of the four corridors.

Chipo, being the only one other than him with a ranged weapon, fired her crossbow. The whip of the bolt shot across the room into one of her oncoming attackers and echoed throughout the palace.

One down.

Dylan took aim with his bow and loosed an arrow.

Two down.

The remaining attackers all charged.

This was it. Dylan readied himself, putting his bow over his shoulder and unsheathing his blade. He didn't have time to fire another shot. It would only weaken his position when he then had to go for his blade anyway. By then the attackers would be upon them. He did as his mother had taught him. Feet firmly planted in a wide stance. Knees bent. Hard to knock over. He faced his attacker side on, giving him as little of his body as possible to poke holes in. Claire pulled her khukuri knife out. Her stifled sobs had stopped. Dylan breathed a small sigh of relief at that. She'd pulled herself together, partially. At the very least, the four of them would give as good as they got, Claire included.

He heard a couple more shots being fired from Chipo's crossbow followed by another body hitting the floor. It was too late to try and count, though.

The attackers entered the central hall in a rush. Dylan's stance held firm as one guy came at him. He ducked his shoulder, giving the attacker the opening, before hitting him with his shoulder as hard as he could. He pushed up with his feet and lifted the bastard off the ground. The guy gasped in surprise as Dylan drove his knife in below the ribs.

From somewhere in the distance, Dylan heard screaming. He looked up to see Luca and his group charging down one of the corridors to enter the fray. A second later Dan and his group appeared down one of the other corridors. Dylan wanted to cheer. The arrival of the rest of the Disconnected somewhat evened the numbers out. At least, they would have. As Dylan ducked a blow and kicked an attacker to the ground, he looked up and saw Dan and his group being cut down from behind. Their flanking manoeuvre had been accounted for. There was nothing he could do except watch for a few infinite seconds as they were killed.

Luca and his group made it to the central hall and joined in the fight, but with Dan and the others dead, the numbers were against them. Dylan was forced to return his attention to his attacker as the guy got back to his feet and picked up the knife he had dropped. There was no way out. He couldn't see the next play in his mind. Their attack had failed. All he could do was try to get out of there, to perhaps draw the fight into another space. Force the remaining Crows to come out from wherever they were hiding. That or find the room with Mia in it. If he could do that, he might be able to switch from a fight to a negotiation. They were all likely in the same room. He remembered the face he'd spotted in the corridor to the left. It was nothing more than a hunch, but it was all he had to go on. 'With me!' He bowled his attacker to the side and charged down the corridor. He heard the pounding of footsteps behind him, unsure of whether it was his own people or his attackers. Either way, he'd know soon enough. 'Mia!' he shouted at the top of his lungs as he ran, hoping to draw a response. *'Mia!'*

He made it as far as the lobby between the corridor and the next room when he heard a sound quite unlike anything he had heard before.

29

Jake didn't look back over his shoulder as his family and the others left. He couldn't. If he did, he knew his resolve would break. He'd only change his mind and ask for someone to stay with him. That or he'd turn and go with them. Either way, it wouldn't work. They needed him to stay. And he needed to do this. For his own sake as much as theirs. He had to draw the other two factions in, keep them by the abbey for as long as possible, so that the others could have a decent chance of freeing Mia and Eloise and getting away to safety. And one of those factions was getting near. He could hear the footsteps pounding down the street.

Time was running out.

His distraction needed to be loud. Loud enough that it could be heard throughout the surrounding area. He remembered a church his mother and father had once shown him when they were scoping the perimeter of their territory back home. It hadn't been much. A small stone building atop a rather insignificant hill. The roof had caved in. A set of bells had fallen and lay cracked upon the floor. His father had explained that in their day, they would have made quite the racket. Loud enough for a whole village to hear from miles away.

This place had to have bells. The sheer size of the place demanded it. If it did, they would be high up, he knew. In one of its towers. There was no telling whether they might still be in working condition, but, lacking any other method of making a noise, save for bellowing at the top of his lungs, he turned from the door and ran for the stairs. He could only hope that the bells were up there.

There was a lot of ground to cover, though, and not much time to cover it in. He moved as fast as his legs would carry him, flying up the stairs and onto the next floor, passing intricately detailed stone tombs and the nave, onwards up the next set of stairs to the tower until he found a room which looked right. It was a small square room with ropes hanging down from the ceiling. Ten or so, by the looks of it. He didn't stop to count the exact number. Not wanting to waste time in attempting to gather his breath, he leapt upon the nearest rope and pulled with all his weight.

It snapped, coiling down on top of him in a cloud of dust as he hit the floor with a thud.

He had not accounted for its age, or its years of neglect. *Idiot.* The state of the abbey in its disrepair should have given him enough warning. He got gingerly back up to his feet, caressing a scraped elbow and a slightly bruised ego.

The next rope he tried more gently, taking a firm stance beneath and pulling down with both hands.

It worked.

Somewhere nearby, a bell began to chime. He pulled again and then moved to the next rope, repeating the task over and over until every rope that hadn't snapped or been cut was ringing its bell above. Jake felt like he'd been caught up in a storm, such was the all-consuming wave of sound. It was at once overpowering yet uplifting, like some part of his soul had risen from within. A dormant spirit awakened. It was wondrous. Each bell chiming just after the other. He felt the hairs on his neck stand on end and his skin prickle like goose flesh. He danced between the ropes, laughing with joy as he kept the orchestra up. He had done it. He'd alerted the bastards to his presence. There was no way that anybody within miles hadn't heard, he was sure of it. Being so close, he felt as if the sound was powerful enough to be heard around the world. It shook his bones from within.

Dylan and his mother had their chance. The chiming bells would certainly have caught the attention of the two factions nearby. Even if it was only for a few moments, they would have stopped to listen. Perhaps they would have discussed a potential approach. Of course they would have decided to approach. Who wouldn't have stopped to investigate? At the very least, they had probably surrounded the abbey. Perhaps the two factions had even run into each other. *Wouldn't that just be perfect if they've killed each other already.* Either way, he was unlikely to escape unnoticed, he knew. He hoped that wherever his brother and mother were, they were taking advantage of the chance he'd afforded them. That his efforts had been worthwhile.

With the bells still ringing above, he left the room, his mind incapable of processing much thought in its numbed state. He rested against a wall for a moment, catching his breath and savouring the sound as it petered out. If this was to be the last sound he ever heard, so be it. At least it was something as magical as this. He could finally be proud of his efforts. He'd atoned for his transgressions. Whatever happened next was of little concern. His family would not doubt his loyalty and would not forget his sacrifice.

Satisfied with his efforts, he headed back down. The peals dwindled and the abbey returned to silence. Almost. As Jake moved to the last staircase, he heard voices nearby. He could not be sure whether they were coming from inside or outside, only that they were close. Unsheathing his blade, he peered out of one of the broken windows. There was no longer any need to be subtle. They knew someone was inside. He just needed to know what he was up against.

Looking out over the window ledge, he couldn't see anyone below. He kept moving downstairs, his back to the wall and his blade out, ready to face anyone coming up, but he didn't run into a single soul. With every step he slowed his pace, trying desperately to maintain control. Of his breathing, of his grip on his blade and, most importantly, of his own conviction.

He smelled them before he saw or heard them. It was the distinct unwashed odour of those who lived in urban environments, away from open spaces and clear streams. A dirty smell. Foul, even. A stench in the truest sense of the word. Like someone had found a rotting carcass and rolled around in it. After weeks in the countryside, his imprisonment by the Silver Eagles had come as a shock to him; the stench as much as the capture itself. They were close by.

He stuck closer to the wall. Like a gecko coming out to hunt for flies, he crept along, inch by inch, staying low.

'They're in here somewhere,' someone whispered. A woman. Pretty old by the sound of her voice. But then again, it might have just been because she was whispering. Jake's family didn't have that kind of luck. They were not the kind to chance upon the weak and infirm. They were the kind to constantly be pitted against rivals more capable and more aggressive. That had been his experience. Always expect the worst. At least that way life didn't disappoint as often. All it could do then was meet expectations.

'Shhh,' another voice said. Male. More youthful. More panicked. 'They could be anywhere in here. The ringing's stopped. Maybe they saw us enter.'

Too fucking right. Encouraged by the fact that they thought his actions had been the efforts of a whole group, Jake crept round a stone tomb and stepped up to his full height. He swung his blade. Caught the old woman unaware. Her face barely registered her shock before his blow slammed her backwards. Jake held onto the knife's handle, watching the blade reappear from the old woman's chest as her body fell back to the floor.

'He's here!' the man shouted.

Jake heard shouts nearby, followed by the pounding of feet. This wasn't the time to stick around. He turned on his heel and ran back to the stairs, retracing his way back up to the next floor. The man gave chase, grunting loudly as he followed Jake up through the abbey.

From outside Jake heard more shouting. The other faction must have heard the commotion. They were entering the fight. All but one of the entrances were barricaded. Jake had no way out. He hadn't a hope of fighting his way through one faction on his own, let alone two. All he could do was climb. So he did. Like a deer being chased by a wolf, he darted this way and that, crossing the floor to the next set of stairs which would take him back to the bell-ringing room, all the while hoping nobody had a bow and arrow trained on him.

Unlike a startled deer, though, he knew that his path was ultimately going to be a dead end. *Unless...*

He made the decision before he had a second to reconsider. It was all or nothing. He kicked through a window and climbed out over the ledge. The man behind him had not been as quick. Jake had a few fleeting moments to move. It was a long way down. Too long. He felt sick again, as he had when climbing the clock tower, the height giving him vertigo. But he had no choice. He lowered himself so that he was hanging by his grip alone, his feet scraping the wall in desperate search of a solid placement. The footsteps of his attackers drew near. With a deep breath and firmly closed eyes, he let go and slid to a sudden stop on the roof, his knees buckling beneath him as he rolled. The fall brought back the memory of his being shot through a window by Chipo not so long ago.

A head appeared above him, then two. 'He's on the roof. He's climbing down!'

Jake ran to the edge of the roof and climbed over. The drop was further this time but thankfully more forgiving. He landed in thick grass and rolled away from the abbey.

The others were on him in seconds. Thankfully not all, though. He could hear the scraping of steel. They were fighting each other. As both factions fought one another, Jake did the only thing he could.

He bolted.

The four who'd been almost on him gave chase.

He couldn't go into the Palace of Westminster, even if it was the closest building and the most obvious place to try and lose them. Dylan and his mother might still be in there. Mia might not yet be safe. Instead he ran along the road, openly drawing the others away from the palace entrance. He got to a small square adjacent to the clock tower at the edge of the palace. The long grass was surrounded by bronze statues. Figures from history, no doubt. At least they weren't alive to witness his terrified face.

He darted behind one just as an object flew overhead. An axe. It clanged against the bronze as he slalomed between another two statues before coming to a stop. The others had stopped running, too. He could hear their panting as his own chest heaved. Balling his hands into fists to stop from shaking, he tried to gather his thoughts. To ready himself for one final showdown. Three against one. It wasn't looking good. Any moment now they would appear round the side of the statue and it would all be over.

Round the side. Of course. Sheathing his blade, he grabbed hold of the stone platform upon which the statue stood and began to climb. To his left Big Ben stood watching over. Time stood still—quite literally, the old clock having stopped working long before.

Jake climbed up the squat bronze figure and peered over its shoulders. The three attackers were just below. They hadn't expected him to come from above. They were doing just as he had suspected: flanking the statue so as to take him from both sides.

Before they had a chance to hear or see him, Jake unsheathed his blade again and jumped, landing on an attacker's shoulders, his blade driving deep into the man's neck.

The man gave out an awful howl as the two of them hit the dirt.

Two against one.

Better odds, at least. Not great, but better.

With his own blade still buried in the guy's neck, Jake picked up his victim's axe just as the other two turned to see what the commotion was. Nobody said a word as they faced each other. They looked as out of breath as he did. Jake gripped his newfound axe and got a sense of its weight as he stared the other two down.

He waited.

Both men looked hesitant. They were both bigger than him. Real men. Big, bearded, menacing guys, taller and heavier than him. Without weapons he wouldn't stand a chance. With weapons, well, that was a different story. All he could do was give his level best.

The guy on his left swung first. His metal pipe was long. It afforded him quite a reach. Jake jumped backwards to avoid it. The other guy had a knife. Nothing special. Deadly, for sure, but at least he couldn't keep Jake beyond arm's length like his mate. Jake went for him first. He raised his axe as if to swing down. The guy ducked and moved to his side. Anticipating the move, Jake spun and swung low, burying the axe in the guy's stomach.

'One on one, finally,' he said, pulling the axe from his victim.

The big bastard with the pipe smiled. 'Just what I was waiting for, kid.'

Jake rolled backwards to avoid a flurry of swings, the guy's pipe whistling through the air like a stormy wind down a stone shaft. Any second now one of the blows would connect, Jake knew. That'd be it. He couldn't afford to get in close. But he couldn't do anything from afar. There was only one play left. Dodging another swing, Jake threw the axe with all his might. He didn't care if it hit the guy with the blunt side. The force alone would be enough to at least injure him. As it was, the axe struck Jake's opponent between the nose and forehead, burying itself in the guy's skull. The man toppled over onto his back.

Jake grabbed the handle and wrenched it free from the corpse. It took two solid pulls to get the thing out. As he wiped the blood and bits of bone on the corpse's chest, he saw movement in the periphery of his vision. In all the commotion he had not seen the others bearing down on him from the abbey.

Shit.

30

Claire stopped in her tracks at the strange sound. Then it came to her. *The bells! Jake's done it. He's drawn the others to the abbey.* But at what cost? She had been so distraught when he'd suggested staying behind that she'd barely been able to get a word out. It was almost as if he had been the parent and she the child as he'd consoled her and then ushered her on her way.

There was no changing Jake's mind when he had that look on his face, though. It had always been that way, ever since he was a little boy. How his little brow would furrow when he dug his heels in over something he'd taken issue with. It usually became a staunch moral stance. His arms would fold firmly across his chest and his chin would stick out defiantly. In those moments he was seriousness personified. It was real serious when his little foot would stomp the ground. Then there really was no messing with the little man. She'd thought it unbearably cute back then. Admirable, even. Today, though, it had scared her to her very core. There was nothing she could do but accept his decision. He'd wanted to stay. She knew why. That same hardline decision-making he'd shown as a toddler had only grown over the years. The occasional struggle he'd faced, though, was that his emotions and his intellect so often ran away with him, causing him to jump to irrational conclusions. Sometimes he might think there was an animal tracking him in the forest, bringing on unbearable paranoia. During such times, nobody would be able to convince him otherwise. Occasionally he might misinterpret someone's words or actions, which would result in him taking a 'moral' stance. Regardless of consequence, he took his stances all the same. Refusing to give an inch. He had his own internal code for right and wrong. Part of her liked to think she'd had a hand in finessing that code, but in fact it had mostly been there since birth. Just as he had felt strongly enough that his family had betrayed him, causing all of this, she knew that his bullheaded thinking would not let him rejoin the family until he'd done something to redeem himself. It was his way.

The chiming bells were almost haunting. They took her back decades, to the years she'd lived in London, back when her biggest concerns were trivial matters. Career progression. Getting on the property ladder. What kind of father her fiancé Matt might someday be. What kind of mother she might someday be. Whether such dreams were even possible with a job as all-consuming as hers.

How pitiful it all seemed now. All the time she'd wasted worrying. She should have enjoyed her time with Matt more. Should have left the office a little earlier each evening. Perhaps they'd have heard the bells of Westminster more often if they'd taken the time to go out in the city together instead of spending their nights at their desks.

The bells ringing meant Jake was alive. At least, she hoped so. *Now get out of there, my baby boy.* She hoped that whatever his need to atone, he'd found his peace and was making his way back to her. Back to where he belonged. Otherwise, what was it all for? She felt powerless to control the situation. It was the worst of all feelings. To be at the mercy of the world, like a small tree alone in the open, unprotected, being forced this way and that by the elements. In moments like this her need to control everything was overpowering, but it was something she was having to learn to let go of. To do only what she could and what was right, and to let the rest take care of itself. It was the only way. But letting go was a hard thing to do, especially when her sons were involved.

While one son was out there, hopefully getting as far from the abbey as possible, her other son and her friends were right here, and they were all under attack. Returning her focus to the fight at hand, she ran after Dylan, who had charged down one of the corridors leading off the central hall. She heard Chipo, Tatenda, Luca and the others following her.

Dylan was caught up in a battle with two others in the lobby at the end of the corridor. He was screaming and shouting for Mia all the while.

Claire ran straight into one of his attackers, burying her khukuri knife in his side, just below the ribs. She pulled the knife across his belly and watched as he grabbed at his guts to prevent them from spilling out, before toppling over onto the floor, dead.

The others arrived from behind and the fighting grew more intense in the smaller space. Claire felt claustrophobic as she ducked and weaved. The lobby stank of warm flesh. A warm, putrid smell that made her gag. She knew they needed to keep moving. The tight space would only lead to mistakes. An accidental blow. A swipe of a blade closer than intended. In the blink of an eye, one of her own could be dead at the hands of an ally. She was surprised by the staunch defence the Crows were putting up in the lobby. Either they were trying to hold Claire and the Disconnected there because they had planned it as their intended kill zone, or there was something else on the other side of the large wooden doors.

Mia.

Dylan seemed to be thinking along the same lines. Having killed his opponent, he looked from Claire to the door and nodded. He kicked it open.

At once Claire recognised the setting in which she'd watched politicians debate before the Blackout. Their sessions had often been played on the news in bite-size chunks. The House of Commons was a large room, with long rows of wooden benches covered in green cushions on either side. Each row behind grew progressively higher, so that the room gave off the same appeal as a stadium. An arena. A place in which gladiators clad in suits battled with words for the prize of the public's approval. In the centre was a large wooden table. She recalled that this was where the politicians had once stood to make their impassioned arguments. The roof above had caved in and a long beam of golden light shone down, illuminating particles of dust that hung in the air like infinitesimal fireflies. And on the other side, sitting in what was once known as the Speaker's Chair, was Mia, with a guard either side of her.

Fear was etched into every pore on her face as she remained frozen to her seat in statuesque horror. In front of her stood a tall, bald man with a sinister expression. His appearance gave Claire the same sickly feeling she'd had when she'd first stumbled upon New Britain and its brutal leader, Frank. And in front of the scary man, with his hand firmly around her little neck, stood Eloise, looking confused and betrayed.

'That's enough,' the scary man said. 'Any more foolishness and they both die.'

Claire placed a hand on Dylan's shoulder to prevent him from lurching into an attack. She felt his muscles tense beneath her palm. Behind her the commotion came to a halt. Looking back over her shoulder, Claire saw her friends being pushed towards her as the remaining Crows surrounded them all. There was nothing more she could do. Not without putting Mia and Eloise in harm's way. She and the Disconnected had the numbers now. The fighting had reduced the odds to an even split, but the two prisoners up front meant Claire couldn't do anything reckless.

'Nobody else needs to die,' she said. 'My name is Claire. What's yours?'

'One.'

'Juan?'

'No, One.'

Claire hoped her face had not betrayed her surprise at his strange title. 'Okay, One, we're not here to fight you for control of the city. We only came to get our people back.'

'Why?'

'Why what?'

'Why do you need your people back? What do these two offer that is so unique that it can't be offered by another?'

'Because they mean something to us.'

'So find new people. These ones are weak. They'll only bring you down. You should leave them.'

'Never.'

'That is why your people will lose. You're too emotional.'

'We will gladly live with our faults. Just give us Mia and Eloise.'

'Eloise?' One looked down at the little girl still in his fierce grip. 'That was your name, Nine? You want it back? You want to go home to that weak group, just to be sent out again to scout like you did before, nothing more than their little pawn?' Eloise struggled against the hold he had on her but was unable to free herself. 'I thought not.' One looked back at Claire. 'She stays, for now.'

Claire looked back over her shoulder at the rest of the Disconnected. She could see the hurt in their eyes. She knew that hurt. 'The last person who refused to return my own people to me paid for that mistake with his life.'

One smiled. It was a menacing smile, one side of his lips curling up far too high for a normal smile. Maniacal, almost. Like smiling was something he didn't quite understand. Like it was something he watched others do and tried to mimic but failed miserably. Still, he seemed to be enjoying the moment. That much was evident in the way he stared Claire down. 'I don't care about your people. And I'm not refusing anything. Not yet. You can have one back. Choose.'

Claire felt her stomach clench. He was so nonchalant the way he said it. So cavalier. She wished she had Chipo's crossbow right now so she could bury a bolt between his eyes. It might even wipe that look off his face. There was no way she could choose between Mia or Eloise. That's what he wanted, she figured. He was trying to divide the group, to make them argue. To be drawn down to his level. Presumably he'd already forced Mia to talk. He probably knew that Claire and Dylan were from outside London. That they weren't technically a part of the rest of the Disconnected. If Claire chose Mia, the rest of the group would feel betrayed. They might even turn on her. If she chose Eloise, Dylan would never forgive her. Ultimately, there was a good chance this guy was just messing with her.

Twisting the knife because he could. 'We'll need both back.'

'You can't have both back. I'll need to keep one, at least for now. When I know you've all left the city for good, I'll let that one go. If I find that you've not left, that you've stuck around and are trying to retaliate, I'll kill whoever it is I have in my possession. See, you can't trust people in this world, Claire. Everybody needs something as leverage. That's how the system works. So, choose. Who gets to go back with you today?'

'How do I know you'll let the second go?'

'You don't. But if you come looking, I'll kill you and everybody else you know. That I promise.'

Claire closed her eyes and tried to think of a way out. How she might play along. Keep the prick happy by agreeing to his terms, just long enough to let some new situation arise whereby she could seize the upper hand. As it was, there was no way she could control the outcome. She could feel the heat of Dylan breathing down the back of her neck. All eyes were on Claire.

When she opened her eyes, they were drawn to the door behind One, just behind the Speaker's Chair. Had it moved?

The door opened slightly. An inch or two at most. Claire wondered if anyone else had seen it. She hoped her expression had not given it away. Her khukuri knife was still in one hand. There was no telling who would come through the door, but she had to be ready to cover Dylan. To make sure at least one of her boys made it out alive.

Before she had a chance to warn him, the door flew open and a young man holding a bow and arrow entered in a flash, pointing it at One.

It took Claire a moment to register what she was seeing. Who she was seeing. 'Jake!' He looked like he'd been through hell. His nose was bleeding. There was a cut across one of his cheeks. And his shirt was ripped. He had an axe tucked into his belt which was dripping blood all down his side. Somebody else's blood. Claire saw too that in the brief commotion of Jake's entrance, Eloise had broken free of One's grasp. She was holding a pistol she'd pulled from her own belt and was pointing it at Jake. Claire wondered whether the gun was a bluff. If anybody had any ammunition left, they'd have used it by now, surely. Unless they were a scared and conflicted child, perhaps, who'd seen some of the people who were once her own fighting against those who were protecting her now.

Whatever it was, everyone in the room was now in a stalemate. She and Dylan were at the table in the centre of the room, too far from anybody to do anything before someone got killed. Behind her, the rest of the Disconnected, including Chipo and Tatenda, were surrounded by Crows. Mia had a guard on either side of her. And now One had Jake pointing an arrow at him but Eloise had her gun pointed at Jake. Claire couldn't bear to see one of her sons threatened like this. 'Eloise, please—'

'Don't call me that.'

'Nine, then.'

'Don't call me that either.'

One turned to face Jake. 'You one of them lot, kid? Where the fuck have you been hiding?'

'I am one of that lot,' Jake said. 'You're going to let them all go, preferably before my arm gets tired.'

'It's not me you have to negotiate with, mate,' One said. He gestured with his head towards Eloise.

Claire's stomach tightened once more.

'Hey, Eloise,' Jake said, his voice becoming gentler. 'I'm Jake. I knew Martin for a little while. You remember him?'

She nodded.

'He was a good man, Martin. It pains me to say that he didn't survive this battle. My mum over there knew him really well. She was an old friend of his, from back before you or I were born. Before the Blackout. Can you believe that?'

Eloise looked momentarily at Claire before returning her cold gaze to Jake. 'So?'

To Claire, Jake looked calm and controlled. Well beyond his years. There was so much of Maxime in him during that moment. Gentle yet firm. Unfazed by the gun pointed in his direction.

'We knew him well enough to know how much you meant to him,' Jake said. 'He thought you were dead. That's what he told us. When he saw you at Buckingham Palace, he only wanted to come get you. To free you. Because he loved you very much.'

Eloise's chin quivered ever so slightly. 'He wasn't mad at me?'

'No. He wanted you to come home to the group. He didn't care about any of the other stuff. I should know. I was like you not so long ago. My family and I got separated. We got into a fight with each other. I was angry and, as a result, I made mistakes. But that's the thing about families: once you're part of one, you're always family. And no matter what, there's always a place for you back home. I know that now. I hope you do, too. All those people over there,' Jake said, pointing towards the group of Disconnected behind Claire, 'who fought to get in here so they could come and save you—they're your family. When you're ready, they'll welcome you back home.'

The room fell into silence as everybody waited with bated breath for Eloise to react.

Claire couldn't take it any longer. She was fit to burst. She stepped closer to the table and cleared her throat. 'One, do you know where we are? Do you remember what the purpose of this room used to be?'

He looked around. 'Yeah, this is the House of Commons. It was where all the posh arseholes pretended to give a shit, standing around and arguing over whatever they thought would net them the most votes. Presumably before they got back in their fancy little cars and fucked off back to their countryside mansions. Never had much time for it, if I'm being honest. Too much posturing. Not enough getting on with it.'

'I don't think it was all posturing,' Claire said. 'Some of them were genuinely trying to get things done. That's why they'd raise their concerns in this room and debate them amongst all in power.'

One shook his head, that unsettling smile of his reappearing once more. 'Game was rigged, though, wasn't it? Complete fucking farce most of the time. They never sorted out half the shit they needed to. It's simpler now. More honest. Us or them. Always. Only one winner.'

'That sounds just as rigged to me,' Claire said. She glanced at Jake for a second, looking at the face she loved so dearly. Drawing strength from his presence, she gave him her best smile before returning her gaze to One. 'The Blackout reset the whole system. We don't have to play by the old rules. It doesn't have to be a case of feast versus famine. People don't have to suffer so that others can succeed. We can design a new system, free from the pressures of legacy. Free from the bias of existing systems. We can take what worked from the old system—and there was some stuff that worked—and replace what didn't with what is right, with what is most likely to result in a peaceful and prosperous society. I didn't intend for my children to be raised in a world where they had to kill to survive. That mentality will be the end of humanity. We've seen it today. Look how few remain standing. This is our chance to learn how to better work together. We can rebuild society the way it should be. I've already seen it happen. A start, at least. The town I came from before arriving here in London was a town that had been under the rule of a tyrant. We ousted him and we opened it up to surrounding areas. Now we help others do well so that they in turn can help us do well. I refuse to give up on that. People do have the potential for greatness. I see it in my sons. But if we force each other to live by a code of fear, it will poison everything we hold dear. We have to believe in each other. Believe we can be greater. This is our fresh start. It's either that or we play this thing out to its natural conclusion whereby everybody dies, until that cycle of death wipes us from the face of the earth.' She stopped to let the point sink in, looking at Eloise as she drew breath. The little girl smiled back, her expression soft and warm. It was the closest to hope that Claire had felt in a long time. 'This doesn't need to be about sides anymore. We can find a way to work together to build something new. To take a line from someone I once knew, the choice is yours.'

Once again the room was silent, only Claire was no longer so tightly wound. She no longer felt the need to control every aspect of the outcome. She'd said her piece. She'd meant every word of it. There was nothing else to control. As she returned Eloise's smile, a great weight, one she had been carrying for the better part of two decades, lifted from Claire's shoulders.

Eloise lowered her weapon.

One grinned again, his lips pulled back so that his teeth

were bare, like a wolf's before the bite. 'Never!' He launched forwards towards the little girl.

The sound of the shot reverberated around the room. Claire's ears instantly began to ring. Realising she'd closed her eyes in reaction to the noise, she opened them. Eloise stood before her, aim still holding fast, arms steady as an old oak. One stumbled to the floor, a small pool of blood appearing through his trousers, just above the knee.

31

Dylan opened his eyes as the warmth of the morning sun woke him. Stretching out on the mattress, he felt an ache in his back. A week after the battle, he was still in pain, but it didn't matter. The ache was a good reminder that he was still alive. He turned over and put his arm around Mia. Big spoon to little spoon. She was warm.

Every morning for the last seven days he'd woken feeling guilty. Had he not been so determined to go out into the world with her, she would not have been put through such an ordeal. Had they only stayed home, everything could have been avoided. All the fighting, the deaths, the injuries: they were all his fault. As much as he had tried to tell himself that safety was never a guarantee and that life would always throw obstacles in one's way, he could not shake the guilt. Even Mia's own attempts to comfort him had failed at first.

Today was the first day he'd woken without the guilt in the pit of his stomach. There was no anger, either. Instead, there was something else. Happiness. Hope, perhaps. Whatever it was, it was a good feeling. He drew Mia closer to him, breathing her scent in.

'Good morning,' she said. She turned over to face him and pressed her nose ever so gently against his. 'Sleep well?'

'I did. You?'

'Yes.' She leaned in and kissed him softly. 'Excited for today?'

'Of course.'

'You think they'll come?'

'I think so. I hope so.'

'Well, we should get going, then.'

She made an attempt to sit up but Dylan put an arm on her shoulder. 'Not yet. This is the best part of my day. Everyone else can wait a little longer.' She rested her head on his chest and curled a leg over his. Dylan knew in that moment that his adventure wasn't a location. It wasn't some path to a distant horizon. It wasn't about where they were going or what they were doing. All that really mattered was that they were together, sharing the experience. So long as he woke up like this, beside Mia, every single day, it was all the adventure he'd ever need. Nothing excited him more.

His blissful reverie was disturbed by a knock at the door. 'Yeah?'

'Everyone's getting up,' Chipo said.

'Coming.' Dylan gave Mia a tight embrace, savouring her scent once more, and then got up. 'You sure you want to do this? We could go back, you know? Or we could continue. We could still find our sandy beach across the ocean, like we always talked about.'

'I'm sure.'

'Okay.' He left her to get changed and went to find Jake. Buckingham Palace was the busiest it had been since they had returned to bury all the bodies. The rest of the Disconnected had been moved from their Underground base to the palace in celebration of the city now being a safe zone. This was where they would rebuild from. Small fires were burning in the quadrangle, with some folks preparing a hearty breakfast before the big day. Some had returned from a hunt and were preparing deer for the feast later that day. Jake and Eloise were overseeing the preparations, the pair having formed a close friendship in the days since the battle. 'How's it looking?' Dylan said as walked up behind his little brother.

'Do you think it's enough?' Jake said.

'It's enough.'

'What if they don't come?'

'Then we'll have spare,' Dylan said, nudging his brother playfully. Upon seeing the concern in Jake's expression, he answered more seriously, 'They'll come.'

'All of them?'

'All of them. I believe it.'

'Do you think they all lived? Some of the survivors we found afterwards were in a pretty bad way.'

'I hope so,' Dylan said. 'Each faction had their own people back at their bases, just as we had left Marie and some of the others back at Liverpool Street. They'll have been taken care of.'

'What are you two talking about?'

Dylan turned to see their mother behind them. 'Jake was just wondering whether everybody had actually survived the week, especially some of the Blades and the Wolves we picked up off the battlefield afterwards. I say they're fine.'

'I think so, too.'

'You all set to go home?' he said to her.

'I am. Tatenda and Chipo are packing their things as we

speak. I'm excited to see what everyone's done with the town while we've been gone.'

'I'm sure they've looked after it well,' Dylan said. 'What about your stop on the way? Do you really think Harry and his crew are going to agree to our suggestion?'

'I do. A trade route running between home and London will work. There will be people and goods passing freely across Harry's path a lot. It'll bring his town back to life, I know it.'

'Good. They need it. I look forward to checking in on him and seeing the town's growth soon. You'll give him my regards when you see him?'

'I will.'

'Thanks.'

'And what about you two? I can't keep chasing after you your whole lives. You've given me enough grey hairs as it is.'

Dylan smiled and put an arm around his brother. 'We're going to be just fine. We'll look out for each other.'

'Glad to hear it.'

AFTER BREAKFAST they all made their way down to Westminster Palace, returning to the site where the battle had ended. Following the ceasefire, it had been agreed that all factions who wanted to join together in one community would meet one week after. The factions had each been given the time to recover from the fighting and to discuss the idea with their people who had stayed back at base. It had been agreed that a week was long enough to think it over, to ensure that nobody joined the new community with any misunderstanding as to what that united future looked like.

Before they entered, Dylan, Jake and Claire stopped in the square outside the palace to pay their respects. There, in the centre of the square, surrounded by the bronze statues of leaders and political figures of the past, lay the body of the man they had all come to love. The finest leader of their age. The grass had been trimmed back and a simple cross stood at the head of the grave. A new wooden sign had been erected at the edge of the green which read 'Martin's Square'.

Dylan watched as Claire knelt down and kissed the tip of the cross before standing back. Despite the bright morning sun, a stiff breeze blew through the square, sending a chill up Dylan's neck.

'Do you think we were right not to bring weapons?' Jake said.

'I do,' Dylan said. 'I trust them.'

A voice shouted behind them, 'Look! They're coming.'

Dylan turned and walked back to the road, arm in arm with Mia, his brother and mother beside him. There, coming down the street, were two of the other factions. *No Crows.* It was just the Wolves and the Blades. Nevertheless, a large grin crept across his face. This was a good result. Much smaller in number than they had once been but a far more impressive sight to behold in their peaceful approach. They too had opted not to bring their weapons.

Dylan checked the street again.

Still nothing.

Then, just as he was getting ready to welcome the two approaching factions, he saw them. Two columns of people were marching into view. 'They actually came.'

'I thought you hadn't doubted them,' Jake said.

'Not for a second.'

The Disconnected formed a tunnel on either side of the road and began to applaud as the three other factions passed through to enter the palace for the first time as one united community.

As the faces passed by, Dylan kept an eye out for One, but his face never appeared. Eventually, wondering whether he'd missed him, Dylan pulled aside one of the Crows, an elderly woman towards the rear of the formation. 'What happened to One?'

'We gave him the option. He chose expulsion. So did a few others.'

'I'm sorry to hear that.'

'Don't be. He doesn't represent us anymore. Just because he was technically our leader, it doesn't mean he represented every one of our views at all times. We all decided together that it was time to try a new strategy, one which some of us had wanted for a long time but did not feel we had enough support to vocalise.'

'So he's gone for good?'

'Perhaps. Perhaps not. There will always be those who disagree. They're entitled to their opinions. We just have to show them what we can do together. That we can build something where everyone benefits if they pitch in, while ensuring that nobody gets left behind. It's our responsibility now to prove that this way will work. If we can do that, they may come back in time.'

'I hope you're right.'

'We'll see soon enough, won't we?' She cupped his cheek and smiled before moving on inside with the others. The group of cheering Disconnected followed them all in. As Dylan turned to enter the palace, Claire pulled him back.

'We're going to head off. We've a long walk ahead of us and much good news to spread.'

'You're not coming in?' he said. 'This is a momentous

day. It'll be talked about the rest of our lives. You won't want to miss this.'

She smiled back at him, caressing his hair as she had when he had been a child. 'I've done my part. My time in charge is done. It's time for you all to lead us into the future. The world is your responsibility now. I hope you do a better job with it than we did.'

START THE QUEEN OF THE UNWORTHY SERIES TODAY

DOWNFALL (QUEEN OF THE UNWORTHY BOOK 1)

A kingdom attacked. A princess on the run. A battle for survival.

In Deepwater, Princess Tempest believes her impending marriage to be the worst of her troubles; but when an attack is made on the king, starting a battle for control between the nations of Nyazere, she must flee the only home she has ever known and form new alliances if she is to survive. But beyond the walls of her city lies a dangerous road, where blades and coin matter more than legacy and titles.

Downfall is the first book in the Queen of the Unworthy series, featuring an engaging sword and sorcery fantasy world, filled with battles, backstabbing and morally ambiguous characters aplenty. If you like fast-paced adventure and thrilling fantasy, then you'll love the first book in G.A. Everett's page-turning series.

Pick up Downfall to discover this thrilling new series today!

THANK YOU ... AGAIN

Wow, you made it to the end of my book!

If you've made it this far, **please consider leaving a review of this book.** It'll only take a minute or two to write but I'll appreciate it forever.

You can visit my website www.gaeverett.com and sign up to the newsletter there to receive a FREE BOOK. The newsletter will keep you up to date with my news regarding all future book releases.

NOVELS BY G.A. EVERETT

Hunted (Disconnected series prequel)

Artificial (Disconnected #1)

Blackout (Disconnected #2)

Redemption (Disconnected #3)

Downfall (Queen of the Unworthy #1)

ACKNOWLEDGMENTS

Years ago, when I first sat down to start on *Artificial,* having decided the idea I'd had for a novel was worth attempting in earnest, I did not know what would become of it. I spent so long working on that first book, learning a lot about the process of writing along the way. It took more effort to finish than I had perhaps anticipated. Turns out, writing a book is hard work!

As a result, I never quite knew whether I had more books in me. But I'm glad I did. After three books in this series—four, if you count the prequel, *Hunted*—I'm happy with my tale. My interest in the themes I wanted to explore within the story, as well as the world and characters I created, was strong enough to power me through to the end, but I could not have done it without the support of a great many people.

Firstly, I'd like to thank my editor, Carrie O'Grady, who I've loved working with again. Any final typos are my own fault!

My thanks also to my cover designer, Stuart Bache, who continues to produce such incredible designs.

I'd like to thank my wife, who put up with the early morning alarms, the late nights, and, of course, the first draft.

I'd also like to thank my friends and family, who've continued to pretend they like my books. Please don't ever stop!

Finally, I'd like to thank you, reading this passage now. If you've stuck with this series to the end, I hope you enjoyed the ride. I'm sorry if any of your favourite characters didn't make it! I hope the journey was worth it. And I hope you'll be with me on the adventures I have planned next.

Printed in Great Britain
by Amazon